LEGENDS DON'T DIE IN CHICAGO

BOOK ONE

BOBBY

BOLOGNA

a novel

JUSTIN LAMPERT

First Paperback Edition

ISBN: 978-1-969709-97-5

Published by Lampert & Sons Publishing

Printed in the United States of America

For Chicago.

For the food. For the sports. For the attitude.

For everyone who ever ate a hot dog standing up.

FOREWORD

First of all, I need to thank Chicago. Not the band—though "25 or 6 to 4" absolutely slaps—but the city. The actual city. The one with the wind and the attitude and the inexplicable pride in a baseball team that didn't win anything for over a century. Chicago taught me that loyalty isn't about logic, it's about love. And also that ketchup on a hot dog is a crime against humanity.

To my family: thank you for pretending not to notice when I mumbled dialogue to myself at the dinner table, acted out fight scenes in the garage, and spent way too many hours researching the proper way to dispose of fictional bodies. Your concerned glances were noted and appreciated.

To my son Gunner: I hope you finally read this one. I know, I know—reading your dad's books is weird. But this one's got mob guys, hot dogs, and a lion. If that doesn't get you, nothing will. Also, thank you for only occasionally rolling your eyes when I explained the plot to you for the fifteenth time. Your tolerance is appreciated. And yes, some of the jokes are actually funny. You'll see.

To my friends: you know who you are. You're the ones who listened to me explain the plot seventeen different times and somehow still pretended to be interested. You're the ones who answered bizarre text messages like "How long would it take a lion to eat a person?" and "What's the Chicago equivalent of sleeping with the fishes?" without calling the authorities. Your restraint is appreciated.

To all my readers: this is my third book, which means some of you came back for more. That's either a testament to my writing or evidence that you need better hobbies. Either way, I'm grateful.

And finally, a confession: like Bobby's crew in this book, I eventually left Chicago for Florida. I know, I know. I can feel the disappointed stares from three states away. But here's the thing—you can take the writer out of Chicago, but you can't take Chicago out of the writer. I still put giardiniera on everything. I still argue about pizza. I still believe, deep in my heart, that the Cubs are going to win it all again next year.

Some things never change. Even when everything else does.

Enjoy the book. Eat something good. And whatever you do, don't put ketchup on that hot dog.

With love, gratitude, and an unhealthy attachment to Italian beef,

Justin Lampert

Boca Raton, Florida

"In Chicago, you either eat or get eaten. Bobby Bologna figured why not do both."

—Overheard at Manny's Deli, 1998

"The thing about legends is nobody remembers if they were actually smart. They just remember if they were loud."

—Detective Frank Delaney, CPD

"My cousin knew a guy who knew Bobby Bologna. Said he once ate three Italian beefs in one sitting. That man was an American hero."

—Anonymous caller, WSCR Sports Radio

PROLOGUE

Salt Lake City, Utah — June 14, 1998 The last thing Bobby Bologna ever saw was Michael Jordan's jump shot.

Which, if you think about it, is a pretty good last thing to see.

Better than a hospital ceiling. Better than the barrel of a gun. Better than the inside of a car trunk on a cold night in January, which is how most people in Bobby's line of work usually went.

No, Bobby Bologna died watching the greatest basketball player of all time sink a seventeen-foot jumper over Bryon Russell to clinch the 1998 NBA Finals. He died in the middle of eighteen thousand screaming fans.

He died courtside, which he'd paid a small fortune and several large favors to secure. He died with mustard on his chin and joy in his heart and a hot dog lodged so deep in his throat that three paramedics couldn't dislodge it.

He died the way he lived.

Eating.

Loudly.

In public.

And nobody in Chicago would ever forget it.

The funny thing about legends is that they start dying the moment they stop talking.

Bobby Bologna had talked every day of his life. He talked about food.

He talked about loyalty. He talked about the Cubs and the Bears and the Bulls with a passion that bordered on religious. He talked about the proper way to order an Italian beef (dipped, with hot giardiniera, eaten leaning forward so the juice runs down your arms instead of your shirt, which is the *only* civilized method). He talked about his grandfather, who came over from Naples in 1892 and never learned more than thirty words of English but somehow built a produce empire that his children promptly ruined. He talked about respect, and tradition, and the fundamental moral bankruptcy of putting *ketchup* on a hot dog.

He talked, and talked, and talked.

And then, on the greatest night in Chicago sports history, he stopped.

But the city kept talking about him.

That's the thing about Chicago. The city doesn't forget. It just gets the story wrong on purpose, because the wrong version is usually better.

Within a week, there were already three versions of how Bobby Bologna died.

The first version said he choked on a hot dog. This was technically true, though it left out the part about Michael Jordan and the standing ovation and the seventeen thousand people who didn't notice a man dying fifteen feet from the court because they were too busy losing their minds over a basketball game.

The second version said he had a heart attack because the Bulls won.

This was romantic but medically inaccurate. Bobby's heart was fine. His windpipe was the problem.

The third version—and this was the one that stuck—said Bobby Bologna was so happy that Chicago finally got its sixth championship that his body simply couldn't contain the joy. His soul left his body at the exact moment Jordan released the ball, floating up through the rafters of the Delta Center and ascending directly to some sort of sports heaven where Ditka was God and the Cubs hadn't broken everyone's heart for ninety years.

This version was completely made up.

But it was Chicago, so people believed it anyway.

This is the story of the last year of Bobby Bologna's life.

It's a story about food and loyalty and the proper way to dispose of a body when the zoo isn't cooperating.

It's a story about Chicago in 1997 and 1998, when the city was drunk on basketball and nobody wanted to think about what came next.

It's a story about a crew of men who were not particularly smart, not particularly careful, and definitely not as smooth as they thought they were.

It's a story about how legends get made.

And it starts, like all good Chicago stories, with an argument about beef.

PART ONE

BOBBY ON TOP

Late Summer — Early Fall 1997

CHAPTER 1

Al's #1 Italian Beef — North Avenue, Chicago

Bobby Bologna believed in three things: Chicago.

Loyalty.

And eating like it might be your last meal.

Which, in retrospect, was maybe not the healthiest philosophy.

The morning sun hit North Avenue like a hangover, bright and unforgiving and entirely too cheerful for a Tuesday in late August. The air smelled like exhaust and cooking grease and that particular Chicago smell that meant the lake was doing something weird again. A bus groaned past, packed with people who had places to be and no intention of enjoying any of them.

Al's #1 Italian Beef sat between a dry cleaner that hadn't been open since Reagan and a check-cashing place that definitely had. The sign was old and faded and missing the 'A' in 'Al's,' but nobody cared because everyone who mattered already knew where it was.

The neighborhood was changing, like every neighborhood in Chicago was always changing, but Al's stayed the same. It had survived disco. It had survived Reagan. It had survived the fire of '89, which was actually just a grease fire in the back that Tony the dishwasher put out with his apron and a lot of profanity. It would survive whatever came next, because places like this didn't die. They just got more authentic.

Inside, the place was small and loud and perfect.

Fluorescent lights that buzzed like angry bees. Laminate counters scarred with decades of elbows and spilled gravy. A menu board that hadn't changed since Kennedy was still not shot yet. The walls were covered with old photos of people nobody recognized anymore—neighborhood guys from the sixties and seventies who had probably all done something interesting before they died or moved to Schaumburg, which was basically the same thing.

The fryers hissed. Beef got chopped with a rhythm that could have been music. Somebody in the back yelled something in Italian that was probably an insult but sounded like opera.

This was sacred ground.

And Bobby Bologna was here for communion.

Bobby stood in line like he owned the place.

He did not own the place.

He had, however, once been politely asked not to lean on the counter so hard after cracking it during an argument about giardiniera ratios. This was three years ago, and the crack was still there, running through the laminate like a scar from a war nobody remembered. Bobby considered it a point of pride that his passion for condiments had left a permanent mark on the establishment.

He was a big man, Bobby Bologna. Not fat—he *would* correct you on this immediately and possibly violently—but substantial. Solid. The kind of big that came from generations of Italian grandmothers who believed that skinny meant sick and that every problem could be solved with more pasta.

He wore a track suit even though he had never tracked anything in his life. The jacket was Sergio Tacchini, navy blue with white stripes, bought at a strip mall in Rosemont from a guy who definitely stole it from somewhere nicer. His hair was dark and slicked back with enough product to waterproof a small boat. His cologne could be detected from approximately thirty feet away and smelled like someone had tried to bottle the concept of "trying too hard."

He was forty-three years old.

He had never left Illinois.

He had never wanted to.

Why would he? Everything he needed was right here. The food. The weather, even when it was trying to kill you, which was most of the time.

The people who understood that being from Chicago wasn't just geography—it was a personality trait. A medical condition. A religion with the Bears as its prophets and deep-dish pizza as its sacrament.

Bobby loved this city the way some men loved their wives.

Actually, more than that.

Bobby's wife had left him in 1994, and he barely noticed because the Bulls were making their first championship run and *priorities were priorities.*

"Two dipped, one wet, one dry," Bobby announced to nobody in particular. "And whatever the hell Nicky gets, but no giardiniera. He cries."

14

Behind him, Vinny 'The Mayor' Capozzi was arguing with a cab driver outside about parking.

Neither of them owned the car in question.

This was not unusual.

Vinny 'The Mayor' Capozzi had earned his nickname not because he had any political ambitions—Vinny's politics consisted entirely of "whoever's less annoying"—but because he had opinions about everything and shared them with the enthusiasm of a man running for office. He had opinions about parking, about traffic, about the proper way to merge onto the Kennedy, about whether the new mayor was better than the old mayor (he wasn't), about the designated hitter rule (an abomination before God and man), about the correct ratio of mustard to onions on a Maxwell Street Polish (two to one, minimum, and if you disagreed you were probably from Wisconsin), and about approximately six hundred other topics that nobody had asked about.

He was five-foot-seven, which he claimed was five-foot-nine, and had a mustache that looked like a caterpillar had died on his upper lip and he'd decided to keep it out of respect. He was wearing a Members Only jacket that had somehow survived from 1986 and refused to die.

Right now, he was explaining to a cab driver why parking in front of a fire hydrant was actually fine if you kept the engine running.

The cab driver disagreed.

This disagreement had escalated to the pointing stage.

"You can't tell me where to park!" Vinny shouted, even though the cab driver was not telling him where to park, because Vinny was not in a car.

"I'm not telling you anything!" the cab driver shouted back. "I'm telling the guy whose car that is!"

"Well, where is he?"

"I don't know! That's your problem!"

Inside, Bobby watched through the window and shook his head.

"Vinny's gonna get arrested before lunch," he said.

Sol 'Numbers' Rosen didn't look up from his newspaper. "Statistically, he gets arrested more often after lunch. The morning is actually our safest window."

Sol was the crew's accountant, which in this case meant he kept track of who owed them money, who they owed money to, and how long until both of those numbers became everyone's problem.

He was forty-three years old, Jewish, and had a degree in economics from DePaul that his mother had framed and hung in her kitchen next to a portrait of Sandy Koufax. He had not used that degree for anything legal since approximately 1987, which was when he'd figured out that the illegal applications paid significantly better and required fewer meetings.

Sol was the only member of the crew who read newspapers. He subscribed to the Tribune and the Sun-Times, because he believed in hearing both sides of any story, even when both sides were wrong. He was currently reading about the Cubs' latest collapse, which he found comforting in its predictability.

He was thin where Bobby was thick, quiet where Bobby was loud, and careful where Bobby was reckless. They had known each other since third grade at St. Alphonsus, where Bobby had beaten up a kid who was making fun of Sol's yarmulke, and Sol had done Bobby's math homework for the next eight years in gratitude.

It was not a traditional friendship.

But it had lasted.

"You're reading about the Cubs?" Bobby asked. "Why do you torture yourself?"

"It's not torture. It's meditation. The Cubs losing reminds me that the universe has order."

"That's sad, Sol."

"Yes. But it's consistent."

Nicky 'Peanuts' Moretti stood near the menu board, staring at it with the intensity of a man trying to decode ancient scripture.

The menu had not changed in thirty years.

Nicky had been coming here for fifteen.

He still stared at it every time like the words might rearrange themselves into something new.

Nicky was twenty-nine years old, though he had the energy of a golden retriever and the attention span of a goldfish. Nobody was entirely sure how he'd ended up in organized crime. Bobby's working theory was that Nicky had wandered into a meeting once looking for a bathroom and just never left.

He was loyal, which counted for something. He was strong, which counted for more. And he was enthusiastic, which occasionally counted against him when that enthusiasm was directed at terrible ideas.

His nickname came from his love of peanuts, which he ate constantly, including at times when eating peanuts was not appropriate. Funerals. Court appearances. That one job where they were supposed to be hiding in a warehouse and Nicky's crunching almost got them all killed.

"Hey, Bobby," Nicky said, without looking away from the menu.

"You think they'd ever add, like, a chicken option?"

The entire restaurant went quiet.

Not silent—there was still the hiss of the fryers and the clatter from the kitchen—but the humans went quiet. Every head turned. Every conversation paused.

Bobby turned slowly, like a man who had just heard something he needed to verify before responding.

"What did you just say?"

"I was just thinking—"

"In a beef place?"

"I know, but—"

"In Chicago?"

Nicky finally looked away from the menu. His face had gone pale. "I didn't mean—"

"You ask about *chicken* in a *beef* place, Nicky. In Chicago. In my presence."

Sol sighed without looking up from his newspaper. "And we were doing so well."

Frankie 'Legit' Petrucci, who had been standing near the napkin dispensers counting cash for reasons nobody understood, finally spoke up.

"He didn't mean anything by it, Bobby. Right, Nicky? You didn't mean anything."

Nicky nodded vigorously, his head bobbing like a dashboard ornament on a bumpy road. "I definitely didn't mean anything. I don't even like chicken. I hate chicken. Chicken is the worst meat. The absolute worst."

Bobby held his gaze for a long moment.

Then he smiled.

"Get him a beef. Dry. No giardiniera. He cries when it's spicy."

"I don't cry," Nicky protested. "My eyes water."

"That's crying," Vinny shouted from the doorway, having apparently won or abandoned his argument with the cab driver. "That's man crying."

17

"It's not the same—"

"Yes it is."

"Eyes watering is like a medical thing—"

"So is crying."

Sol turned a page in his newspaper. "We are going to die because of this conversation."

Frankie 'Legit' Petrucci was thirty-six years old and had earned his nickname because he was constantly trying to run legitimate businesses.

This never worked.

He'd tried a car wash that was just a front for stolen car parts. He'd tried a pizza place that was just a front for stolen pizza. He'd tried a dry cleaning business that was just a front for money laundering, but then he'd actually started caring about the dry cleaning and nearly lost the whole operation because he couldn't stop giving people discounts.

Frankie wanted desperately to be a normal businessman. He wanted to pay taxes and attend chamber of commerce meetings and complain about zoning regulations like a real American. But every time he got close, something went wrong. A supplier turned out to be connected. A customer turned out to be a cop. A building inspector turned out to be taking bribes from the other crew.

Chicago wasn't set up for legitimate business.

So Frankie kept doing what he knew, and he kept counting cash near napkin dispensers, and he kept hoping that someday, somehow, he'd find a way out that didn't involve a body bag or a witness protection program.

He was also the most nervous member of the crew, which was saying something, because they were all nervous about different things. But Frankie was nervous about everything. He was nervous about cops. He was nervous about other crews. He was nervous about cholesterol, which seemed irrelevant given his profession but which he still thought about every time he ate a beef sandwich.

"The counter guy looks stressed today," Frankie whispered to nobody.

"You think he's a cop?"

Sol didn't look up. "Counter Marco has worked here for twenty-seven years."

"That's a long cover."

"That's dedication to beef, Frankie. Try to focus."

The guy behind the counter was indeed named Marco, though everybody called him 'Counter Marco' to distinguish him from 'Back

Marco,' who worked in the kitchen and had not spoken to Counter Marco since an incident at a family barbecue in 1994 that neither of them would discuss.

Both Marco's were sixty-something and built like fire hydrants, with forearms that suggested they had been slicing beef since before most of the people in line were born. Counter Marco had a scar on his left hand from an incident with a meat slicer in 1978, and he showed it to new customers as a warning about respecting the equipment.

He slid the sandwiches down the counter with the practiced efficiency of a man who had done this approximately four million times.

"Two dipped, one wet, one dry, one pathetic."

"Hey," Nicky said. "That's mean."

"You ordered a dry beef with no giardiniera. What do you want me to call it? Heroic?"

Bobby picked up the sandwiches and distributed them to his crew like a priest handing out communion at Easter mass. There was a ritual to it. A reverence. This was not just food. This was tradition. This was identity.

This was Chicago, on bread, with gravy.

"To health," Bobby said, raising his sandwich.

Sol muttered, "We're going to prison."

They took their first bites in silence.

This was rare.

This was spiritual.

The beef at Al's #1 was not the best beef in Chicago. That was a matter of heated debate among people who took such debates seriously, which in Chicago was approximately everyone. Some said Mr. Beef on Orleans was better. Some swore by Johnnie's in Elmwood Park. Some claimed that Portillo's had gone corporate but was still secretly the best, and these people were usually from the suburbs and could not be trusted.

But Al's #1 was Bobby's spot.

It had been his father's spot before him.

It had been his grandfather's spot before that, back when the neighborhood was different and the beef was probably the same because the recipe hadn't changed since Eisenhower.

Bobby's grandfather had come over from Naples in 1892, part of the great wave of Italian immigration that transformed whole neighborhoods of Chicago from German and Irish to Italian in the span of a generation.

He had worked on the railroads, then in the stockyards, then in produce, building something from nothing through a combination of hard work and practices that his grandchildren would later call "entrepreneurial" and law enforcement would call "a conspiracy to commit extortion."

Bobby's father had inherited the produce business and run it into the ground through a combination of gambling, drinking, and a genuine inability to understand basic accounting. By the time Bobby was old enough to take over, there was nothing left to take over except debts and grudges.

So Bobby had done what generations of Chicago men had done before him: he'd figured out how to make money in ways that didn't show up on tax returns.

And he'd kept coming to Al's, because some things were sacred.

Sol ruined it.

He always ruined it.

"We got problems," Sol said, still holding his sandwich but no longer eating it, which for Sol was the equivalent of screaming.

Bobby chewed thoughtfully. "Define problems."

"North Side's moving into northwest territory. Schaumburg, mostly. And they're not being quiet about it."

Vinny scoffed. "They don't own the mall. That's like a pigeon claiming it owns the parking lot."

"They think they do," Sol said. "And Tony Smiles doesn't think you're good for business."

Tony 'Smiles' Caravelli was the head of the North Side crew, which operated out of a bar in Lincoln Park that served cocktails with ingredients nobody could pronounce and charged prices that would make a mortgage broker blush. The place was called something pretentious—Bobby could never remember what—and attracted the kind of people who thought organized crime was something that happened in movies and Martin Scorsese was exaggerating. Tony himself drank kombucha. *In public.* He had been seen ordering a quinoa bowl at his own bar, which, as far as Bobby was concerned, was a bigger crime than anything Tony had actually done. Tony also pronounced "giardiniera" *wrong* on purpose because he thought the correct pronunciation was pretentious, which was the *most pretentious reason in the world* to mispronounce something.

Tony was called 'Smiles' because he smiled constantly. When he was happy, he smiled. When he was angry, he smiled. When he was threatening to have someone's kneecaps *redesigned*, he smiled. This was unsettling in a way that made even experienced criminals uncomfortable.

A smiling man is dangerous because you can never tell what he's really thinking. A man who smiles while describing how he's going to dispose of your body is dangerous because he's clearly thought about it enough to enjoy the process.

Bobby wiped his mouth with a napkin. "Tony Smiles can smile at my ass."

Frankie whispered, "I just think—maybe—please don't say that in public."

"Why? Everyone here knows me."

"That's why you shouldn't say it in public."

Nicky raised his sandwich. "I think Tony Smiles is creepy. Right? Tell me I'm right."

"That's because he smiles when he shouldn't," Sol explained, finally taking a bite of his beef. "That's not a friendly trait. Studies show that inappropriate smiling is associated with psychopathy, narcissism, and *real estate sales*."

Vinny pointed his sandwich at Sol. "I knew a real estate guy once. Smiled like that. Tried to sell my grandmother a condo in Boca."

Frankie frowned. "What happened?"

"She bought it."

"That's not a story about psychopathy, Vinny. That's a story about your grandmother."

"My grandmother lives in Boca now. Her husband doesn't. You tell me which one's the psychopath."

Bobby leaned back against the counter, careful not to crack it again.

"Look. We eat. We breathe. We handle our business. Nobody tells Bobby Bologna where he can stand."

Vinny nodded aggressively. "Yeah! That's like—" He searched. "That's like a guy telling a bear where it can crap. That's the energy."

Nicky raised his sandwich. "To standing! Right, Bobby? Right?"

Everyone stared at him.

"What?" Nicky said.

Sol rubbed his temples. "We are going to die because of *enthusiasm*."

That's when Bobby noticed the guy.

Two spots down the counter. Tourist, probably—you could tell by the clean shoes and the bewildered expression and the way he held his hot dog like he wasn't sure which end was up.

He was maybe thirty, dressed in the kind of khakis and polo shirt combination that suggested middle management at a company that made something boring. His hair was too neat. His posture was too good. He had probably never been punched in his life, and it showed.

And he was drowning his hot dog in ketchup.

Bobby froze.

He stared.

The ketchup kept coming, a red flood that would have been appropriate for a crime scene but was absolutely criminal on a Chicago-style hot dog.

Slowly, like a man watching a car accident in slow motion, Bobby turned to his crew.

"You seeing this?"

Vinny followed his gaze. "Oh, come on."

Nicky whispered, "Is that allowed?"

Frankie said, "I don't think there's a law—"

Bobby was already walking.

There are certain things you don't do in Chicago.

You don't root for the Packers. Ever. Not ironically. Not because your spouse is from Wisconsin. Not because you lost a bet. The Packers are the enemy, and cheering for them is treason punishable by social exile.

You don't call it Willis Tower. It's the Sears Tower. It will always be the Sears Tower. You can pry that name from Chicago's cold, dead, architecturally proud hands.

You don't claim that New York has better pizza. New York has good pizza—thin, foldable, acceptable in an emergency—but it's not better pizza. It's different pizza. And anyone who says otherwise has never experienced the religious transcendence of a proper Lou Malnati's deep dish, where the cheese stretches like a dream and the sauce sits on top like God intended.

And you absolutely, under any circumstances, for any reason, no matter how lost you are or how much you think you know about condiments, put ketchup on a hot dog.

This isn't a preference. It's a moral position.

The National Hot Dog and Sausage Council, which is a real organization that exists for reasons nobody questions, has officially declared that ketchup on a hot dog is unacceptable after the age of eighteen. The Chicago History Museum has exhibits about the Chicago-style hot dog that do not mention ketchup except to condemn it.

There are restaurants in this city that will refuse to serve you if you ask for ketchup on your dog, and these restaurants are considered pillars of the community.

A Chicago-style hot dog has rules. An all-beef frankfurter on a poppy seed bun. Yellow mustard. Chopped white onions. Bright green sweet pickle relish. A dill pickle spear. Tomato slices or wedges. Sport peppers.

A dash of celery salt.

No ketchup.

Never ketchup.

Ketchup is a child's condiment, suitable for French fries and the insecure. On a hot dog, it's a declaration that you don't understand what you're eating, that you don't respect the craft, that you have no business being in this city.

Bobby Bologna knew all of this.

He lived by it.

And now, in his spot, in his neighborhood, some tourist was committing crimes against Chicago food culture.

This could not stand.

Bobby leaned over the man's shoulder. "Hey, buddy."

The guy looked up and smiled nervously, ketchup still dripping from the squeeze bottle in his hand. "Yeah?"

"You from around here?"

"Uh—yeah." The guy nodded. "Grew up in Naperville. Just moved back to the city a few months ago."

Naperville. That explained it. Naperville was a suburb about thirty miles west, technically part of the Chicago metropolitan area but spiritually about as Chicago as Orlando. People from Naperville said "pop"

instead of "soda" and thought that counted as local flavor.

Bobby pointed at the hot dog. "Then why are you committing crimes?"

The man blinked. "It's just ketchup."

That's when the entire line turned on him.

"You don't put ketchup on a hot dog!" an old guy shouted, his face red with decades of accumulated condiment opinions.

"That's disrespectful!" someone else yelled.

A woman in a Bears jersey shook her head in disgust. "My grandfather would rise from his grave."

"This is exactly what's wrong with this country," announced a man who had not been part of the conversation until now and would probably continue announcing things about what was wrong with this country for the foreseeable future.

The guy from Naperville looked around with growing horror. "I just wanted—"

"Nobody cares what you wanted," Bobby said, not unkindly. "What you wanted was wrong."

Before anyone could fully process what was happening, Vinny grabbed the man by the collar and dragged him backward.

Nicky tripped over a chair trying to help.

Frankie screamed, "WE ARE NOT DOING THIS AGAIN."

Sol closed his eyes.

The guy went down under a flurry of righteous Chicago fury. Not a real beating—nobody wanted to actually hurt him—but a ceremonial humiliation, a correction, a lesson delivered through the medium of controlled chaos.

His hot dog flew through the air and landed on the floor, where it belonged.

The ketchup bottle rolled under a table.

Not one employee intervened.

Counter Marco just shook his head. "Every week, I swear."

Back Marco poked his head out from the kitchen, saw what was happening, and retreated. He had his own problems.

Afterward, Bobby crouched next to the man and patted his shoulder.

"Learn from this," he said, genuinely meaning it.

The man groaned something that might have been an apology or might have been a request for medical attention.

"You're not hurt. You're educated. There's a difference." Bobby stood up and brushed off his knees. "Now, you're gonna get up, you're gonna order another dog, and you're gonna do it right this time. Mustard. Onions. Relish. The whole Chicago. And then you're gonna eat it like a man from this city."

The guy looked up at him with something like terror.

"And if I see ketchup near your face again," Bobby continued, "we're gonna have a longer conversation. You understand?"

The man nodded.

"Good." Bobby offered him a hand up. "Welcome back to Chicago."

Outside, Bobby stepped into the sunlight and took a deep breath.

The morning was heating up, the August humidity settling in like a guest who'd overstayed their welcome. Traffic crawled past. A bus honked at a car that had stopped for no apparent reason. Somewhere, a dog barked at something only dogs could see.

This was his city.

Every block of it. Every corner. Every cracked sidewalk and rusted fire escape and grease-stained storefront.

"That was unnecessary," Sol said, appearing beside him.

"It was educational."

"It was assault."

"Light assault. Motivational assault."

Sol sighed. "We have actual problems, Bobby. Tony Smiles is not going to be handled with condiment enforcement."

Bobby watched the traffic for a moment. "You know what my grandfather used to say?"

"Something about beef?"

"He used to say that a man who can't protect what he loves doesn't deserve to love anything. He meant the neighborhood. The family. The food." Bobby turned to look at Sol. "You think I'm gonna let Tony Smiles, who drinks cocktails with fruit in them, tell me where I can and can't do business?"

Sol was quiet for a moment. "Tony Smiles has more men. More money. More connections downtown. We're not in the same weight class, Bobby."

"Then we fight smarter."

"Do we? Do we fight smarter? Because what I saw in there was not smart."

Bobby grinned. "That was community outreach."

Vinny emerged from the restaurant, brushing off his jacket. "That guy definitely peed himself a little."

"That's learning," Bobby said. "Fear is the first step to wisdom."

Frankie came out next, pale and sweating. "I need to lie down."

"You always need to lie down."

"I have anxiety, Bobby. Documented anxiety."

"Then get undocumented. We got work to do."

Nicky bounded out last, somehow still holding half a sandwich. "That was fun! We should do community outreach more often."

Sol rubbed his temples. "I'm going to die surrounded by *idiots*."

They walked to the car—a black Lincoln Town Car that Bobby had won in a poker game and Frankie had somehow managed to register legally, which was maybe the most legitimate thing he'd ever done.

Bobby slid into the back seat with the comfort of a man who knew his place in the world. Vinny took the wheel because he liked driving and nobody else trusted him not to give a running commentary if he was in the passenger seat. Frankie sat shotgun, nervously checking the mirrors. Nicky and Sol squeezed into the back with Bobby.

"Where to, boss?" Vinny asked.

"Gino Giorgetti's. We got a meeting."

Sol straightened. "With who?"

"People who matter." Bobby leaned back into the seat. "Time to talk business."

Vinny pulled away from the curb, nearly hitting a cyclist who shouted something that probably wasn't a compliment.

"I hate cyclists," Vinny announced.

"Everybody hates cyclists," Nicky agreed.

"They think they own the road."

"They don't own anything."

"Exactly."

Sol looked at Bobby. "This meeting—is this about Tony Smiles?"

Bobby watched the city roll past. The bodegas and the barber shops and the old buildings that had seen a hundred years of arguments about territory and respect and who got to stand where.

"This meeting is about making sure Tony Smiles knows where he belongs. And where he doesn't."

Sol nodded slowly. "And where's that?"

Bobby smiled.

"Not in my city."

CHAPTER 2

Gino Giorgetti's — The Loop

Gino Giorgetti's didn't serve food.

It served statements.

The kind of place where men with too much money and not enough conscience went to feel respectable while discussing things that were neither legal nor polite.

The restaurant occupied the ground floor of a building on a side street off Michigan Avenue, close enough to the Magnificent Mile to feel important, far enough to avoid the tourists. The exterior was understated—just a brass plaque and a burgundy awning—but the interior was all dark wood and white tablecloths and the kind of hushed elegance that whispered "we don't take reservations from just anyone."

Bobby loved it.

Not because he fit in—he absolutely did not, and the maitre d' made this clear every time through the slight tightening of his smile—but because he could afford it anyway.

Money was its own kind of elegance.

They arrived at noon precisely, because noon was when Gino's opened for lunch and Bobby liked to be first. First meant best seats. First meant respect. First meant the waiters hadn't started their shift already exhausted by difficult customers, so they still had enough energy to pretend that serving you was a privilege.

The maitre d' was a man named Pierre who was definitely not French and whose real name was probably Pete, but who had committed to the bit so thoroughly that even his own mother probably called him Pierre now.

"Mr. Bologna," Pierre said, with exactly enough warmth to be polite and exactly enough distance to be clear that he wished Bobby would stop coming here. "Your usual table?"

"No. The back room. We got business."

Pierre's smile tightened another quarter inch. "Of course. Right this way."

They followed him through the main dining room, past tables of lawyers and bankers and the occasional minor celebrity who was not quite famous enough for anywhere nicer. Sol nodded at a man he recognized from a real estate deal that had gone sideways in 1994. Vinny glared at a waiter who had once given him a look he didn't like. Nicky stared at everything like he'd never been inside a building with cloth napkins before.

The back room was small, private, and had no windows. This was intentional. The walls were paneled in dark oak, the lighting was dim, and the table was round, because round tables meant nobody sat at the head, which meant nobody was technically in charge, which meant everyone could pretend they were equals even when they obviously weren't.

There were already two men at the table.

Johnny "No Thumbs" Carbone sat on the far side, nursing a glass of red wine that cost more than Nicky's monthly rent. He was sixty-two years old, had been in the business since Nixon, and had earned his nickname through a combination of a carpentry accident and strategic rumor-spreading. He actually had both thumbs. But the name stuck, and names that stuck were names that worked.

Johnny ran a crew on the South Side, mostly construction and union work, with some gambling on the side. He was old school in the truest sense—more interested in making money quietly than making noise loudly—and he had survived three different federal investigations through a combination of good lawyers and better timing.

He nodded at Bobby. "Bobby Bologna. You're late."

"I'm first."

"Then everyone else is later."

Beside him sat a younger man named Marco Benedetti—not to be confused with either of the Marco's from Al's—who was in his late thirties and dressed like someone who had read about Italian fashion in a magazine and tried too hard to replicate it. He was Johnny's nephew, being groomed for something, though nobody was entirely sure what.

"Gentlemen," Bobby said, taking his seat. "We eating first or talking first?"

"Eating first," Johnny said. "Always eating first. Talking on an empty stomach leads to bad decisions."

"Words of wisdom."

"Words of experience."

The food arrived without anyone ordering, because Bobby had called ahead and because the kitchen at Gino's knew exactly what men in back rooms wanted: steak, thick and rare, with potatoes that had been prepared by someone who understood that potatoes were serious business.

They ate in relative silence for the first few minutes, the only sounds being the clink of cutlery and Sol's quiet sigh of appreciation at a properly cooked ribeye.

Bobby watched Johnny eat. There was information in how a man handled his food. Johnny cut his steak with precision, small pieces, chewing thoroughly, never talking with his mouth full. This was a man who planned ahead, who didn't rush, who understood that patience was its own form of aggression.

"So," Johnny said finally, setting down his knife and fork in parallel lines—the international symbol for "I'm done eating, let's talk business."

"Tony Smiles."

Bobby leaned back. "What about him?"

"He's moving northwest. Schaumburg, Oak Brook, the malls. Territory that used to be—" Johnny paused meaningfully. "—open."

"Open means available. Available means I can operate there too."

"Tony don't see it that way."

"Tony can see it any way he likes. Doesn't change the geography."

Johnny picked up his wine glass, swirled it thoughtfully. "Tony's got connections downtown. City hall. The aldermen. He's made himself useful to people who make decisions."

Sol spoke up for the first time. "We know. We've been tracking his political investments."

Johnny looked at him with interest. "The accountant speaks."

"Rarely. But accurately."

Bobby smiled. "Sol's my secret weapon. While everyone else is counting guns, he's counting money. And money tells the real story."

"What story is that?"

"That Tony Smiles is overextended. He's spending on politicians like they're investments, but politicians aren't investments. They're rentals. You pay and pay and the moment you stop paying, they find someone else."

Johnny considered this. "You think he's vulnerable?"

"I think he's confident, which is worse. Vulnerable men are careful. Confident men make mistakes."

"And you're going to wait for him to make a mistake?"

Bobby smiled. "I'm going to help him make one."

The conversation continued for another hour, covering territory and percentages and the delicate calculus of how much to push and when to pull back.

They discussed the Schaumburg mall situation, where Tony had been muscling into protection arrangements that Bobby's crew had been eyeing.

They discussed the union situation on the West Side, where loyalties were shifting and old alliances were fraying. They discussed the upcoming city council elections, where three seats were in play and the outcomes could reshape who had influence over what.

Johnny was cautious, as old men tended to be. He'd seen too many young hotshots flame out, too many sure things collapse, too many confident plans end in federal indictments. He advised patience.

Observation. Letting Tony overextend himself and then picking up the pieces.

Bobby listened respectfully.

Then he ignored most of it.

Between the main course and dessert, Bobby casually ordered a beating.

"There's a guy on Fullerton," he said, cutting into a slice of tiramisu that had cost eighteen dollars and was worth every penny. "Name's Deluca. Owns a body shop. Owes us thirty-two hundred from a loan last March."

Sol nodded, confirming the numbers.

"He's been dodging calls. Making excuses. Told Frankie's guy that he's got cash flow problems and needs another month."

Johnny raised an eyebrow. "Thirty-two hundred? That's hardly worth the trouble."

"It's not about the money. It's about the thirty-seven other guys who also owe us money and are watching to see what happens to the one who doesn't pay."

Johnny nodded slowly. "The math of fear."

"Exactly." Bobby took a bite of tiramisu. "Vinny, you and Nicky handle it. Nothing permanent. Just educational."

Vinny grinned. "My specialty."

Nicky perked up. "Can we stop for food after?"

"You just ate."

"That was an hour ago."

The violence and the fine dining. The business discussions and the casual orders for broken bones. The way he could talk about art and culture one minute—he had opinions about the Art Institute, about Chicago architecture, about the proper way to appreciate a Monet—and the next minute send his men to beat a mechanic with a pipe.

Some people thought this was hypocrisy.

Bobby thought it was balance.

The city was built on both. The beauty and the brutality. The museums and the meatpacking plants. The Magnificent Mile and the midnight alleyways.

You couldn't love Chicago without loving all of it.

And Bobby loved all of it.

The meeting ended with handshakes and promises to stay in touch, which in this business meant actual communication rather than the usual polite fiction.

Johnny left first, his nephew trailing behind like a well-dressed shadow. Bobby's crew stayed for coffee—espresso, properly made, not the watered-down garbage you got at chain restaurants—and a final review of the situation.

"That went well," Frankie said, nervously.

"It went," Bobby corrected. "Whether it went well depends on what happens next."

Sol pulled out a small notebook—he still preferred paper, claiming that electronics could be seized and subpoenaed while paper could be burned. "We need to move on Schaumburg within the next two weeks. Tony's consolidating his position there. If we wait too long, it'll cost three times as much to push back."

"Then we don't wait."

"And the thing with Deluca?"

"Handle it tonight. Make sure the right people see. Make sure the right people talk."

Vinny cracked his knuckles. "With pleasure."

They left Gino's into the afternoon sun, the Loop bustling with office workers on lunch breaks and tourists who had wandered away from

31

Michigan Avenue looking for something authentic and had instead found a Potbelly's.

Bobby stood on the sidewalk for a moment, watching the city move.

"You know what I love about Chicago?" he said.

"The food?" Nicky guessed.

"The weather?" Vinny tried. "I hate the weather."

"Then why would I love the weather?"

"I don't know how you think."

Sol sighed. "Nobody does."

Bobby smiled. "I love that it's honest. Cold in the winter, miserable in the summer, beautiful for about three weeks in between. It doesn't pretend to be something it's not. It doesn't apologize for being hard. It just is what it is, and you either deal with it or you leave."

Frankie blinked. "That's... surprisingly philosophical."

"I contain multitudes."

"Do you know what that means?"

"Not really. I heard it somewhere." Bobby clapped his hands.

"Alright. Vinny, Nicky—Deluca tonight. Sol—start working on Schaumburg. Frankie—do whatever it is you do when you're not having anxiety."

"I have anxiety while doing other things."

"Then do those other things."

Bobby started walking toward the car, his crew falling in behind him like ducklings following a particularly well-dressed mother duck.

"Tomorrow we're going to the Art Institute," he announced. "I feel like looking at paintings."

Sol closed his eyes. "Please tell me there's a business reason for that."

"There's a cultural reason. Culture is business. Everything is business."

"That's not comforting."

"It's not supposed to be."

They reached the car, piled in, and pulled away from the curb.

Behind them, Gino Giorgetti's returned to its quiet elegance, waiters clearing tables and preparing for the dinner crowd.

And somewhere on Fullerton Avenue, a man named Deluca was about to have a very bad evening.

Bobby's Apartment — The Morning After

Bobby lived in a condo in Lincoln Park.

Not flashy. Not modest. Somewhere in between.

The kind of place that said its owner had money but did not need to prove it. The kind of place that was comfortable without being ostentatious.

The morning after Game Five, Bobby woke up early.

This was unusual.

Bobby was not a morning person. He believed that any activity requiring consciousness before ten AM was fundamentally uncivilized.

But today was different.

Today he needed to prepare.

The apartment was quiet.

Bobby lived alone. Had lived alone since his divorce. Had grown to appreciate the silence in a way he never expected.

Silence meant no arguments. No compromises. No having to explain yourself to someone who would never understand.

Silence meant freedom.

He made coffee.

Strong. Black. The way his father used to make it.

Stood by the window and watched the city wake up.

Lincoln Park was beautiful in the morning. Trees and joggers and people walking dogs and the general bustle of a neighborhood that took itself seriously but not too seriously.

Bobby had lived here for twelve years.

Knew every block. Every restaurant. Every face that mattered.

This was home.

The phone rang.

Sol.

"You're awake early."

"Couldn't sleep. Too excited."

"About Utah?"

"About everything. This feels important, Sol. This feels like the end of something."

"The end of the season."

"More than that. The end of an era. Jordan isn't coming back after this. Pippen is leaving. Phil is leaving. Everything we've watched for the last decade is about to be over."

"That's surprisingly melancholy for a man who just watched his team win."

33

"I contain multitudes."

Bobby hung up and went back to the window.

The city was fully awake now.

Traffic building. People rushing. The ordinary chaos of an ordinary Wednesday in an ordinary neighborhood.

Except it was not ordinary.

Not to Bobby.

Every day was a gift. Every moment was borrowed time. Every sunrise might be the last one you see.

That was what the life taught you.

To appreciate what you had.

Because it could disappear at any moment.

He showered. Dressed. Made breakfast.

Eggs and bacon and toast. The same breakfast he made every morning. The ritual that grounded him. That reminded him who he was and where he came from.

His mother used to make this breakfast.

Every morning before school.

Standing in the kitchen of their house in Bridgeport, wearing an apron that had seen better days, humming songs from the old country.

Bobby missed her.

Missed her every day.

Hoped she could see him now.

Hoped she was proud.

The crew gathered at noon.

Same place as always. Frankie's office above the dry cleaner.

They sat around the table that had seen a thousand meetings. A thousand plans. A thousand arguments about things that seemed important at the time and would be forgotten within weeks.

"Utah," Bobby said. "Tomorrow. First flight out."

"Who is going?" Frankie asked.

"Me. Sol. Vinny. Nicky. You can stay here, Frankie. Someone needs to hold down the fort."

Frankie looked relieved.

Everyone pretended not to notice.

They spent the afternoon making arrangements.

Flights. Hotels. Transportation.

The logistics of traveling to another city to watch a basketball game that might be the most important basketball game of their lives.

Bobby handled none of it.

That was Sol's job.

Bobby's job was to believe. To maintain faith. To hold the vision of victory that would carry them through whatever came next.

"What if they lose?" Nicky asked quietly.

Everyone stopped.

"They won't lose," Bobby said.

"But what if they do?"

Bobby looked at him.

"Then we come home. We wait. We hope. And we believe that Game Seven will be different. Because that's what fans do. We believe even when believing is stupid. We hope even when hope is foolish. We love even when love breaks our hearts."

Nicky nodded.

"I just wanted to know."

"Now you know."

That night, Bobby didn't sleep.

He lay in bed, staring at the ceiling, thinking about everything that had led to this moment.

The years of watching. The years of hoping. The years of believing that this team, this city, this impossible collection of talent and will and desire, could do something that had never been done before.

Six championships.

In eight years.

A dynasty that would never be repeated.

A legacy that would last forever.

And he would be there to see it end.

Would be there when the final buzzer sounded.

Would be there when the confetti fell.

Would be there.

That was all that mattered.

Being there.

Bearing witness.

Living the moment that would become memory.

He fell asleep sometime after three.

Dreamed of basketball and hot dogs and a father who had taught him to love this game.

And when he woke up, it was time to go to Utah.

Time to watch history happen.

Time to become legend.

Even if he did not know it yet.

INTERLUDE: 3 AM

Bobby's Apartment — Lincoln Park Bobby Bologna couldn't sleep.

This happened more often than anyone knew. The crew saw him as a force of nature—loud, certain, unstoppable. They didn't see the nights when he lay in bed staring at the ceiling, counting the cracks in the plaster like they were the years he had left.

Fifty-three.

Fifty-four if he made it to October.

His father had died at fifty-one. Heart attack. Too much stress, the doctors said. Too much weight. Too much of everything that made life worth living and simultaneously shortened it.

Bobby got out of bed and walked to the kitchen.

The apartment was nice. Nicer than anywhere he'd lived as a kid. Two bedrooms, even though he only used one. A view of the park, even though he rarely looked at it. Art on the walls that Angela had picked out before she left, which he kept because taking it down would mean admitting she wasn't coming back.

She wasn't coming back.

He knew that.

He'd known it for years.

But the art stayed.

In the kitchen, he opened the refrigerator and stared at its contents.

Leftover beef from Al's. Half a pizza from Gino's. Containers of things he'd meant to eat and never did. The refrigerator of a man who lived alone and pretended he didn't.

He wasn't hungry.

That was the strange part. Bobby Bologna was always hungry. Hunger was his defining characteristic, his reason for being, the engine that drove everything he did.

But at 3 AM, in the blue light of the refrigerator, he felt nothing.

Just empty.

He closed the refrigerator and walked to the window.

Chicago spread out below him. Streetlights and traffic signals and the distant glow of downtown. Somewhere out there, people were sleeping.

Somewhere out there, people were living lives that didn't involve territory disputes and loyalty oaths and the constant calculation of who was going to betray whom.

Normal people.

Bobby had never been normal.

He'd tried, once. Right after Angela left. He'd thought about getting out. Moving somewhere warm. Florida, maybe. Opening a restaurant.

Being just another guy who made sandwiches and watched the sunset.

He'd lasted three days.

Three days of quiet. Three days of nobody needing him. Three days of waking up without purpose.

He came back to Chicago on the fourth day and never mentioned it again.

The phone rang.

At 3 AM, a ringing phone meant trouble.

Bobby answered. "Yeah."

"Bobby. It's Marco. From the barbershop."

"Marco. It's three in the morning."

"I know. I'm sorry. But I heard something. Something you should know."

Bobby listened.

When Marco was done, Bobby hung up and stared at the phone for a long moment.

Tony Smiles was making moves. Quiet moves. The kind that wouldn't show up until it was too late to stop them.

Bobby should call Sol. Should wake up the crew. Should start planning countermeasures.

Instead, he sat down at the kitchen table and did nothing.

There was a photo on the table.

His parents. Wedding day. 1952.

His mother in a dress she'd made herself. His father in a suit he'd borrowed from his brother. Both of them smiling like they knew exactly how their lives would go and were happy about it.

They hadn't known, of course.

Nobody ever did.

His father would work himself to death in jobs that didn't appreciate him. His mother would clean houses for people who barely noticed she existed. They'd raise three sons in a two-bedroom house in Bridgeport, and two of those sons would die young—one in Vietnam, one in a car accident that might not have been an accident—and the third would become Bobby Bologna, who everyone knew and nobody really understood.

"What would you think of me?" Bobby asked the photo.

The photo didn't answer.

It never did.

The thing nobody understood about Bobby Bologna was that he didn't actually want any of this.

Not the territory. Not the respect. Not the constant performance of being Bobby Bologna, the man who was always on, always loud, always certain.

What he wanted was simpler.

He wanted to matter.

He wanted to wake up in the morning and know that his existence meant something. That he had built something. That when he died—and he knew he would die, probably sooner than he'd like—people would remember him as more than just a fat guy who loved food and yelled a lot.

He wanted to be loved.

Actually loved. Not respected. Not feared. Loved.

Angela had loved him once. Or he'd thought she had. But love, it turned out, couldn't survive the life he'd chosen. Couldn't survive the secrets and the absences and the constant fear that one day she'd get a phone call saying he wasn't coming home.

She'd left before that phone call could come.

Smart woman, Angela.

Smarter than him.

Bobby looked at the clock. 4:17 AM.

In three hours, he'd have to be Bobby Bologna again. Loud. Certain. Unstoppable.

But for now, in the quiet of his apartment, he was just Robert Bologna Jr., fifty-three years old, alone in the dark, wondering if any of it had been worth it.

He didn't have an answer.

He suspected he never would.

At 4:30, he finally went back to bed.

At 7:00, his alarm went off.

At 7:15, he was Bobby Bologna again, calling Sol about Tony Smiles, planning countermeasures, performing certainty he didn't feel.

Nobody knew about the night.

Nobody would ever know.

Some things you carried alone.

That was the price of being who he was.

And Bobby paid it.

Every night.

In the dark.

Where nobody could see.

CHAPTER 3

Gene & Jude's — River Grove

Two days later, Bobby decided the crew needed a field trip.

"Gene & Jude's," he announced at the morning meeting, which was really just everyone standing around Frankie's office drinking coffee that had been burnt since the Carter administration. "It's been too long."

Sol looked up from his laptop—he had finally given in to technology, though he kept his paper backups. "We were there three weeks ago."

"Like I said. Too long."

Vinny grinned. "I could eat a dog."

"I could eat six dogs," Nicky said.

"That's concerning."

"I'm a growing boy."

"You're thirty."

"Internally, I'm growing."

Gene & Jude's was a legend.

Not a legend like Bobby was trying to become—loud and memorable and probably ending badly—but a quiet legend, the kind that accumulated over decades of doing one thing perfectly and never apologizing for it.

The place had been operating in River Grove since 1946, which meant it had been serving hot dogs for longer than most of its customers had been alive. It was small, crowded, and had exactly one thing on the menu: hot dogs. Technically they also had tamales and fries, but nobody ordered tamales and the fries came with the dogs whether you asked for them or not.

There was no ketchup.

There was no seating.

There was no patience for people who didn't know what they wanted.

Bobby loved it.

They arrived at 11:30, which was early enough to avoid the worst of the lunch rush but late enough that the crew working the line had hit their rhythm.

The smell hit them first—grilling meat and frying potatoes and that particular combination of mustard and onion that was basically a controlled substance.

"God," Vinny breathed. "I missed this smell."

"We were here three weeks ago," Sol repeated.

"I missed it."

Bobby approached the counter with the confidence of a man who knew exactly what he was doing. The woman working the line—somewhere between fifty and seventy, it was impossible to tell—didn't look up.

"Four dogs, extra everything," Bobby said.

"Fries?"

"Obviously."

She still didn't look up as she started working. "You the guy who cracked the counter at Al's?"

Bobby blinked. "That was years ago."

"News travels."

Bobby turned to Sol. "How does she know about that?"

Sol shrugged. "Chicago's a small town pretending to be a big city. Everyone knows everyone's business."

"That's unsettling."

"That's networking."

They stood against the wall with their dogs and their fries, eating in that slightly hunched-forward posture that the paper wrapping demanded.

There were no plates at Gene & Jude's. No napkins, technically, though they kept a stack of tiny squares that served more as psychological comfort than actual function.

The dogs were perfect.

Depression-style, which meant they were steamed and then grilled, giving them that specific snap that Chicago dogs were famous for. The toppings were piled high—mustard, onion, relish, sport peppers—and the fries were dumped directly on top of everything, creating a combination that shouldn't work but absolutely did.

"This is why I stay in Chicago," Nicky said, his mouth full.

"Don't talk with food in your mouth," Frankie muttered. "It's disgusting."

"You're eating too."

"But I'm not talking."

"You're talking now."

"That's different."

Sol ate in silence, as he did most things, observing the other customers. Regular people. Working people. People who had never committed a crime more serious than speeding and who would be horrified to learn that the five men in track suits standing against the wall had collectively broken more laws than most prison populations.

Bobby watched a man about his own age at the counter, ordering for himself and what looked like two kids. Normal family. Normal life.

Normal everything.

He wondered, sometimes, what that would be like.

Then he took another bite of his hot dog and the wondering stopped.

That's when the guy walked in.

Early twenties. Suburban haircut. The kind of polo shirt that screamed "my parents pay for everything." He looked around with the slightly confused expression of someone who had seen this place on a food show and had driven out from wherever to experience it.

He approached the counter with the nervous energy of a man who wasn't sure if he was allowed to be somewhere.

"Hi," he said. "Could I get a hot dog with, um, ketchup?"

The woman behind the counter didn't even blink. "No."

"No?"

"We don't have ketchup."

"But it's a hot dog place."

"It's a Chicago hot dog place. We don't have ketchup."

The guy laughed nervously, like maybe this was a joke he wasn't getting. "Seriously though. Everyone has ketchup."

"Not here."

Bobby had stopped eating.

Vinny had stopped eating.

The entire restaurant had gotten very quiet.

The guy pressed on, apparently immune to the social cues that were screaming at him to stop.

"I just want a little ketchup. Just a little."

"We don't have it."

"That's crazy. Every restaurant has—"

Bobby stepped forward.

Not aggressively—he was still holding his hot dog, after all, and you don't waste a dog—but with enough presence that the guy noticed and turned.

"Hey, buddy."

"Yeah?"

"She said they don't have ketchup."

"Yeah, but—"

"So they don't have ketchup."

The guy looked around at the other customers, seeking support. He found none.

"Look, I just drove forty-five minutes to get here—"

"Then you should've done some research."

"I read about this place! It's supposed to be great!"

"It is great. And part of what makes it great is that they don't serve ketchup to people who don't understand what they're eating."

The guy's face was getting red now. "Who are you to tell me what to eat?"

Bobby smiled. Not the friendly smile. The other one.

"I'm nobody. But I'm nobody who's been eating here since before you were born, and I'm nobody who's going to stand here and watch you disrespect this place because you can't appreciate what's in front of you."

"It's just a hot dog!"

"Nothing is just anything."

The guy made a mistake.

He pointed at Bobby's chest.

"Listen, pal, I didn't come here to get lectured by some guy in a track suit about condiments—"

Vinny moved first.

Not Bobby—Vinny—because Vinny had been waiting for an excuse and this was better than any excuse he was going to manufacture himself.

He grabbed the guy's arm and twisted, spinning him around and slamming him face-first against the wall with a force that was probably more than necessary but definitely satisfying.

Nicky knocked over his own food trying to help, which was sad because he'd only eaten half.

Frankie screamed, "NOT AGAIN."

Sol closed his eyes.

The woman behind the counter sighed with the exhaustion of someone who had seen this exact scenario play out more times than she could count.

"Every week."

The other customers joined in, not because they wanted to fight—most of them had never been in a fight in their lives—but because this was Chicago and some instincts were deeper than civilization.

An old guy threw a punch that missed by three feet.

A woman in a Cubs jersey kicked at the guy's shins while yelling something about respecting tradition.

Someone's kid started crying, which seemed appropriate.

Bobby just stood there, still holding his hot dog, watching the chaos unfold with something approaching paternal pride.

"This is beautiful," he said to Sol.

"This is assault."

"Tomato, tomahto."

"That's not how that works."

It was over in less than a minute.

The guy was on the floor, covered in mustard and onion and what was probably someone else's fries. His polo shirt would never recover. His dignity had preceded the shirt into oblivion.

Bobby crouched down next to him.

"Learn from this."

The guy groaned.

"You're going to get up, you're going to leave, and you're going to think about what you did. And the next time you go to a Chicago institution, you're going to respect it."

Another groan.

"Or don't. And see what happens."

Bobby stood up and finished his hot dog in one triumphant bite.

"Let's go," he said to the crew. "I feel like visiting a museum."

They walked out into the sunlight, leaving behind a scene of mild devastation and a guy who would probably see a therapist about this later.

"That was unnecessary," Sol said.

"That was community service."

"That was battery."

"Light battery. Medicinal battery."

Vinny was grinning. "I love Gene & Jude's."

"Everyone loves Gene & Jude's," Nicky agreed. "Except that guy."

"He doesn't count."

They piled into the car, Vinny behind the wheel as usual.

"Where to, boss?" he asked.

"Art Institute," Bobby said. "I want to look at paintings."

Sol stared at him. "Please tell me you're joking."

"Culture, Sol. A man needs culture."

"You just orchestrated a beating over mustard."

"And now I want to see some Monets. The human spirit is vast."

Sol rubbed his face as the car pulled away.

Behind them, Gene & Jude's continued serving hot dogs to people who understood them.

The guy from the suburbs eventually picked himself up, found his car, and drove back to wherever he came from.

He never asked for ketchup again.

How Vinny Became The Mayor Nobody called Vinny Capozzi "The Mayor" because he had political ambitions.

They called him that because he had opinions about everything, shared them constantly, and somehow made you feel like you should have asked for his input even when you definitely had not.

He was born in 1954 in Bridgeport, which was the most Chicago thing you could be. Bridgeport produced mayors—actual mayors, not just nickname mayors—and aldermen and cops and priests and exactly the kind of people who made the city run through a combination of patronage, stubbornness, and knowing whose cousin was connected to whose uncle.

His father had worked at the stockyards until the stockyards closed, and then he'd worked construction until his back gave out, and then he'd worked the door at a bar on Halsted until he died of a heart attack at fifty-two, which was young but not unusual for men who had spent their lives lifting things that were too heavy and eating things that were too salty.

His mother had raised six kids in a three-bedroom house and had never once complained, at least not out loud, which was the Bridgeport way. You suffered in silence or you didn't suffer at all. Complaining was for people who had time for complaining, and nobody in Bridgeport had time for anything except work and church and the occasional Sox game.

Vinny was the fourth of six. Middle children learned early that you had to fight for attention or you'd disappear into the background. Vinny had never been good at disappearing.

He met Bobby Bologna in 1978, at a card game that was definitely not legal and was being held in the back of a bar that definitely didn't have the right permits.

Vinny was twenty-four and working as an "assistant" to a guy who ran numbers out of a dry cleaner in Pilsen. The pay was decent, the hours were flexible, and the moral considerations were things he had learned not to examine too closely.

Bobby was twenty-three and already making a name for himself as someone who got things done. He wasn't the smartest guy in the room—that was Sol, who Vinny met the same night—but he had a quality that was harder to define. Presence. Confidence. The sense that wherever Bobby Bologna was, that was where things were happening.

The card game went badly for Vinny. He lost approximately three hundred dollars, which was two weeks' pay and which he absolutely did not have.

Bobby covered it.

Not as a loan. Not as a favor. Just... covered it. Threw the money on the table and said, "Now you owe me loyalty, which is worth more than cash."

Vinny had been loyal ever since.

The nickname came in 1983.

They were at a bar—a different bar, not the one from the card game, which had been shut down after someone made certain complaints to certain officials—and Vinny was explaining to everyone who would listen why the Bears' offensive line was fundamentally flawed and why the coaches should be fired and why he, Vinny Capozzi, could do a better job even though he had never played football at any level and didn't entirely understand the rules.

"You're like a mayor," someone said. "You got opinions about everything but you're not actually responsible for any of it."

The name stuck.

Vinny pretended to hate it.

He didn't.

Twenty years later, he was still at Bobby's side.

He had been married twice—the first time to a woman named Donna who had left him after two years because she said she "couldn't live with the uncertainty," and the second time to a woman named Marie who had somehow made peace with the uncertainty and was now lighting candles for him every Sunday at St. Alphonsus.

He had a daughter from the first marriage who didn't speak to him and a son from a relationship that didn't quite count as a marriage who did.

He had arthritis in his right knee from an incident in 1991 that nobody talked about anymore.

He had high blood pressure and a doctor who kept telling him to eat better and a complete inability to follow that advice because what was the point of being alive if you couldn't enjoy food.

And he had Bobby.

After everything—after the marriages and the incidents and the years of doing things that would shock his mother if she were still alive—Bobby was the one constant. Bobby was family in a way that family wasn't always family.

Bobby was the reason Vinny got up in the morning.

Bobby was the reason Vinny was still here.

And if Bobby asked him to do something—anything—Vinny would do it.

No questions.

No hesitation.

That was loyalty.

That was Bridgeport.

That was The Mayor.

CHAPTER 4

The Art Institute — Michigan Avenue

The Art Institute of Chicago sat on Michigan Avenue like a temple to things that mattered.

The bronze lions out front—nicknamed North and South, though Bobby always called them "the boys"—had been guarding the entrance since 1894. They were decorated with wreaths for the holidays, laurels for championships, and nothing at all for regular days, which made their presence feel even more eternal.

Bobby loved those lions.

He'd come here with his grandfather as a kid, back when the museum was free on certain days and Italian families from the neighborhood would pile onto the L and make a day of it. His grandfather didn't understand art—the man had never finished sixth grade and thought Picasso was a kind of pasta—but he understood that important places demanded respect.

"You stand up straight in here," his grandfather had said. "This is culture."

Bobby still stood up straight.

"Why are we here?" Vinny asked, staring at a painting of some flowers like it might attack him.

"Because art is important."

"For who?"

"For everyone. For civilization. For people who want to be more than just animals eating and fighting."

Sol looked at him. "We literally just participated in a fight over hot dog toppings."

"And now we're participating in culture. Balance."

They moved through the galleries in a loose formation—Bobby in front, Sol beside him, Vinny and Nicky trailing behind like confused bodyguards, and Frankie bringing up the rear, nervously checking exits.

The place was quiet at this hour, mid-afternoon on a Tuesday, mostly populated by tourists speaking languages that Nicky couldn't identify and art students sketching in notebooks.

Bobby stopped in front of a Monet.

Water lilies. Soft colors. The kind of painting that looked like a blur up close but became something beautiful from a distance.

"You know what I love about the Impressionists?" he said.

"Please don't tell us," Sol muttered.

"They were rejected. The establishment called them frauds. Said they weren't real artists because they didn't paint things exactly like they looked. But they kept going. They created their own movement. Their own galleries. Their own legacy."

Vinny squinted at the painting. "It looks like a swamp."

"It's a garden pond."

"What's the difference?"

"About fifty million dollars."

They drifted through room after room. French Impressionists. American Modernists. That one section with the tiny medieval miniatures that always made Bobby feel like a giant.

He stopped at a Hopper painting—Nighthawks, the famous one with the diner and the lonely people and the empty street.

"This is Chicago," he said.

Sol leaned in. "It's New York. The diner is based on a place in Greenwich Village."

"No, it's not. Look at the light. Look at the loneliness. Look at the feeling of it. That's Chicago energy."

"It's literally documented that Hopper—"

"Documents can be wrong, Sol. This is a Chicago painting. I've decided."

Sol opened his mouth to argue, then closed it. Some battles weren't worth fighting.

In the Asian Art section, Nicky discovered jade.

"Bobby. Bobby, look at this. It's a tiny horse. Made of rock."

"It's jade."

"It's beautiful."

"It's three thousand years old."

Nicky's eyes went wide. "No way."

"Way. It was made before Jesus. Before Rome. Before pretty much everything."

Nicky stared at the tiny horse like he was having a religious experience.

"I want one."

"You can't have that one."

"I know. But like. A different one."

Bobby smiled. This was why he brought the crew to places like this.

Not because they appreciated art—they didn't, not really—but because everyone deserved to feel the weight of history sometimes. Everyone deserved to stand in front of something ancient and beautiful and feel small in a way that was also, somehow, encouraging.

"We'll find you a jade horse, Nicky."

"Really?"

"Really. There's a guy in Chinatown who sells them. Probably not three thousand years old, but close enough."

That's when Bobby saw the guy.

Same guy from Gino Giorgetti's two days ago. Tony Smiles' nephew.

The one who was being groomed for something.

He was standing in front of a Seurat, pretending to appreciate pointillism but clearly waiting for something.

Or someone.

Bobby's good mood evaporated.

"Sol."

Sol followed his gaze. "I see him."

"That's not a coincidence."

"Nothing is a coincidence anymore."

Bobby moved toward the nephew with the casual confidence of a man who had every right to be wherever he wanted to be.

"Hey. Marco, right?"

The nephew turned, surprise flickering across his face before being replaced by carefully practiced calm. "Mr. Bologna. What brings you to the Art Institute?"

"Culture. You?"

"The same."

They stood in silence for a moment, both looking at the Seurat. It was a beach scene, French, composed of thousands of tiny dots that somehow became waves and sand and people when you stepped back far enough.

"You know what I like about Seurat?" Bobby said.

"No."

"He understood that the big picture is made up of tiny details. Lots of tiny decisions, one after another, until you've got something beautiful. Or something ugly. Depends on the details."

The nephew's smile was thin. "That's very philosophical."

"I'm a philosophical guy." Bobby turned to face him directly. "You here alone?"

"Just looking at art."

"In the same museum where I'm looking at art. On the same day. At the same time."

"It's a popular museum."

"It is. But popular doesn't mean coincidental."

The nephew held Bobby's gaze for a long moment. "My uncle says hello."

"Tell him I say the same."

"He also says the Schaumburg situation is non-negotiable."

Bobby smiled. Not the friendly smile.

"Tell him everything is negotiable. That's what makes it business."

They left the museum without incident, though Sol's blood pressure suggested otherwise.

"That was a message," Sol said as they walked past the lions.

"Obviously."

"They're watching us. Following us. They wanted you to know that they're watching."

"I know."

"And?"

Bobby stopped on the steps, looking out at Michigan Avenue, at the traffic and the tourists and the great gray expanse of a city that had been built on exactly this kind of standoff.

"And now they know that I know. Which means we're past the polite part."

Vinny cracked his knuckles. "So we're in the rude part now?"

"We're in the interesting part."

Nicky looked confused. "I thought we were looking at art."

"We were. And now we're done looking. Now we're making art."

Sol closed his eyes. "Please never say that again."

Bobby laughed and started down the steps toward the car.

"Tomorrow we go to the Museum of Science and Industry. I want to show you boys some history."

"More museums?" Vinny groaned.

"Education, Vinny. A man is nothing without education."

"I have education. I graduated high school."

"Barely."

"Still counts."

They piled into the car, leaving the Art Institute and its lions behind.

Somewhere across the city, Tony Smiles was probably smiling.

But Bobby was smiling too.

And his smile had teeth.

Bridgeport — Where Bobby Grew Up Bobby Bologna was born in Bridgeport, which meant he was born into a particular kind of Chicago.

Not the Chicago of tourists and postcards. Not the Chicago of the Magnificent Mile and fancy restaurants where people paid forty dollars for pasta that their grandmothers would have made for two.

Bridgeport Chicago.

The Chicago of politicians and precinct captains. Of union halls and corner bars. Of families who had been there for generations and would stay for generations more because leaving Bridgeport was like leaving part of your soul behind.

The house on Emerald Avenue where Bobby grew up was still there.

He drove past it sometimes, when nostalgia hit harder than usual, when the present felt too complicated and the past felt like the only thing that made sense.

Red brick. Two stories. A front porch where his father used to sit in summer evenings, drinking beer and commenting on everyone who walked past.

"That's Mrs. Kowalski. Husband's a drunk."

"That's Jimmy from the hardware store. Good kid. Bad taste in women."

"That's the alderman. Everybody smile and wave."

Bobby learned more about politics sitting on that porch than he ever learned in school.

"Why are we here?" Sol asked, as Bobby pulled the car to a stop across from the old house.

"Just looking."

"At what?"

"At where I started. Sometimes you need to remember where you started to understand where you're going."

Sol looked at the house. It was ordinary. Completely ordinary. The kind of house that existed in every neighborhood in every city, housing families who were trying their best and usually falling short.

"It's a nice house."

"It was a loud house. My parents fought constantly. My brothers fought constantly. The neighbors fought constantly. There was always yelling."

"That doesn't sound nice."

"It wasn't nice. It was alive. There's a difference."

Bobby's father had worked at the stockyards until the stockyards closed.

Then he worked at a packing plant until the packing plant moved. Then he worked wherever would take him, which wasn't many places by the time the eighties came around.

His mother cleaned houses for people on the North Side. Rich people.

People who had things that needed cleaning because they had too much to keep track of themselves.

She used to come home with stories.

"Mrs. Patterson has a chandelier in her bathroom. A bathroom! Who needs a chandelier in a bathroom?"

"Mr. Reilly keeps his money in a coffee can in the pantry. Doesn't trust banks. Must be thousands in there."

"The Hendersons are getting divorced. I can tell. They sleep in separate rooms and the only thing they say to each other is 'excuse me.'"

Bobby learned more about the rich from his mother's cleaning stories than from any other source. He learned that money didn't make you happy.

That big houses were just bigger spaces to be lonely in. That the people who had everything often appreciated nothing.

"My father used to say that Bridgeport was the only honest place in Chicago," Bobby said, still looking at the house. "He said everywhere else was pretending to be something it wasn't. But Bridgeport? Bridgeport knew what it was and didn't apologize."

"What was it?"

"Working class. Political. Stubborn. The kind of place where everybody knew everybody and nobody forgot anything."

"That sounds exhausting."

"It was. But it was also safe. In its own way. You knew where you stood. You knew what was expected. The rules made sense."

Sol nodded. "And now?"

"Now I make my own rules. Which is better in some ways and worse in others."

Bobby started the car again.

"Let's go. I'm getting hungry."

"You're always hungry."

"That's because food is one of the few things that still makes sense."

They drove away from Emerald Avenue, past the church where Bobby had been baptized, past the school where he had learned to read and fight and understand that the world was not a fair place but that didn't mean you stopped trying.

Behind them, the house stayed where it had always been.

Patient.

Permanent.

Waiting for someone else to grow up and leave and maybe come back someday to stare at it from a parked car.

That was Bridgeport.

That was where Bobby Bologna started.

And somewhere, deep in his bones, that was where Bobby Bologna would always be.

Wrigley Field — September 1979 Nineteen years before Bobby Bologna died at a basketball game, he watched his father die at a baseball game.

The Cubs were losing.

This was not unusual. The Cubs were always losing. That was part of their charm, if charm was the right word for chronic disappointment.

Bobby was nineteen years old, home from a semester of college he was definitely going to drop out of, sitting next to his father in the bleachers at Wrigley Field. They had been coming to games together since Bobby was six. Same seats. Same routine. Same beautiful pointless hope that this year might be different.

His father, Salvatore Filoni, was fifty-two years old and looked sixty-five. A life of hard work and harder drinking had carved deep lines into his face. His hands were rough from decades of labor — the stockyards, the packing plants, the loading docks, whatever work was available when work was scarce.

But at Wrigley, none of that mattered.

At Wrigley, Sal Filoni was just a man watching baseball with his son.

"You want another dog?" his father asked, already standing.

"I'm good, Pop."

"You're always good. That's your problem. You don't want enough."

"I want the Cubs to win."

His father laughed — a big, rough sound that Bobby would remember for the rest of his life. "Then you want the impossible. That's good. Always want the impossible. That way you're never disappointed by the ordinary."

Sal Filoni walked toward the concession stand.

Bobby watched him go.

He would replay this moment ten thousand times. The way his father walked. The slight hitch in his step from the knee he'd blown out in '71.

The way he turned back once to smile at Bobby, a smile that said everything was fine, everything was normal, this was just another day at the ballpark.

It was not just another day.

Bobby heard the commotion before he understood it.

Shouting. Someone calling for help. A woman's scream that cut through the crowd noise like a knife.

He stood up. Looked toward the concession area.

Saw the crowd forming. Saw people backing away from something on the ground.

Saw his father's shoes.

Bobby ran.

Pushed through the crowd. Knocked people aside. Didn't care.

His father was on the ground. Face gray. Eyes open but not seeing.

Someone was doing CPR. Badly. The compressions were too fast, too shallow, the kind of CPR you learned from television and forgot the moment you needed it.

Bobby dropped to his knees.

"Pop. Pop, look at me."

His father's eyes didn't move.

"POP."

Nothing.

The paramedics came. They worked on Sal Filoni for eleven minutes.

Eleven minutes of chest compressions and defibrillator shocks and controlled urgency that Bobby would dream about for years.

They pronounced him dead at 3:47 PM.

Bottom of the seventh inning.

Cubs down by four.

Bobby's whole world, collapsed in the time between pitches.

His father had been going to get a hot dog.

That was the part that stayed with Bobby. Not the death. Not the CPR.

Not the eleven minutes that felt like eleven hours.

The hot dog.

His father had stood up, walked toward food, and never came back.

And Bobby, who had said "I'm good," had let him go.

After that, Bobby was never "good."

After that, Bobby always wanted the hot dog.

After that, Bobby ate like every meal might be his last. Not because he was afraid of dying — he wasn't, not really — but because he was afraid of not living. Afraid of saying "I'm good" and missing something. Afraid of letting the moment pass without consuming it completely.

His therapist, years later, would call this "complicated grief manifesting through oral fixation."

Bobby called it being hungry.

Same thing, really.

The Cubs lost that day.

Bobby never went back to college.

And somewhere in the grief and the rage and the desperate need to feel something other than loss, Bobby Filoni started becoming Bobby Bologna.

The man who ate.

The man who lived out loud.

The man who would rather die with mustard on his chin than live with regret in his heart.

Nineteen years later, at another arena, during another game, Bobby would make the same walk his father made.

Toward food.

Toward joy.

Toward an ending that felt, in its own strange way, like coming home.

But that was later.

First, Bobby had to learn how to live.

The Debt — March 1989 The first time Bobby Bologna saved Sol Rosen's life, neither of them expected it.

Sol owed money to people who did not accept payment plans.

This was, he would later admit, a predictable consequence of gambling on sports he did not understand with money he did not have. The math had seemed sound at the time. The math was always sound at the time. That was the seductive lie of gambling — it felt like calculation when it was really just hope with numbers attached.

The debt was forty-seven thousand dollars.

Sol had about three hundred in his checking account and a car that might be worth two thousand if the buyer didn't look too closely at the transmission.

The men who held his debt were not interested in cars with bad transmissions.

They were interested in making examples.

They found him in his apartment on a Tuesday evening.

Three of them. Professional. Calm in the way that only people who hurt others for a living could be calm.

The leader was a man named Victor, who had no last name that anyone used and no patience for excuses.

"Mr. Rosen," Victor said, sitting uninvited at Sol's kitchen table. "You owe Mr. Castellano forty-seven thousand dollars. You have owed this for ninety-three days. Interest has accumulated. The current balance is sixty-one thousand, four hundred dollars."

Sol felt his stomach drop. "I can get it. I just need more time."

"Time has been extended twice. Mr. Castellano is not a patient man."

"A week. Just one more week."

Victor smiled. It was not reassuring.

"Mr. Castellano has instructed us to collect what we can. If the full amount is not available, we are to collect... pieces."

One of the other men produced a pair of bolt cutters.

Sol's bladder nearly failed him.

The knock on the door saved his fingers.

Victor paused. Gestured for one of his men to check.

The man opened the door.

Bobby Filoni stood in the hallway, holding a paper bag that smelled like Italian beef.

"Hey," Bobby said, like this was the most normal situation in the world. "I heard there was a math problem."

Victor stood. "Who the hell are you?"

"I'm the guy who's going to pay Mr. Rosen's debt. If you'll let me in."

"This is not your business."

"I'm making it my business." Bobby walked past the man at the door, set the bag on the counter, and started unpacking sandwiches. "You guys hungry? I got extra."

Victor stared at him. "You have sixty-one thousand dollars?"

"I have sixty-five. The extra's for your trouble." Bobby pulled out a thick envelope and tossed it on the table. "Count it if you want. I'll wait."

Victor counted.

It was all there.

He looked at Bobby with the confused respect of a predator encountering something it didn't quite understand.

"Why?" Victor asked.

Bobby shrugged. "I heard this guy's good with numbers. I need someone good with numbers. Seemed simpler than interviewing candidates."

"You paid sixty-five thousand dollars to hire an accountant?"

"I paid sixty-five thousand dollars to hire an accountant who owes me everything." Bobby smiled. "That's worth more than money."

Victor and his men left.

Sol stood in his kitchen, shaking, staring at the man who had just saved his life like it was a casual errand.

"I don't understand," Sol said.

"What's to understand? You owed money. Now you owe me instead. The terms are better, I promise."

"You don't even know me."

Bobby handed him a sandwich.

"I know you're smart. I know you're scared. And I know you're going to be loyal to me for the rest of your life, because that's what people do when you save them." He took a bite of his own sandwich. "Eat. You look like you're going to pass out."

Sol ate.

Because what else could he do?

And somewhere between the first bite and the last, he understood what had just happened.

Bobby Filoni had not just paid his debt.

Bobby Filoni had bought his soul.

And strange as it seemed, Sol was okay with that.

Because the alternative was losing fingers to a man named Victor.

And because, against all logic, he actually liked this strange, hungry man who had walked into his apartment like he owned the world.

"So," Bobby said, finishing his sandwich. "You start Monday. Any questions?"

"What exactly will I be doing?"

"Numbers. Money. Making sure I don't get audited by the IRS or killed by people I forgot to pay."

"That sounds illegal."

"It sounds like job security." Bobby smiled. "Welcome to the family, Sol. I think we're going to be friends."

They were.

For nine years.

Until a hot dog in Utah ended everything.

But Sol never forgot that first night.

Never forgot the man who had saved him for no reason except that he could.

Never forgot the sandwich that tasted like mercy.

And when Bobby died, Sol cried harder than he had ever cried in his life.

Not for the boss.

For the friend.

The only real friend he had ever had.

January in Chicago — A Love Letter January in Chicago was not a month.

It was a test.

A test of will, of endurance, of the fundamental human capacity to survive in conditions that God clearly never intended humans to experience.

The temperature dropped below zero and stayed there, like the weather had decided to make a point and wouldn't stop until everyone agreed that the point had been made.

The wind came off the lake with a malice that felt personal, cutting through jackets and scarves and every layer you thought would be enough, finding the gaps, the weaknesses, the places where warmth tried to hide.

The snow fell and fell and fell, and then fell some more, piling up on sidewalks and streets and cars until the whole city looked like it had been buried and was waiting to be excavated in spring.

And through it all, Chicagoans went about their business.

Because that's what Chicagoans did.

"I hate January," Vinny announced, stomping into the office with snow falling off his shoulders like dandruff from a particularly aggressive scalp.

"Everyone hates January," Sol replied, not looking up from his calculations.

"I hate it more than everyone."

"That's not possible. January is universally hated. Your hatred is not special."

"My hatred is always special."

Bobby stood by the window, watching the snow fall.

He didn't hate January.

He understood why other people hated it—the cold, the gray, the way every day felt like a fight against the elements—but for Bobby, January was honest.

January didn't pretend to be pleasant.

January showed you exactly what it was, and you either dealt with it or you didn't.

There was something pure about that.

Something almost refreshing.

"You know what I love about winter in Chicago?" Bobby said.

Sol sighed. "Here we go."

"I love that it doesn't apologize. Other cities get cold and everyone acts like it's a tragedy. Chicago gets cold and everyone just puts on another layer and keeps moving."

"That's called survival instinct."

"It's called character. The weather shapes the people. You can't live through fifty Chicago winters and be weak. The city won't let you."

Vinny shook snow off his coat. "The city doesn't care about character. The city just wants us to freeze."

"The city wants us to earn it. Everything good has to be earned. That's the Chicago way."

The crew had developed winter routines over the years.

Longer meals, because nobody wanted to go back outside.

More meetings in places with heaters, because frostbite was bad for business.

Different routes, because some streets got plowed and some streets became ice rinks that even experienced Chicago drivers approached with fear.

Bobby made sure everyone had good coats.

This wasn't generosity—it was practicality.

You couldn't run an operation if your people were too cold to function.

"Remember that winter in ninety-three?" Nicky asked, apropos of nothing.

"Which part?" Sol asked.

"The part where we had to do that thing and my ears almost fell off."

"Your ears didn't almost fall off."

"They felt like they were going to fall off. There's a difference but also not really."

"That doesn't make sense."

"Cold doesn't make sense. Cold just happens."

Bobby watched the snow continue to fall.

Somewhere out there, Tony Smiles was probably warm and comfortable, plotting moves from a heated office with good coffee and no frost on the windows.

Somewhere out there, police were patrolling streets that had become obstacle courses, trying to maintain order in a city that didn't want to be maintained.

Somewhere out there, regular people were living regular lives, dealing with regular problems, worrying about regular things like paying bills and raising kids and getting through another day.

And here was Bobby Bologna, standing at a window, thinking about weather like it meant something.

Maybe it didn't.

Maybe he was just getting old and philosophical, which was what happened when you spent too much time indoors waiting for the temperature to become survivable.

But maybe it did mean something.

Maybe the cold was part of what made Chicago Chicago.

Maybe you couldn't understand this city without understanding what it meant to be freezing and still functioning.

Maybe the weather was the first test, and passing it was how you earned the right to call yourself a Chicagoan.

"Alright," Bobby said, turning from the window. "Let's get to work. The cold isn't going anywhere, and neither are we."

The crew assembled around the table.

Outside, January continued its assault.

Inside, business went on.

Because that's what Chicago did.

It kept going.

No matter what.

PART TWO

THINGS GET WEIRD

Late Fall 1997

INTERLUDE: THE KID

Maxwell Street — 2:47 AM Bobby Bologna found the kid behind a dumpster.

This was not how he'd planned to spend his Tuesday night.

The plan had been simple: meet with a guy about a thing, collect what was owed, go home, watch the end of the Bulls game on tape delay.

Normal Tuesday.

But the kid changed that.

He was maybe sixteen, maybe younger—hard to tell with the dirt and the bruises and the way he was curled up like he was trying to disappear into the brick wall.

Bobby almost walked past.

Almost.

"Hey."

The kid flinched. Looked up. Eyes wide with the particular fear of someone who'd learned that attention usually meant pain.

"I'm not gonna hurt you."

"Everyone says that."

"Everyone lies. I don't."

Bobby crouched down, which was harder than it used to be because his knees weren't what they were. Sol kept telling him to see a doctor.

Bobby kept telling Sol that doctors were for people who didn't have better things to do.

"What's your name?"

Silence.

"Okay. Don't tell me. That's fine." Bobby looked at the bruises. Fresh ones, layered over old ones. The kind of pattern that told a story without words. "Who did this?"

More silence.

"Let me guess. Somebody at home. Somebody who should be protecting you instead of—" Bobby made a vague gesture at the kid's face.

The kid's jaw tightened.

That was answer enough.

Bobby stood up. Reached into his pocket. Pulled out a roll of bills that would have made a normal person's eyes bulge.

"Here."

The kid stared at the money like it was a bomb.

"Take it."

"Why?"

"Because you need it and I don't."

"Nobody gives away money."

"I'm not nobody. Take the money."

The kid took the money. Slowly. Waiting for the catch.

"There's a diner on Halsted. Donna's place. Tell her Bobby sent you. She'll give you food, let you clean up, maybe find you somewhere to sleep that isn't behind a dumpster."

"What do you want?"

Bobby looked at him.

"What?"

"For this. The money. The help. What do you want? What do I have to do?"

And Bobby understood.

Because this kid had learned, the hard way, that nothing was free.

That every kindness came with a price. That the world was full of people who gave things just so they could take things later.

Bobby had known people like that.

Bobby had been people like that.

But not tonight.

"Listen to me." Bobby's voice dropped, losing the casual tone and finding something harder underneath. "What you have to do is survive. That's it. You survive tonight. You survive tomorrow. You keep surviving until surviving gets easier. And when it gets easier, you remember that somebody helped you once, and you help somebody else."

"That's it?"

"That's it."

"You don't want anything?"

"I want the Bulls to win the championship. I want my knees to stop hurting. I want a beef sandwich from Al's, which is closed, so I can't have it." Bobby shrugged. "What I don't want is anything from you. I don't even know your name."

The kid was quiet for a long moment.

Then: "Marcus."

"Marcus. Good name. Strong name." Bobby nodded. "Go to Donna's, Marcus. Get some food. Get some sleep. And then figure out the next thing. One thing at a time. That's how it works."

He turned to leave.

"Hey."

Bobby looked back.

"Why?" Marcus asked. "Really. Why help me?"

Bobby thought about it.

About his grandfather, who came to Chicago with nothing and built something.

About his father, who inherited everything and lost it.

About himself, who had done things he couldn't take back and made choices he couldn't explain.

"Because somebody should have helped me once, and nobody did. And I can't go back and fix that. But I can do this."

Marcus didn't respond.

Bobby didn't expect him to.

In the car, Vinny was waiting.

"Everything okay, boss?"

"Everything's fine."

"Who was that kid?"

"Nobody."

"You gave him money."

"You were watching?"

"I'm always watching. It's my job."

Bobby settled into the passenger seat. "Then you should know better than to ask questions."

Vinny pulled away from the curb.

"Can I ask one question?"

"No."

"I'm gonna ask anyway." Vinny glanced at him in the rearview.

"Why'd you help him? Some random kid? Doesn't make sense."

Bobby watched the city roll past. The streetlights. The closed storefronts. The occasional figure moving through shadows.

"Vinny. You know what the difference is between us and them?"

"Who's them?"

"Tony Smiles. The feds. The politicians. Everyone who thinks they're better than us because they wear nicer suits and use bigger words."

"What's the difference?"

"The difference is we remember where we came from. We remember what it was like to have nothing. And when we see somebody who has nothing, we don't look away. We don't pretend they don't exist. We help. Because that's what Chicago does. That's what we do."

Vinny was quiet.

"That's actually kind of beautiful, boss."

"Don't tell anyone I said it. I have a reputation."

"Secret's safe with me."

"It better be. Now drive. I want to see if Portillo's is still open."

"It's three in the morning."

"So?"

"So Portillo's closes at midnight."

Bobby sighed heavily. "This is the worst night of my life."

"You just did a really nice thing for a kid."

"And I'm going to bed without a beef sandwich. The universe is unfair."

Vinny laughed.

Bobby didn't.

But somewhere behind his scowl, something that might have been a smile was hiding.

Three months later, Donna called.

"That kid you sent me? Marcus?"

"I remember."

"He's working here now. Busing tables. Kid's good. Hard worker. Doesn't complain."

Bobby nodded, even though she couldn't see it.

"Good."

"He asked about you. Wanted to know your last name. I didn't tell him."

"Good."

"He wants to thank you proper."

"Tell him the thanks is working hard. The thanks is surviving. He doesn't owe me anything else."

"You're a good man, Bobby Bologna. Whatever else anyone says about you."

Bobby hung up without responding.

Because he wasn't a good man.

He was a man who did bad things for complicated reasons.
But sometimes, rarely, he did a good thing too.
And maybe that was enough.
Maybe it had to be.

INTERLUDE: WHY VINNY IS ANGRY

Why Vinny Is Angry Everyone knew Vinny Capozzi was angry.

Not everyone knew why.

Vinny had a son once.

Marco.

Six years old.

Bright eyes. Big smile. The kind of kid who waved at strangers and believed in Santa Claus until the very last possible moment.

Vinny loved him more than anything he had ever loved.

More than money. More than respect. More than the life he had chosen and the crew he had sworn himself to.

Marco was the best thing Vinny had ever done.

And then Marco got sick.

Leukemia.

The word sounded like nothing—just syllables, just sounds—until it was attached to your son's name.

Then it sounded like the end of everything.

Marco fought for eighteen months.

Vinny spent every dollar he had. Every dollar he could borrow. Every favor he had ever earned.

It wasn't enough.

Nothing was ever enough.

Marco died on a Tuesday morning in March, while Vinny was in the hallway arguing with a doctor about experimental treatments that insurance wouldn't cover.

He wasn't there when it happened.

He had stepped away for five minutes.

Five minutes.

He would never forgive himself for those five minutes.

Vinny's wife left him six months later.

She said she couldn't look at him anymore.

She said he reminded her of everything they had lost.

She said she needed to start over somewhere that didn't smell like hospitals and grief.

Vinny didn't argue.

He didn't have anything left to argue with.

After that, Vinny was angry.

Not sometimes.

Always.

Every parking spot was a war. Every insult was a declaration. Every moment of silence was an opportunity to remember a boy who waved at strangers and believed in things that weren't true.

Bobby knew.

Sol knew.

They never talked about it.

Some wounds were too deep for words.

Some wounds just needed space to bleed.

When Bobby died, Vinny cried harder than anyone expected.

Not for Bobby.

For Marco.

For the five minutes.

For everything he had lost and would never get back.

Some people are angry because they're cruel.

Vinny was angry because he had loved something too much, and the world had taken it anyway.

That was the worst kind of angry.

The kind that never heals.

CHAPTER 5

Museum of Science and Industry — Hyde Park

The Museum of Science and Industry made Bobby Bologna feel smart.

This was dangerous.

Hyde Park was a different Chicago than Bobby's Chicago.

Bobby's Chicago was all diners and dive bars and streets where everybody knew your name because knowing names was survival. Hyde Park was the University of Chicago and bookstores and coffee shops where people argued about philosophy instead of about who owed who money.

Bobby drove through it like a tourist in his own city, pointing out buildings he half-recognized and making up facts he completely invented.

"That's where Harold Washington used to live," he said, pointing at a random brownstone.

Sol looked at his newspaper. "Harold Washington lived in Hyde Park. That's a different neighborhood."

"Same general area."

"Not really."

"Close enough for government work."

"What does that even mean?"

Bobby ignored him. "And that's where they invented the nuclear bomb."

Sol lowered his paper. "That's actually true."

"See? I'm educational."

"One accurate statement doesn't make you educational."

"It makes me more educational than Nicky."

In the back seat, Nicky perked up. "Hey, I know things."

"Name one thing you know."

"I know that... the Bulls are good."

"That's not knowledge. That's observation."

"Observation is knowledge."

Sol sighed deeply. "This is going to be a long day."

72

The Museum of Science and Industry sat like a palace on the shore of Jackson Park, the last surviving building from the 1893 World's Columbian Exposition. It had originally been the Palace of Fine Arts, which Bobby found hilarious because now it housed a German submarine and a model coal mine.

"This place was built for the World's Fair," Bobby announced as they approached the entrance. "Eighteen ninety-three. My grandfather came through here when he first got to America. Right off the boat from Naples. No English, no money, just vibes and determination."

Vinny nodded like he understood. "That's inspirational."

"It's heritage. This city is built on immigrants who came here with nothing and took what they could. That's tradition."

Sol muttered, "I think the Native Americans might have a different perspective on that tradition."

Bobby waved his hand. "Semantics."

"It's not semantics. It's genocide."

"Fine. Semantics and genocide. But also tradition. Multiple things can be true."

Inside, the museum was vast and echoing, filled with schoolchildren on field trips and retirees reliving their youth and tourists who had come to Chicago for reasons nobody understood because why would you leave wherever you're from to come somewhere colder.

Bobby led the crew through the exhibits like he owned the place.

He didn't own the place.

But he acted like it, which was basically the same thing.

"This here," he said, stopping in front of a display about the World's Fair, "is where America showed the world what it could do. Electricity. Machines. Progress. All of it happened right here."

Frankie looked at a photo of the original exhibition. "It looks like a wedding cake exploded."

"It was the White City. Everything was white. Symbolism or something."

"Symbolism for what?"

"I don't know. Progress? Cleanliness? White is a color that symbolizes."

Sol stared at him. "Your educational narration is not reassuring."

"I'm not here to reassure. I'm here to inspire."

They moved through exhibit after exhibit.

The coal mine, where you rode a fake elevator down into fake darkness and pretended to be a fake coal miner for approximately six minutes.

The submarine, which was real—captured from the Germans in World War II—and which made Vinny deeply uncomfortable because of something he called "boat anxiety" that nobody wanted to ask about.

The baby chicks, which hatched every day in an incubator and which Nicky wanted to take home until Sol explained that stealing from museums carried enhanced penalties.

Through it all, Bobby kept talking.

About history. About Chicago. About what it meant to be from a place that had built itself from scratch, burned down, and built itself again.

"You know what I love about this city?" he asked, standing in front of a model of the 1893 fairgrounds.

"The food?" Nicky guessed.

"Yes, but also no. I love that it's stubborn. New York thinks it's the center of the universe. LA thinks it's the future. Chicago doesn't think anything. It just keeps going. Cold winters? We keep going. Corrupt politicians? We keep going. Cubs losing for a hundred years? We keep going."

Vinny nodded. "The Cubs are really bad."

"That's not the point."

"But they are."

"The point is resilience. The point is that this city has been through everything and it's still here. Still standing. Still feeding people and housing people and making people feel like they belong somewhere."

Sol looked at him with something approaching surprise. "That was almost poetic."

"I contain multitudes."

"You keep saying that."

"Because it keeps being true."

They reached the Bodies exhibit.

Bobby stopped.

The exhibit was one of those traveling shows that displayed preserved human bodies, sliced and arranged to show the muscles and organs and all the things that usually stayed inside where they belonged.

It was educational.

It was disturbing.

It was, Bobby thought, oddly beautiful in a way that made him uncomfortable.

"What the hell," Vinny breathed, staring at a body that had been sliced into cross-sections like a medical textbook come to life.

"It's anatomy," Sol said. "They preserve the bodies somehow and pose them. It's science."

"It's creepy is what it is."

Nicky couldn't stop staring. "That guy used to be alive."

"All of them used to be alive. That's the point."

Bobby moved through the exhibit slowly, studying each display with an intensity that worried Sol.

There was something calculating in his gaze.

Something that Sol recognized from planning sessions.

"Bobby," Sol said carefully. "What are you thinking?"

Bobby stood in front of a body that had been posed like a soccer player, muscles exposed and frozen mid-kick.

"I'm thinking," Bobby said slowly, "that I know some guys we should do this to."

Vinny laughed nervously. "That's a joke, right?"

"Mostly."

"What does 'mostly' mean?"

"It means let's get out of here. This place is giving me ideas."

They left the exhibit quickly, Frankie looking pale and Nicky looking fascinated in a way that concerned everyone.

"I didn't like that," Frankie announced.

"Nobody asked you to like it," Bobby said. "But you have to admit it's impressive. The human body, I mean. All those systems working together. All those pieces that have to function perfectly or everything falls apart."

Sol watched him carefully. "You're being philosophical again."

"I'm being observant. Big difference."

"And what are you observing?"

Bobby stopped in the middle of the main hall, surrounded by exhibits about space and trains and the wonders of the modern world.

"I'm observing that everything is more complicated than it looks. That something that seems simple—a body, a business, a city—is actually thousands of tiny pieces that all have to work together. And if you understand the pieces, you can understand how to make them work. Or how to make them stop."

Sol absorbed this. "That's either very wise or very concerning."

"Why not both?"

"That's not how wisdom works."

Bobby started walking toward the exit. "It is for me."

They emerged into the afternoon sun, the lake stretching out to the east like a gray reminder that Chicago was always, at its heart, a city between two forces: the prairie behind it and the water in front.

"I'm hungry," Nicky announced.

"You're always hungry."

"This is true."

Bobby checked his watch. "Manny's. I feel like pastrami."

Vinny grinned. "Now you're talking."

They piled into the car, leaving the museum and its preserved bodies and its history lessons behind.

But Bobby kept thinking about those bodies.

About systems.

About pieces.

And about how easy it was to take something apart when you knew where all the pieces connected.

INTERLUDE: TONY SMILES

What Tony Smiles Did to Mickey Flowers Nobody talked about what happened to Mickey Flowers.

Not because they forgot.

Because they were afraid to remember.

Mickey Flowers ran a small book out of a bar in Cicero. Nothing major.

Sports bets, mostly. Cubs fans who thought this year was different. Bears fans who knew it wasn't but bet anyway.

Mickey made a mistake.

He skimmed from Tony Smiles.

Not much. Maybe eight hundred dollars over three months. Enough to cover his kid's braces. His wife's car payment. The kind of small, desperate theft that small, desperate men committed when the math didn't work and the bills kept coming.

Tony found out.

Tony always found out.

They found Mickey in his own bar.

The door was unlocked.

The lights were on.

The jukebox was playing "My Way" by Frank Sinatra, because Tony Smiles had a sense of humor that made people want to vomit.

Mickey was seated at his own bar. His hands were on the counter. His drink was in front of him—untouched, the ice long melted.

His eyes were open.

On the bar in front of him, arranged in a neat row, was the message Tony had wanted everyone to read.

You did not need to ask what it was.

You only needed to look at Mickey's face once and decide to never make Mickey's mistake.

The official cause of death was heart failure.

Which was technically true.

His heart failed because someone had hurt him so badly that his body simply gave up.

Bobby heard about it three days later.

Sol told him, voice flat, face carefully neutral.

"Mickey Flowers. From Cicero."

Bobby stopped eating. That never happened.

"Tony?"

Sol nodded.

"Over what?"

"Eight hundred dollars. Maybe less."

Bobby set down his fork.

For a long moment, he said nothing.

Then: "That's not business. That's performance."

Sol agreed. "He's sending a message."

"To who?"

"Everyone. Anyone thinking about crossing him. Anyone thinking he's soft because he smiles."

Bobby looked out the window.

"The smile is the worst part," he said quietly. "He smiled the whole time, didn't he."

Sol didn't answer.

He didn't have to.

After that, Bobby understood something he hadn't before.

Tony Smiles wasn't just a rival.

Tony Smiles was a warning.

The kind of man who pulled teeth from a living person over eight hundred dollars wasn't fighting for territory.

He was fighting because he liked it.

And that made him more dangerous than any businessman with a gun.

That made him a monster.

Bobby still wouldn't back down from Schaumburg.

But he started sleeping with a gun under his pillow.

Just in case the monster came smiling in the night.

INTERLUDE: WHAT TONY DOES

Cicero — 11:47 PM The man's name was Danny Pulaski.

He was forty-three years old. He had a wife named Marie and two daughters, ages twelve and nine. He coached his younger daughter's softball team. He went to church most Sundays. He had worked for Tony Smiles for six years, managing a laundromat that cleaned more money than clothes.

None of this would save him.

Tony Smiles sat in a folding chair, watching Danny sweat.

The warehouse was cold—December cold, the kind that seeped through walls—but Danny was sweating anyway. Fear did that. Fear made the body forget how temperature worked.

"Danny." Tony's voice was soft. Almost gentle. "You know why you're here."

"Mr. Caravelli, I can explain—"

"I didn't ask you to explain. I said you know why you're here."

Danny swallowed. His hands were zip-tied behind him. His knees ached from the concrete floor. Ricky "The Coat" Mantelli stood behind him like a shadow with bad intentions.

"The money," Danny whispered.

"The money." Tony nodded. "Thirty-two thousand dollars. Missing from the laundromat over the past four months. A little here, a little there. You thought nobody would notice."

"My daughter—she's sick—the insurance doesn't cover—"

"Danny." Tony leaned forward. The smile never wavered. That was the terrifying part—the smile stayed exactly the same whether he was ordering dinner or ordering something else entirely. "Do I look like a man who cares about your daughter's medical bills?"

Danny started to cry.

Tony let him.

The thing about Tony Smiles was that he never raised his voice.

He never had to.

Volume was for people who needed to prove something. Tony had nothing to prove. Tony had power, and power spoke in whispers.

"Here's what's going to happen," Tony said, once Danny's crying had subsided to sniffles. "You're going to tell me where the money is. All of it. Every dollar you haven't already spent on whatever your daughter needed."

"I spent it. All of it. The treatments—"

"Then you're going to tell me how you plan to pay it back."

"I don't—I can't—"

"You can. You will. Because if you don't, Danny, I'm going to visit Marie."

Danny's head snapped up.

"I'm going to visit Marie," Tony continued, still smiling, still soft, "and I'm going to explain to her that her husband made some very poor decisions. And then I'm going to explain what those decisions cost. Not in dollars. In other ways."

He let the sentence land.

He did not need to finish it.

Danny started sobbing in the way men sob when they have understood something they cannot un-understand.

Tony watched without expression.

Without pity.

Without anything at all.

This was what Bobby Bologna didn't understand.

Bobby thought respect came from loyalty. From shared meals and shared history and the bonds between men who had been through things together.

Bobby was a romantic.

Tony was a businessman.

And business, real business, was built on one thing: the credible promise of consequences. Not anger. Not passion. Not the volcanic eruptions that Bobby mistook for strength.

Just the quiet certainty that crossing Tony Smiles meant losing everything you loved.

Danny would pay back the money.

He would sell his house if he had to. He would work three jobs. He would do whatever it took, because now he understood—truly understood—what Tony Smiles was capable of.

That understanding was worth more than the thirty-two thousand dollars.

That understanding was worth everything.

"Ricky," Tony said, standing. "Take Danny home. Make sure Marie sees him like this. Make sure she understands."

"What about the money?"

"He'll find it. Won't you, Danny?"

Danny nodded frantically. "Yes. Yes. I'll find it. I'll pay you back. Every dollar. I swear. I swear on my daughters' lives."

Tony smiled.

"That's exactly what you're swearing on, Danny. Don't forget it."

He walked out of the warehouse into the December night.

The cold felt good.

The cold felt clean.

Behind him, he could hear Danny's sobs echoing off the concrete walls.

Music, almost.

The sound of a lesson being learned.

Tony's driver was waiting with the car.

"Where to, boss?"

"Home. I'm tired."

The driver nodded and pulled away from the warehouse.

Tony looked out the window at the Chicago skyline. The lights. The buildings. The city that everyone thought belonged to Bobby Bologna just because Bobby was loud about loving it.

Bobby didn't understand.

The city didn't belong to people who loved it.

The city belonged to people who were willing to do what was necessary.

And Tony Smiles was always willing.

That was the difference.

That was everything.

Three weeks later, Danny Pulaski delivered thirty-two thousand dollars in cash to one of Tony's associates.

He had sold his house.

His family was living in a two-bedroom apartment in Berwyn.

His daughter was still getting her treatments, but now Danny worked fourteen-hour days and never complained about anything.

Marie didn't look at him the same way anymore.

Something had broken in their marriage that night. Something that wouldn't heal.

But they were alive.
Their daughters were alive.
And Tony Smiles had made his point.
That was how you built an empire.
Not with passion.
With fear.

INTERLUDE: WHY SCHAUMBURG MATTERS

Why Schaumburg Matters Schaumburg wasn't just a suburb.

Schaumburg was the future.

Sol explained it to Bobby over breakfast at Manny's, drawing diagrams on napkins because Bobby learned better when food was involved.

"It's about the malls," Sol said. "Woodfield is the biggest shopping center in the Midwest. Bigger than anything in the city. And malls mean cash."

"Cash from what?"

"Everything. Parking lot deals. Loading dock access. Security contracts. The vending machines alone clear six figures a year—and that's just the legitimate stuff."

Bobby chewed his pastrami. "So it's about money."

"It's about supply chains. Woodfield gets deliveries from every major distributor in the region. Trucks in and out, twenty-four hours a day. You control the loading docks, you control what comes in and what goes out. Electronics. Clothing. Jewelry. All of it passes through, and all of it can fall off the back of a truck."

"And Tony wants that."

"Tony has half of it already. He's been working the unions—Teamsters, loading crews, warehouse workers. Another year and he owns the whole pipeline from the port to the parking lot."

Bobby stopped chewing.

"That's not a territory grab. That's an empire."

Sol nodded. "The city is dying, Bobby. Industry's leaving. The neighborhoods are shrinking. But the suburbs are growing. Schaumburg, Naperville, Oak Brook—that's where the money's going. That's where the future is."

"Schaumburg was never anybody's."

"Exactly. The Outfit had Cicero. The North Side had Lincoln Park. Schaumburg has been wide open since the eighties because nobody from the old neighborhoods wanted to drive that far for less prestige. Tony figured out that's the bug, not the feature. Nobody's there. So he's going."

"And if Tony gets it—"

"Then we're irrelevant. We're fighting over scraps in a city that doesn't need us anymore while he builds something that will last for decades."

Bobby stared at his sandwich.

This wasn't about pride anymore.

This was about survival.

"So what's the play?" Bobby asked.

Sol sighed. "We have three options. One: we take Schaumburg from him. War. Blood. Probably prison for some of us. Two: we make a deal. Split the territory. Accept that the best we can do is a percentage."

"And three?"

Sol met his eyes. "We get out. Liquidate everything. Move somewhere warm. Retire before it's too late."

Bobby laughed. "You know I can't do that."

"I know." Sol folded his napkin diagram. "That's what worries me."

Bobby chose option one.

Of course he did.

Bobby always chose the fight.

That was what made him Bobby Bologna.

It was also, Sol would later realize, what killed him.

Not the hot dog.

The hot dog was just the ending.

The beginning was Schaumburg.

The beginning was refusing to accept that some fights weren't worth winning.

CHAPTER 6

Manny's Deli — South Jefferson Street

SMASH CUT:

Metal screaming.

A blade chewing through flesh.

Thick, wet slices collapsing onto each other like dominoes made of meat.

Steam rising from surfaces that had been cold moments ago.

The sound alone could turn a man's stomach.

Fast.

Relentless.

Mechanical.

DING.

An order bell.

Pull back.

It's a deli slicer.

Pastrami stacking up in perfect, glistening folds, pink and black and beautiful in that specific way that only cured meat can be beautiful.

Manny's Deli was loud and alive and holy ground.

The place was a Chicago institution in the truest sense—it had survived recessions, scandals, and the fundamental shift from a city that made things to a city that just talked about making things. It had fed mayors and mobsters and everyone in between, often at the same table, because Manny's was neutral territory.

Not neutral in the official sense. There was no treaty, no agreement, no formal declaration.

Just an understanding that had built up over fifty years of serving the best corned beef in the city: you don't start trouble at Manny's.

Sol Rosen loved this place more than he loved most people.

They took their usual booth in the back, the one with the tear in the vinyl that nobody had fixed since the first Bush administration. Bobby ordered for the table because Bobby always ordered for the table.

"Pastrami, corned beef, brisket, and whatever Nicky's eating, which is apparently everything."

The waitress, a woman named Gloria who had been working here since Carter and would probably outlive them all through sheer stubbornness, didn't write anything down.

"Drinks?"

"Cream sodas. Celery soda for Sol because he's being difficult."

"I like celery soda."

"Nobody likes celery soda. They tolerate it."

"I actively enjoy it."

"Then you're broken."

The food arrived in waves, piled high on plates that sagged under the weight of decades of tradition.

For a few minutes, nobody talked.

This was the protocol.

At Manny's, you ate first and discussed second, because talking while eating was disrespectful to the food and because anything important enough to discuss could wait until you'd at least made a dent in your pastrami.

Bobby worked through his sandwich with the focus of a man performing a religious ritual. The bread was fresh. The meat was perfect.

The mustard was that specific yellow that existed nowhere else in nature but somehow tasted exactly right.

"Okay," he said finally, setting down the last quarter of his sandwich.

"Let's talk."

Sol wiped his mouth. "The Schaumburg situation is accelerating. Tony's been making calls to the union reps out there. Trying to lock down the construction side before we can get a foothold."

"What's our timeline?"

"Two weeks. Maybe less. Once he's got the unions, we're looking at a much bigger fight to get in."

Bobby nodded. "Then we move faster."

"How fast?"

"This weekend. I know a guy at Woodfield—one of the managers, owes us from that thing with his brother-in-law. We use him to set up a meet with the other players."

Sol considered this. "A meeting at a mall is risky. Public. Cameras."

"Public is the point. Nobody does anything stupid at a mall. Too many witnesses. Too many kids."

Vinny snorted. "You'd be surprised what people do at malls."

"I would not, actually. I've been to the Wisconsin Dells outlet mall. I've seen things."

Frankie leaned in, nervous as always. "What about the police? They've got eyes on Tony's crew already. If we're both at the same location at the same time—"

"Then we're two groups of guys who happened to be shopping at the same mall. Coincidence. Circumstance. The beauty of public spaces."

Sol shook his head. "The police aren't stupid, Bobby. They're understaffed and underpaid and they have to pick their battles, but they're not stupid."

"I'm not saying they're stupid. I'm saying they're realistic. They're not going to waste resources on a maybe. They want to catch people doing something, not talking about doing something."

"And if the talking turns into doing?"

Bobby smiled. "Then we make sure we're the ones doing the leaving."

They finished their food while discussing logistics.

The details were boring but essential: who would approach who, what they would say, what they would offer, what they would threaten (implicitly, because explicit threats were for amateurs and federal recordings).

Bobby listened more than he talked, which was unusual for him. He was thinking about the bodies at the museum. About systems and pieces.

About how everything connected to everything else.

Tony Smiles was a system.

His crew. His connections. His money. His relationships.

All pieces.

All connected.

And if Bobby could understand those connections well enough, he could find the places where pressure would have the most effect.

"There's something else," Sol said, as they were finishing up.

Bobby looked at him. "What kind of something else?"

"Vinny's thing. The Deluca thing."

"What about it?"

"He's talking."

Vinny went still. "What do you mean, talking?"

"I mean he's been seen with people. At a bar on Division Street. Telling stories about what happened to him. Making threats about payback."

Vinny's face darkened. "He owes us money and he's making threats?"

"He's not making threats to us. He's making them to whoever will listen. Which, right now, is whoever buys him drinks."

Bobby absorbed this. "Is he connected to anyone?"

"Not that I can tell. But talking is talking. Word spreads. People start wondering if we're as serious as we say we are."

Bobby set down his glass. "Then we remind them."

"How?"

"Vinny. You and Nicky. Tonight. Make sure Deluca understands that talking is worse than not paying."

Vinny smiled. It was not a nice smile.

"With pleasure."

Nicky looked nervous. "Are we talking about, like, heavy reminding or light reminding?"

"Medium. Enough to make a point. Not enough to make headlines."

"Okay. I can do medium."

Sol sighed. "This is going to be my life, isn't it? Tracking violence on a scale from light to heavy."

"You're an accountant. This is just another kind of math."

"It's really not."

They paid in cash, as always, leaving a generous tip for Gloria, who had seen worse and would see worse again and who would continue serving pastrami through all of it.

Outside, the city was settling into that gray November afternoon that Chicago did better than anywhere else. Not quite cold enough for winter coats, but cold enough to remind you that winter was coming and it would be merciless when it arrived.

Bobby breathed it in.

"You know what I love about this city?" he said.

"You keep asking that," Sol said. "You keep not waiting for an answer."

"Because I already know the answer. I love that it's real. No pretense. No bullshit. You are who you are in Chicago, and the city either accepts you or it chews you up and spits you out."

"Which one are we?"

Bobby smiled. "Right now? We're being accepted. But acceptance is temporary. You have to keep earning it."

They walked to the car, past the lunch crowds and the office workers and the endless parade of Chicago humanity doing Chicago things.

Behind them, the deli slicer kept running.

Metal screaming through meat.

Just another day in the food business.

Just another day of putting one piece next to another and calling it a sandwich.

The L Train — Chicago in Motion Bobby Bologna rarely took public transportation.

This was not about status. It was about control.

On the L, you were at the mercy of schedules and strangers and the particular chaos of Chicago public transit. Bobby preferred to be in charge of his own movement.

But sometimes, when he needed to think, he would ride the Brown Line.

Just ride.

All the way around the Loop and back.

Watching the city pass by.

The Brown Line was Bobby's favorite because it went through neighborhoods that meant something.

Ravenswood. Lincoln Square. The Loop.

Past buildings he had known his whole life. Past restaurants where he had eaten. Past corners where things had happened that could not be discussed in public.

The train was a time machine. Each stop a memory. Each memory a reminder that time kept moving whether you wanted it to or not.

"You know what I love about the L?" Bobby asked Sol once, during one of their thinking rides.

"The delays?"

"The perspective. When you drive, you only see what's in front of you. When you ride the L, you see everything. The rooftops. The windows. The lives being lived in all those apartments you would never notice otherwise."

"That's surprisingly poetic."

"I contain multitudes, Sol."

The L train at rush hour was a study in Chicago character.

People packed tight. Nobody making eye contact. Everyone pretending they were alone even though they were pressed against strangers.

That was Chicago.

A city of people who valued their privacy so much they could maintain it even when physically touching other humans.

Bobby respected that.

He understood boundaries even when he didn't respect them.

There was a particular spot on the Loop where the train turned and you could see the whole city spread out.

The Sears Tower reaching up like it was trying to escape.

The lake glittering in whatever light was available.

The endless grid of streets stretching to horizons you couldn't quite see.

Bobby would stand at that spot and feel small.

Not in a bad way.

In the way that reminded him there was something larger than himself.

Something worth protecting.

Something worth fighting for.

"Why do you do this?" Sol asked, on one of their rides. "Just ride around?"

"Because sometimes you need to be in motion to think clearly. The movement helps. The noise helps. The not being anywhere specific helps."

"That doesn't make sense."

"Most true things don't make sense. That's how you know they're true."

Bobby's last L train ride was three days before he flew to Utah.

He rode the Brown Line all the way around.

Watched the city he loved pass by.

Thought about what was coming.

The game. The championship. The possibility that this was the last time he would see Jordan play.

He didn't know, of course, that it was the last time he would see anything.

But maybe some part of him suspected.

Because when the train reached his stop, he stood on the platform for a long time.

Looking at the tracks.

Listening to the trains.

Breathing the Chicago air that smelled like everything and nothing at once.

"Goodbye," he whispered.

To the train.

To the city.

To the life he had built and was about to lose.

Then he walked home.

To pack for Utah.

To meet destiny.

To eat his last meal in the city that had made him who he was.

How the Crew Came Together — 1987 Every crew has an origin story.

Most of them are boring.

This one was also boring, but it involved more food.

Bobby Filoni—he wasn't Bobby Bologna yet, wouldn't be for another three years—met Sol Rosen in a holding cell at the Cook County Jail in the spring of 1987.

Bobby was there for what he maintained was a misunderstanding about a card game. Sol was there for what he admitted was tax fraud, though he preferred the term "creative accounting."

They had six hours to kill before their lawyers showed up.

"What do you do?" Bobby asked, because he asked everyone that.

"I'm an accountant."

"A criminal accountant?"

"All accountants are criminal accountants. Some just haven't been caught yet."

Bobby laughed—a real laugh, not the polite kind—and decided immediately that he liked this guy.

Vinny Capozzi came next.

Bobby found him working as a bouncer at a club on Rush Street.

Vinny was terrible at the job because his temperament was "constantly angry about everything" and bouncers were supposed to de-escalate.

"You're terrible at this job," Bobby observed.

"I know. But it pays."

"I pay better."

Vinny thought about it for three seconds. "When do I start?"

Frankie Petrucci was an accident.

He ran a dry cleaning business that Bobby used for laundering money through a laundry-adjacent business.

One day, Bobby came to pick up his shirts and found Frankie crying in the back office.

"What's wrong with you?"

"Everything. The business is failing. My wife is angry. My mother-in-law moved in."

Bobby sat down. "Tell me about the business problems."

Two hours later, Bobby made him an offer he couldn't refuse.

Nicky Moretti was the last to join.

Bobby was eating at a restaurant in Bridgeport when a young guy at the next table caught his attention. He was eating spaghetti with such pure, uncomplicated joy that Bobby couldn't help but watch.

"You like that spaghetti, Nicky Moretti?"

"It's amazing."

"It's decent. The sauce is from a can."

Nicky shrugged. "It still tastes good."

Bobby hired him the next week. Not because Nicky was talented, but because Nicky had genuine happiness—and that kind of happiness was contagious.

So that was the crew.

Bobby, the boss who loved Chicago more than sense.

Sol, the accountant who could find loopholes in physics.

Vinny, the muscle with opinions about everything.

Frankie, the legitimate businessman gone illegitimate.

And Nicky, the simple soul who reminded everyone what joy looked like.

Five men. One city. Infinite problems.

But they were a crew.

And crews stuck together.

Terry — A Running Problem Terry Mancini owed Bobby Bologna three thousand dollars.

This had been true for four years.

Every time Bobby saw him, Terry ran. In diners. At Cubs games.

Once at a funeral, which was impressive commitment to cowardice.

"TERRY!" Bobby would shout.

And Terry would vanish.

He hid in bathrooms claiming to be "not Terry." He jumped over stadium seats with surprising agility. He once disguised himself as a waiter at a restaurant Bobby was eating at, which almost worked until he tried to take Bobby's order and his voice cracked.

"You sound like Terry," Bobby said.

"I'm not Terry."

"Terry, I can see your face."

"...It's a common face."

Bobby never got his three thousand dollars.

Terry eventually disappeared completely. Some said Florida. Some said witness protection. Some said he faked his own death, which seemed excessive for three grand but was also very Terry.

"Pulling a Terry" became crew slang for disappearing when you owed someone.

The man became a legend.

Not for anything he did.

Just for running.

The Chair Frankie bought new chairs for the office.

Swedish chairs. The kind that came in flat boxes with wordless instructions and approximately nine thousand small screws.

"How hard can it be?" Vinny asked.

Four hours later: Vinny had hit his thumb with a hammer eleven times.

Nicky had eaten three screws, thinking they were mints.

Frankie was breathing into a paper bag.

Sol was calculating their productivity losses and announcing them every fifteen minutes.

And the one chair they'd managed to assemble was leaning forty degrees to the left with several pieces clearly upside down.

"It works," Bobby said. "Watch."

He sat down.

The chair immediately collapsed.

Bobby lay on the floor, surrounded by Swedish engineering, staring at the ceiling.

"I hate Sweden," he said.

They hired a guy to assemble the other four chairs. He did it in eleven minutes and charged them two hundred dollars.

"You could have done this yourselves.

"Get out," Bobby replied.

CHAPTER 6.5

The Parking Situation

Tuesday, 2:47 PM

"I'm not paying it."

Bobby stared at the parking ticket like it had personally insulted his mother.

"It's forty dollars," Sol said.

"It's not about the money. It's about the principle."

"What principle?"

"The principle that I was parked there for six minutes. SIX MINUTES, Sol. I went in, I got my coffee, I came out. Six minutes."

"The sign said no parking."

"The sign was wrong."

Sol pinched the bridge of his nose. "Signs can't be wrong. They're signs. They just... are."

"This one was wrong. And I'm going to prove it."

THE PLAN (as conceived by Bobby Bologna): Step One: Go to City Hall. Step Two: Explain the situation. Step Three: Get the ticket dismissed. Step Four: Victory.

"That's not really a plan," Frankie observed. "That's just... going somewhere."

"Going somewhere with PURPOSE, Frankie. That's what makes it a plan."

City Hall — 3:15 PM City Hall looked like democracy had given up halfway through construction.

Gray stone. Gray windows. Gray people shuffling through gray hallways toward gray offices where gray decisions were made about gray matters that affected everyone but interested no one.

Bobby hated it immediately.

"Which office handles parking tickets?" he asked the security guard.

"Third floor. Room 312. But they close at four."

"It's three-fifteen."

"Better hurry."

Bobby did not hurry. Bobby Bologna did not hurry for anyone. He walked at a dignified pace that communicated his importance to the universe.

This would prove to be a mistake.

Room 312 — 3:47 PM The line had fourteen people in it.

"We're not going to make it," Sol observed.

"We're going to make it."

"There are fourteen people ahead of us and thirteen minutes until they close."

"Math is not destiny, Sol."

"Math is literally destiny. That's what math is for."

Bobby pushed past the line to the front counter, where a woman with glasses and an expression of profound exhaustion was explaining to an elderly man that no, he could not pay his ticket in commemorative coins.

"Excuse me."

The woman looked up. "Sir, there's a line."

"I see the line. I'm choosing to ignore it."

"You can't ignore the line."

"I'm ignoring it right now. Watch." Bobby gestured at the line. "Ignored."

The fourteen people in line began to murmur.

THE SITUATION ESCALATES:

"Sir, if you don't go to the back of the line, I'll have to call security."

"Call security. I'll wait."

"You just said you wouldn't wait in line."

"I won't wait in LINE. I'll wait for SECURITY. There's a difference."

"There really isn't."

A large man in the line—construction worker, by the look of him—stepped forward. "Hey, buddy. Back of the line."

Bobby turned slowly. "Are you talking to me?"

"Yeah, I'm talking to you. We're all waiting. You wait too."

"Do you know who I am?"

"Do I care?"

Bobby considered this. In his world, everyone knew who he was. In this world—the world of parking tickets and commemorative coins and women with exhausted expressions—he was nobody.

This was unacceptable.

"Vinny."

Vinny stepped forward, cracking his knuckles.

The construction worker stepped forward too.

His four construction worker friends also stepped forward.

"Ah," said Sol. "This is going poorly."

City Hall — 3:52 PM

"EVERYBODY CALM DOWN."

Nobody calmed down.

The construction workers were squaring up. Vinny was squaring up.

Nicky was looking for something to eat. Frankie was having what appeared to be a small cardiac event near the water fountain.

The woman behind the counter had, in fact, called security.

Security arrived in the form of two men who were clearly too old for this and one man who was clearly too young and eager.

"What's going on here?" the eager one asked.

"This man—" the construction worker pointed at Bobby "—cut in line."

"I didn't cut. I repositioned."

"That's cutting."

"It's repositioning with intent."

"THAT'S CUTTING."

THE SITUATION ESCALATES FURTHER:

The eager security guard reached for Bobby's arm.

This was a mistake.

Not because Bobby did anything violent. Bobby was, at this moment, attempting to be civil.

But Vinny saw someone reaching for Bobby.

And Vinny had instincts.

City Hall — 3:54 PM

"WHY IS THERE A SECURITY GUARD ON THE FLOOR?"

"He fell."

"He didn't fall. You pushed him."

"He fell AFTER I pushed him. The falling was his choice."

The two older security guards had drawn their weapons, which seemed excessive for a parking ticket dispute but was technically within protocol.

The construction workers had formed a protective circle around their fallen comrade, who had been accidentally elbowed by Vinny while Vinny was pushing the security guard.

The woman behind the counter was on the phone with what sounded like the actual police.

And Bobby Bologna was still holding his parking ticket, which remained unpaid.

"Sol."

"Yes, Bobby?"

"I think we should leave."

"I think we should have left eleven minutes ago."

"Your hindsight is not helpful."

THE ESCAPE:

They did not escape cleanly.

They escaped through a fire exit, which triggered an alarm, which caused everyone in the building to evacuate, which created a crowd of several hundred people on the street outside City Hall, which attracted news cameras, which meant that Bobby Bologna's face was briefly on the five o'clock news under the headline "CHAOS AT CITY HALL: PARKING DISPUTE TURNS VIOLENT."

In the car, speeding away from downtown, Vinny was apologetic.

"I didn't mean to push him that hard."

"You pushed him through a door, Vinny."

"The door was already open."

"It was not already open. It was closed. You opened it. With his body."

"That's one interpretation."

THE AFTERMATH:

The parking ticket was not dismissed.

In fact, Bobby now had:

The original parking ticket ($40).

A citation for disturbing the peace ($250).

A citation for inciting a riot ($500).

A bill for the door Vinny broke ($340).

A bill for the security guard's medical expenses ($1,200).

Total cost of contesting a $40 parking ticket: $2,330.

Plus legal fees.

"We should have just paid the ticket," Sol observed, later that evening.

Bobby was staring at the itemized bill.

"It's not about the money."

"It was never about the money. That was the problem."

"It was about the principle."

"What principle? What principle costs two thousand dollars and gets us on the news?"

Bobby was quiet for a long moment.

"The principle that Bobby Bologna does not pay unjust tickets."

"The ticket was completely just. You parked illegally."

"The sign was in the wrong place."

"THE SIGN WAS WHERE THE CITY PUT IT."

"And the city was WRONG."

Sol stood up.

"I need a drink."

"Get me one too."

"Get your own drink. I'm billing you for the door."

One Week Later Bobby paid the ticket.

He also paid the citations, the door, and the medical expenses.

He did not admit he was wrong.

He simply said he was "choosing to allocate resources toward more productive conflicts."

Sol translated this as: "Bobby was wrong and is pretending he wasn't."

Vinny translated this as: "We won because we didn't go to jail."

Nicky translated this as: "Can we get lunch now?"

Frankie didn't translate anything. Frankie was still recovering from the cardiac event.

And somewhere in City Hall, a woman with glasses and an expression of profound exhaustion told her coworker about "the parking ticket guy"

and they both laughed.

Which, in its own way, was the worst defeat of all.

CHAPTER 7

Lincoln Park Zoo — After Hours

Bobby Bologna did not like animals.

He respected them.

But he did not like them.

"They got dead eyes," he explained, peering through the fence. "No soul. Just hunger."

Vinny adjusted his coat against the November cold. "You're describing us."

"That's unfair. We have souls."

"Do we though?"

The night was cold and clear and entirely too quiet for what they were about to do.

Lincoln Park Zoo sat dark and still, its exhibits closed for the night, its animals sleeping or prowling or doing whatever animals did when nobody was watching. The city lights glowed orange on the horizon. Somewhere nearby, traffic hummed along Lake Shore Drive, oblivious to the five men standing at a service entrance with a duffel bag that was suspiciously heavy.

"I don't like this plan," Frankie whispered.

"You've said that six times," Sol noted. "The repetition doesn't make it more convincing."

"It should. Repetition is how you establish patterns. This is a terrible pattern."

Bobby turned to him. "What's terrible about it?"

"We're at a zoo. After midnight. With a... with a bag. At a zoo."

"You keep saying 'at a zoo' like that explains something."

"It does! Zoos have security. Cameras. Animals that eat things."

"Animals that eat things is the point, Frankie. That's literally why we're here."

The bag contained what was left of someone who had made very poor decisions.

Bobby didn't know the guy's name. Didn't want to know. Johnny No Thumbs had called three days ago with a problem and an offer: make the problem disappear, and there would be consideration in the Schaumburg negotiations.

Bobby had said yes because consideration was valuable and because disposal was, in its own way, a kind of service industry.

"The big cats are this way," Bobby said, leading them along the fence line.

Sol looked at him. "How do you know that?"

"I bring my goddaughter here sometimes. Nice kid. Likes the lions."

"You bring your goddaughter to the same zoo where you're now planning to feed someone to the lions?"

"It's a multi-use facility, Sol. That's just good urban planning."

They found the big cat exhibit after fifteen minutes of wandering.

The area was dark, but not completely—emergency lights provided just enough illumination to see the outlines of enclosures and paths and the occasional sign warning visitors not to feed the animals.

"Ironic," Nicky muttered.

"What?"

"The sign. 'Don't feed the animals.' And we're here to..."

"I get it, Nicky."

Vinny was already at the fence, testing its strength. "This isn't going to be easy to get over."

"We're not going over. We're going through the service gate. Sol has a key."

Sol held up a key that he had acquired through channels Bobby preferred not to think about.

"This opens the maintenance access. We go in, find the back area of the lion enclosure, make the delivery, and leave."

Frankie's voice was very small. "What if the lions don't... cooperate?"

"Lions are opportunistic feeders. They'll cooperate."

"But what if—"

"Frankie. Have you ever seen a lion turn down meat?"

"I've never seen a lion."

"Then trust me. They're very motivated eaters."

The service gate opened with a quiet click.

They moved through in single file—Bobby first, then Sol, then Vinny carrying the bag, then Nicky, then Frankie bringing up the rear and regretting every decision that had led him to this moment.

The zoo at night was different from the zoo during the day.

Quieter, obviously.

But also stranger.

Without the crowds and the noise and the constant motion of families and school groups, the place felt like what it actually was: a collection of cages containing things that would kill you if given the opportunity.

"I don't like this," Nicky whispered.

"Nobody asked you to like it."

"I'm just saying."

"Say it quieter."

They reached the back of the lion exhibit.

A tall fence separated the service area from the enclosure proper. On the other side, darkness moved in ways that suggested something large and hungry and very much awake.

Bobby peered through the fence.

"Hello, babies."

A low rumble answered him.

"That's encouraging," he said. "They're interested."

Sol was checking the area for cameras. "We need to move fast. Security makes rounds every thirty minutes. We've got maybe fifteen before the next one."

"Then let's not waste time." Bobby turned to Vinny. "The bag."

Vinny hoisted the duffel over his shoulder and approached the fence.

"How do we actually... you know... get it in there?"

Bobby pointed to a feeding hatch—a small door in the fence that zookeepers used to slide food into the enclosure without actually entering.

"Through there."

Vinny blinked. "That's tiny."

"Then we make multiple trips."

"Multiple—" Vinny's face went pale. "Bobby, I don't know if I can—"

"You can. Because the alternative is explaining to Johnny No Thumbs why we didn't do what we said we'd do. And I don't want to have that conversation. Do you?"

Vinny swallowed. "No."

"Then unzip the bag and let's get to work."

What happened next would feature in Nicky's nightmares for the rest of his life.

But it worked.

Kind of.

The lions were initially skeptical—they'd been asleep, and being woken up to receive unexpected packages through a small hatch was not their normal routine. But lions were, as Bobby had noted, *motivated eaters.*

Once they understood what was being offered, they became enthusiastic participants.

Maybe too enthusiastic.

"It's not working fast enough," Sol said, watching the enclosure.

"They're playing with it instead of eating it."

"What do you mean, playing?"

"I mean one of them is batting it around like a cat toy."

Bobby stared through the fence. "That's not playing. That's... hunting behavior. They're practicing."

"On something that's already dead?"

"Lions aren't philosophers, Sol. They do what they do."

Frankie had his back to the fence, refusing to look. "I can hear it. I can hear them."

"That's dinner sounds, Frankie. That's the sound of a problem being solved."

"It doesn't sound like problem-solving. It sounds like—"

A flashlight beam swept across the ground.

Everyone froze.

Security.

The guard was maybe fifty feet away, doing exactly what Sol had predicted: making rounds, checking exhibits, being professional in that bored way that suggested he'd done this a thousand times and never found anything interesting.

Until now.

"Hey!" the guard shouted. "Who's back there?"

Bobby dropped flat like he'd been training for this his whole life.

Vinny dove into a bush.

Nicky just stood there, frozen.

Sol grabbed him and yanked him down.

Frankie made a sound that was half whimper, half prayer.

The guard's flashlight swept the area. It passed over the bush where Vinny was hiding. It passed over the spot where Bobby lay pressed against the ground. It passed over the fence, and the feeding hatch, and—

The lions, who had stopped eating and were now watching the flashlight with the interest of animals who recognized the beginning of something new and potentially entertaining.

The guard frowned. "What the hell is that."

He was looking at the bag.

What was left of the bag.

What was visible of the bag, through the fence, illuminated by his flashlight.

"Nope," the guard said, backing away. "Nope, nope, I'm not paid for this."

He turned and walked quickly in the opposite direction, already reaching for his radio, already deciding that this was someone else's problem.

Silence fell.

Then Vinny emerged from the bush, covered in dirt and looking deeply unhappy.

"That was close."

"Too close," Sol agreed. "We need to leave. Now."

They retreated the way they'd come, moving fast but not running—running attracted attention, running looked guilty.

Behind them, the lions returned to their meal.

Behind them, a security guard was probably calling someone who would probably call someone else who would probably decide that whatever had happened was not worth investigating at three in the morning.

And behind them, a problem was being solved in the most natural way possible.

Nature was efficient like that.

In the car, nobody spoke for a long time.

They drove north on Lake Shore Drive, the city lights reflecting off the lake, the skyline glittering like something out of a postcard that definitely didn't mention midnight zoo visits.

Finally, Nicky spoke.

"That lion looked at me."

Bobby glanced at him in the rearview. "What?"

"At the end. One of them stopped what it was doing and looked at me. Like... like it was memorizing my face."

"Lions don't memorize faces."

"This one did."

Sol sighed. "We are going to need therapy. All of us. Professional, ongoing therapy."

Bobby laughed. "We're not going to therapy. We're going home, we're going to sleep, and tomorrow we're going to pretend tonight never happened."

"Can we do that?"

"We can do anything, Sol. That's what being professionals means."

Frankie whispered, "I want a *normal* job."

"You have a normal job. You run a dry cleaner."

"I want a normal normal job. One without lions."

"Then you're in the wrong business."

They drove on through the Chicago night.

Behind them, the zoo settled back into silence.

The lions finished their meal.

And nothing that had happened left any trace that couldn't be explained away as an animal's natural appetite.

Some problems solved themselves.

You just had to know where to take them.

Sol Rosen and the Mathematics of Survival Sol Rosen had always been good at math.

Not just good—exceptional. The kind of good that made teachers uncomfortable and other students resentful. He could look at a page of numbers and see patterns that other people needed calculators to find.

By fourth grade, he was doing his older brother's algebra homework.

By eighth grade, he was helping his father—an accountant at a meatpacking plant—find errors in financial reports.

By college, he was being recruited by firms that promised him a future full of spreadsheets and stability and a office with a window if he just kept his head down and did what he was told.

He had done what he was told for approximately six months.

Then he met Bobby Bologna.

It was 1979. Sol was twenty-three, working at a small accounting firm in the Loop that handled accounts for businesses that were, in retrospect, obviously not legitimate.

He didn't know that at first.

He was young. He was naive. He believed that columns should balance and that numbers didn't lie.

The numbers didn't lie.

But they didn't tell the whole truth either.

One of the firm's clients was a restaurant supplier that seemed to move an awful lot of product to restaurants that didn't appear to exist. Sol noticed. Sol always noticed. That was his gift and his curse.

He mentioned it to his supervisor.

His supervisor told him to stop noticing.

He kept noticing.

And then Bobby Bologna walked into his office.

"You're the numbers guy," Bobby said, not as a question.

"I'm an accountant."

"Same thing. I hear you've been asking questions."

Sol felt something cold settle in his stomach. "I was just—"

"You were doing your job. I respect that. Most people in your position would keep their head down and their mouth shut and collect their paycheck."

"I thought about doing that."

"But you didn't."

"No."

Bobby smiled. It was a good smile. Warm. The kind of smile that made you want to trust the person wearing it, even when you probably shouldn't.

"Here's the thing, Sol. I could threaten you. I could tell you that asking questions is dangerous and that you should stop. But I'm not going to do that."

"Why not?"

"Because I'd rather have you asking questions for me than for someone else."

That was how it started.

Sol left the accounting firm three weeks later. He went to work for Bobby Bologna, handling the numbers that legitimate accountants couldn't handle, finding patterns in cash flow and expenditure that kept them one step ahead of competitors and two steps ahead of the law.

He told himself it was temporary.

He told himself he could leave whenever he wanted.

He was still telling himself that twenty years later.

The thing about Sol was that he understood the math of survival.

Not just financial math—though he was excellent at that—but the broader mathematics of staying alive in a business that regularly produced corpses.

He calculated odds.

He assessed risks.

He built contingency plans that had contingency plans that had contingency plans.

And when things went wrong—as they always did, eventually—he was the one who figured out how to make them go right again.

"You're my brain," Bobby told him once.

"You have a brain," Sol replied.

"I have instincts. That's different. Instincts tell you what to do. Brains tell you how to do it without getting killed."

It was, Sol had to admit, an accurate distinction.

He never married.

He came close once, with Rachel, the lawyer who couldn't understand why he stayed.

After she left, he dated occasionally—women he met through legitimate channels, women who didn't know what he did, women who eventually figured it out and left, or who didn't figure it out and whom he left because lying was exhausting.

Now he was forty-seven and alone.

But not lonely.

That was the strange thing.

He had Bobby. He had the crew. He had a purpose that got him out of bed every morning and a challenge that kept his mind sharp and a sense of belonging that he had never found in the legitimate world.

Was it worth it?

He didn't know.

But he was too deep to get out now.

The math of that was very clear.

Sometimes, late at night, he would sit with a glass of wine and think about parallel universes.

The universe where he had kept his head down and his mouth shut.

The universe where he had become a partner at some prestigious firm, with a corner office and a wife and two kids in a suburb where nothing ever happened.

The universe where he hadn't met Bobby Bologna.

Would that Sol be happier?

Would that Sol be alive?

He didn't know.

But he knew this: that Sol would be bored.

And Sol Rosen had never been bored a single day of his current life.

That had to count for something.

Right?

The Crew Plans a Birthday Party It was Nicky's birthday.

Nobody knew how old Nicky was.

Including Nicky.

"Thirty-something," he said, when asked. "Maybe forty? My mom keeps track."

This was concerning for many reasons, but the crew had long ago stopped being concerned about Nicky.

The point was: it was his birthday, and Bobby decided they should throw a party.

"A party," Sol repeated. "For Nicky."

"Yeah. Why not?"

"We're criminals. Criminals don't throw birthday parties."

"Says who? Criminals are people. People throw parties."

"Bobby—"

"We're throwing a party, Sol. End of discussion."

EVERYONE'S PARTY PLAN

BOBBY'S PLAN:

Rent out a whole restaurant. Get a band. Make it classy. "Nicky deserves class."

Estimated cost: Eight thousand dollars.

Sol vetoed this immediately.

SOL'S PLAN:

Cake. In the office. Thirty minutes maximum. Then back to work.

"That's not a party," Vinny said. "That's a meeting with frosting."

"Meetings with frosting are underrated."

VINNY'S PLAN:

Strip club.

"It's not that kind of party," Bobby said.

"All parties can be that kind of party."

"Nicky's mom might come."

Vinny considered this. "Different strip club?"

"NO."

FRANKIE'S PLAN:

He didn't have a plan.

Frankie never had plans.

Frankie had anxiety and the constant sense that something was about to go wrong.

These were not the same as plans.

NICKY'S PLAN:

"What do you want for your birthday, Nicky?"

"I don't know. Food?"

"What kind of food?"

"The eating kind?"

"Nicky, all food is the eating kind."

"Oh. Then that kind."

They argued for two days about the party.

During this time, the following compromises were suggested and rejected:

A barbecue (rejected because Frankie was "emotionally allergic" to outdoor cooking).

A bowling party (rejected because Vinny was banned from three bowling alleys).

A dinner cruise (rejected because Bobby got seasick and refused to admit it).

Just giving Nicky money (rejected because "that's not a party, Sol, that's a transaction").

THE PARTY

In the end, they did something nobody planned.

They went to Nicky's mom's house.

She had been planning her own party the entire time.

Because she was a mother.

And mothers plan.

The party was in the backyard.

There were streamers.

There was a cake shaped like a hot dog, because Mrs. Moretti knew her son.

There were approximately forty relatives, none of whom knew what Nicky actually did for a living.

("He's in logistics," Mrs. Moretti told everyone. "Very important logistics.")

Bobby stood in the corner, holding a paper plate of food, watching Nicky get hugged by seventeen different aunts.

"This is nice," he said.

Sol raised an eyebrow. "You spent two days planning a party that was already planned."

"I spent two days caring enough to plan. That's what matters."

"That's not—" Sol stopped. "You know what? Fine. That's what matters."

Vinny got into an argument with one of Nicky's uncles about the Bears.

Frankie ate so much lasagna he had to lie down.

Sol calculated the exact cost per slice of the hot dog cake and announced it to no one.

And Bobby watched it all, happy in a way he couldn't quite explain.

"Hey Bobby," Nicky said, walking over with frosting on his face.

"Yeah?"

"Thanks for coming."

"It's your birthday, Nicky. Of course I came."

"My mom said you called her. To make sure there was enough food."

Bobby shrugged. "I didn't want to show up empty."

"She also said you paid for the cake."

"She wasn't supposed to tell you that."

"And the decorations."

"Nicky—"

"And the DJ."

Bobby looked over at the DJ, who was playing Italian music and looking confused about his life choices.

"That guy cost me four hundred dollars," Bobby admitted.

"He only knows three songs."

"I'm aware."

Nicky hugged him.

This was unexpected.

Nicky was not a hugger.

Bobby patted his back awkwardly.

"You're a good boss," Nicky said.

"I'm an okay boss."

"You're a good person."

"Let's not go crazy."

The party went until midnight.

The DJ ran out of songs by nine.

But nobody cared.

Because it was Nicky's birthday.

And the crew was together.

And sometimes, that was enough.

"Next year," Bobby said, as they left, "we're doing the restaurant."

"This was perfect," Nicky said.

"This was your mom's backyard."

"My mom's backyard is perfect."

Bobby couldn't argue with that.

Maxwell Street — The Old Market

Before the university took over, Maxwell Street was the greatest open-air market in Chicago.

Maybe the greatest in the country.

Vendors selling everything imaginable. Food from every culture.

Music drifting from corners where blues legends played for tips. The particular chaos of commerce that happened when people gathered to buy and sell and live.

Bobby remembered it.

"My father used to bring me here on Sundays," Bobby told the crew, driving past where the market used to be. "We would walk through the stalls. He would haggle for things we didn't need. I'd eat Polish sausages until my stomach hurt."

"That sounds nice," Nicky said.

"It was perfect. The kind of perfect you don't appreciate until it's gone."

The university had demolished most of it in the nineties.

Progress, they called it.

Expansion. Development. The forward march of civilization.

Bobby called it something else.

Words that shouldn't be repeated in polite company.

"You know what Maxwell Street taught me?" Bobby asked.

"What?" Sol said.

"That everything is negotiable. Price. Value. Truth. Everything. You walk through that market, you see people making deals that shouldn't be possible. Trading things that have no obvious connection. Creating value out of nothing but conversation and nerve."

"That's capitalism."

"That's humanity. Capitalism is just the name we give it when we want to sound sophisticated."

The Polish sausage stands were mostly gone now.

A few remained. Holding on. Refusing to accept that the world had moved on without them.

Bobby went to one every few months.

Ordered the same thing his father used to order.

Stood in the same spot where they used to stand.

Remembered what Chicago used to be.

"Do you think it was better?" Nicky asked once. "The old days?"

Bobby thought about it.

"No. Different. Not better. We romanticize the past because we know how it ended. But when you were living it, you didn't know. You were just as confused and scared as you're now. Just with different problems."

"That's surprisingly wise."

"I've moments."

The last time Bobby went to Maxwell Street was two weeks before he died.

He didn't know it was the last time.

Nobody ever knows when the last time is the last time.

That's what makes last times so painful.

And so precious.

He ordered a Polish with everything.

Stood on the corner where his father used to stand.

Watched the traffic go by on streets that used to be market stalls.

And for a moment, just a moment, he could almost hear the vendors calling.

Almost smell the smoke from grills that no longer existed.

Almost feel his father's hand on his shoulder, pointing at something interesting.

Then the moment passed.

And Bobby was alone again.

With his sausage and his memories and the particular sadness of watching a city erase its own history.

"Goodbye, Maxwell Street," he said quietly.

To nobody.

To everybody.

To a place that existed now only in the minds of people who remembered.

Then he walked back to his car.

And drove toward whatever came next.

Which would be Utah.

And then eternity.

But he didn't know that yet.

He just knew he was tired.

And hungry.

And glad that some things, at least, still tasted the way they were supposed to.

CHAPTER 8

Woodfield Mall — Schaumburg

Bobby Bologna hated malls.

Too bright.

Too many teenagers.

Too many smells fighting each other for dominance.

And worst of all—too much walking.

"Why does everything in this place look like it's for sale and nobody looks happy?" he muttered, surveying the food court like a general inspecting enemy territory.

Vinny adjusted his jacket, trying to look casual and failing entirely.

"This is neutral territory."

"Neutral territory should feel neutral. This feels aggressive. This feels like capitalism attacking my eyeballs."

Sol was scanning the crowd, counting exits, calculating escape routes.

"There are cameras everywhere."

Frankie whispered, "Why are there so many stores that only sell socks?"

Nicky was already eating a pretzel. "This mall's huge."

Bobby stopped. "Why do you have food already?"

Nicky froze mid-bite. "It was calling me."

Woodfield Mall was one of the largest shopping centers in the country, a sprawling monument to American consumerism that occupied more square footage than some small towns. It had department stores and specialty boutiques and one of those weird stores that only sold candles and another weird store that only sold magnets and a food court that offered cuisines from around the world, all of which tasted vaguely like the same industrial fryer.

It was also, for reasons nobody could fully explain, considered neutral ground for certain conversations.

Maybe because the presence of three thousand shoppers made violence impractical.

Maybe because the security guards were numerous and nervous.

Maybe because there was something fundamentally absurd about conducting criminal negotiations next to a Cinnabon.

Whatever the reason, Woodfield was where you went when you wanted to talk but didn't want to trust.

They found the North Side crew near the food court, sitting at a cluster of tables next to a fake palm tree that looked deeply unhappy about its circumstances.

Tony "Smiles" Caravelli stood when he saw them. Still smiling, of course. The smile was as constant as gravity and twice as unsettling.

Beside him: Ricky "The Coat" Mantelli, who was—shockingly—still wearing the coat. A long leather thing that made him look like he'd gotten lost on his way to a Tarantino audition.

Dom "Radio" Pescatore, already talking to a stranger about something that sounded confidential.

Lou "Dot Com" Battaglia, explaining the internet to nobody.

And Angie Marino, sitting calmly, stirring a soda like she was waiting for a meeting that actually mattered.

Bobby leaned in to Sol. "This already feels like a bad idea."

"We can still leave."

"No we can't."

"Why not?"

"Because I'm already mad."

Bobby stepped forward. "Tony Smiles. Nice mall you got here."

Tony spread his hands. "Relax, Bobby Bologna. We're just talking business."

"Business smells like Orange Julius."

Angie looked up from her soda. "Let's keep this simple. You stay out of Schaumburg. We stay out of your neighborhoods."

Sol nodded. "That's reasonable."

Bobby frowned. "Nobody asked you."

Angie looked at Sol with interest. "You should talk more."

Vinny stepped in. "You don't tell our people what to do."

Tony sighed. "Here we go."

Ricky shifted his weight, and Bobby noticed for the first time that his hand was inside that stupid coat.

Nicky dropped his pretzel.

Dom leaned in, apparently unable to stop himself from commenting on everything. "You hear about that zoo thing last night—" Sol snapped. "WHY WOULD YOU SAY THAT."

Everything went quiet.

Bobby turned slowly to look at Dom. "You been talking about us."

Dom raised his hands. "I talk about everybody."

"That's not comforting."

A mall security guard started walking toward them.

Sol whispered, "We are about to ruin this man's pension."

Ricky reached into his coat.

Vinny moved first.

He slammed Tony into the table with enough force to send trays flying.

Sodas exploded.

Teenagers screamed.

Nicky tackled the wrong guy—a random shopper who had just been trying to enjoy a Sbarro slice—and immediately started apologizing.

Frankie tripped over a chair and disappeared under a pile of napkin dispensers.

Sol dove behind a pretzel stand that offered exactly zero cover.

Someone yelled, "GUN!"

Which was rude and unnecessary because nobody had actually drawn yet.

Ricky finally pulled his gun and immediately lost it when a kid on a skateboard crashed into him.

The gun skidded under a table.

Everyone went for it.

Bobby slipped on spilled Orange Julius and fell into a Cinnabon display.

"WHY DOES EVERYTHING HERE SMELL LIKE SUGAR," he screamed.

Angie grabbed Tony and dragged him backward. "WE ARE DONE HERE."

Dom ran directly into a group of nuns.

Nobody knew why there were nuns at Woodfield Mall.

Nobody questioned it.

Some things just happened in the suburbs.

Mall security finally arrived in force and immediately got overwhelmed by the chaos.

"EVERYONE CALM DOWN," yelled a security guard whose voice suggested he was absolutely not calm.

Sirens started outside.

Sol crawled toward Bobby. "WE HAVE TO GO NOW."

Vinny grabbed Nicky—who was still apologizing to the Sbarro guy—and started running.

Frankie reappeared holding a decorative sock like it was evidence.

"WHY DO YOU HAVE THAT," Bobby yelled.

"I DON'T KNOW."

They sprinted through the mall, knocking over holiday kiosks and very expensive candles.

Bobby looked back as they ran. "I HATE THIS PLACE."

They burst out into the parking lot and dove into the car.

Frankie slammed the door. "I ALMOST DIED BY PRETZEL."

Sol was shaking. "We just started a war in a shopping center."

Vinny laughed. It was the laugh of a man who had lost contact with appropriate emotional responses.

"That was kind of fun."

Bobby stared out the windshield, breathing hard.

Then he smiled.

"They wanted quiet. They shoulda picked a library."

The car peeled out into traffic.

Behind them, mall security was establishing a perimeter around a crime scene that nobody quite understood.

The nuns were giving statements.

The Sbarro guy was getting a free breadstick for his trauma.

And Tony Smiles, for once, was not smiling.

INTERLUDE: CHICAGO POLICE DEPARTMENT

Area Central

Chicago Police Department — Area Central Detective Frank Delaney hated paperwork almost as much as he hated malls.

He stared at the incident report and rubbed his face.

"So let me get this straight," he said. "We got overturned tables, multiple injuries, food court property damage, and a nun filed a statement?"

His partner, Detective Carla Ruiz, sipped burnt coffee. "Two nuns."

Delaney blinked. "Of course it was two."

The Area Central station was a monument to institutional exhaustion, a building that had been modern once and was now just tired. The fluorescent lights buzzed. The coffee was always burnt. The air had that particular staleness that came from too many stressed-out people breathing the same recycled oxygen.

Delaney had been a detective for fifteen years, which meant he'd seen everything and been surprised by none of it. He was fifty-two, divorced twice, and had the kind of face that looked tired even when he was well-rested.

Ruiz was younger—thirty-eight—and still had enough energy to pretend the job didn't slowly destroy everyone who did it. She was sharp, careful, and had the kind of instincts that couldn't be taught.

They made a good team.

Not a happy one, necessarily.

But good.

Photos were spread across the desk—blurry faces, overturned displays, Christmas decorations mixed with police tape. Bobby Bologna showed up in exactly none of them, which somehow made Delaney more certain it was him.

"You don't get this kind of public stupidity without a conductor," Delaney said.

Ruiz nodded. "We've got matching descriptions at Woodfield. Two groups. Both dressed nice. Both yelling like lunatics."

Delaney sighed. "Bobby Bologna."

"Also known as Bobby Filoni. Been quiet-ish for the last few months."

"Quiet people don't flip Cinnabon displays."

Ruiz flipped a page. "And this guy. Tony Caravelli. Goes by Tony Smiles."

"I know Tony." Delaney rubbed his eyes. "Great. So Christmas came early."

Delaney leaned back in his chair.

"What's the endgame here?" he asked.

"Territory. Same as always. North Side's been expanding into the suburbs. Bobby's crew doesn't like it."

"So they have a showdown at a mall."

"Appears that way."

"In front of nuns."

"The nuns were coincidental."

"Nothing is coincidental with these people."

Ruiz shrugged. "Sometimes nuns are just nuns."

Delaney stood up and walked to the window, looking out at the city he'd spent his whole life trying to protect from itself.

"You know what I hate about organized crime?"

"The crime part?"

"The stupidity part. These guys think they're smart. They think they're running sophisticated operations. And then they have a brawl in a food court over territory that's probably worth less than a nice condo."

Ruiz joined him at the window. "You think this is going to escalate?"

"With Bobby Bologna? Always. The man doesn't know how to do anything quietly."

"So what's the play?"

Delaney turned back to his desk. "We watch. We wait. We gather intel. And we let them make mistakes, because they will. They always do."

"That's not very proactive."

"Proactive gets cops shot. Patience gets convictions."

Ruiz considered this. "And if they hurt civilians?"

"Then we stop being patient."

Delaney sat back down and started reading the reports again.

Somewhere out there, Bobby Bologna was probably planning his next move.

119

Somewhere out there, Tony Smiles was probably smiling about something sinister.

And somewhere out there, two nuns were probably still confused about why they'd been asked to describe a man in a tracksuit.

This was Chicago.

Things only got weirder from here.

INTERLUDE: THE KID AT GENE & JUDE'S

The Kid at Gene & Jude's Bobby saw him through the window.

Fifteen, maybe sixteen. Skinny in the way kids are when they're growing faster than their bodies can keep up. Standing outside Gene & Jude's, staring at the menu board like it was written in a language he couldn't quite understand.

Counting coins in his palm.

Counting again.

Coming up short.

Bobby excused himself from the crew and walked outside.

"Hey."

The kid looked up, startled. Scared, maybe. Not of Bobby specifically—scared in the general way that poor kids are scared of adults who might tell them to move along.

"You hungry?"

The kid shrugged. Which meant yes.

"Come on." Bobby held the door open. "My treat."

The kid's name was David.

He was a junior at Lane Tech. His dad had left when he was nine. His mom worked two jobs and still couldn't make rent most months. He was supposed to be at school, but he'd skipped because he hadn't eaten since yesterday and it was hard to focus when your stomach was eating itself.

Bobby listened.

Didn't interrupt.

Didn't offer advice.

Just listened while the kid ate three hot dogs and two orders of fries.

When David was done, Bobby reached into his wallet and pulled out five twenties.

"I can't take that," David said.

"You're not taking it. I'm giving it. There's a difference."

"But—"

"Here's the deal." Bobby leaned forward. "You take this money. You go back to school tomorrow. You graduate. You do something with your life that doesn't involve standing outside restaurants counting nickels. That's the deal."

David looked at the money.

Looked at Bobby.

Looked at the money again.

"Why?" he asked.

Bobby shrugged. "Because somebody did it for me once. Long time ago. And you can't pay back that kind of thing. You can only pay it forward."

David took the money.

Bobby never saw him again.

Never knew if he graduated, or what he did with his life, or if that moment mattered at all in the long run.

But that wasn't the point.

The point was the doing.

The point was being the kind of person who saw a hungry kid and fed him.

Loudmouth. Glutton. Bad husband. Worse enemy.

But every now and then, when nobody was watching, he was also kind.

And that counted for something.

Even if nobody remembered it but him.

Tony Smiles Plans His Next Move Tony Caravelli had been smiling since he was a child, and it had been freaking people out for just as long.

His mother used to say he came out of the womb grinning. His teachers thought he was mocking them. His first girlfriend told him it was "creepy, but like, good creepy?" which he had chosen to take as a compliment.

The truth was simpler.

Smiling was power.

When you smiled, people couldn't tell what you were thinking. When you smiled, people assumed you knew something they didn't. When you smiled while telling someone that bad things were going to happen to them unless they cooperated, that smile was the scariest part.

Tony had figured this out early.

He had been using it ever since.

He sat in his office above the bar in Lincoln Park—a nice office, with actual furniture and actual art on the walls, because Tony believed in aesthetics—and reviewed the reports from Woodfield.

"That was a disaster," he said, still smiling.

Angie Marino sat across from him, her face revealing nothing. "It was a miscommunication."

"Ricky pulled a gun in front of children."

"Ricky panicked."

"Ricky is an idiot. I've been saying this for years."

"He's loyal."

"Loyalty without competence is a liability." Tony set down the reports. "Bobby Bologna walked away from that looking like the reasonable one. Bobby. The man who once cracked a counter arguing about giardiniera. He looks reasonable compared to us."

Angie considered this. "We need to reframe the narrative."

"We need to do something more than reframe. We need to demonstrate that Woodfield was an aberration, not a pattern."

"And how do we do that?"

Tony's smile widened.

"We do something quiet. Something professional. Something that reminds everyone that the North Side doesn't make scenes—we make results."

Tony had grown up on the North Side, in a neighborhood that had been Italian when his grandparents arrived and was now a mix of everything, which was what happened to neighborhoods in Chicago. They evolved or they died.

His father had run a small operation—gambling, mostly, some loan sharking—and had made enough money to send Tony to a decent school and give him opportunities that his father had never had.

Tony had taken those opportunities and run with them.

By thirty, he had expanded beyond his father's operation, building connections with politicians and businessmen who preferred not to examine too closely where certain donations came from.

By forty, he was running the North Side with an efficiency that his father would have admired and possibly feared.

Now he was forty-five, and he wanted more.

Not because he was greedy—though he was, a little—but because standing still was the same as falling behind. The world didn't wait for people who were satisfied with what they had.

Bobby Bologna understood this.

That was why Bobby was dangerous.

"What about the zoo situation?" Angie asked.

Tony frowned. "What zoo situation?"

"There are rumors. Something happened at Lincoln Park Zoo a few nights ago. Security found... irregularities."

"What kind of irregularities?"

"The kind that suggest someone was disposing of something."

Tony's smile flickered. "Bobby?"

"Unknown. But the timing is suspicious."

"If Bobby's gotten sloppy enough to be disposing of things at public zoos, he's gotten sloppy enough to make mistakes."

"Or he's gotten desperate enough."

Tony considered this. "What's our source?"

"A security guard who likes to talk after a few drinks. He doesn't know who he's talking to, obviously. But he mentioned finding evidence of nighttime visitors near the big cat enclosure."

"Big cats."

"Lions."

Tony leaned back in his chair. "That's either brilliant or insane."

"With Bobby, it's usually both."

The plan took shape over the next few hours.

Angie was good at plans. That was why Tony kept her close. He had the vision; she had the details. Together, they had built something that was more than just an operation—it was an organization, with structure and rules and a clarity of purpose that Bobby Bologna's crew would never achieve.

Bobby ran things on instinct and loyalty.

Tony ran things on strategy and discipline.

One of those approaches was sustainable.

One of them was a ticking clock.

"Christmas is coming," Angie said, near the end of their meeting. "The city will be distracted. Everyone focused on shopping and family and holiday obligations."

"You're thinking about the Michigan Avenue situation?"

"I'm thinking about opportunities. People are careless during holidays. They make assumptions. They let their guard down."

Tony nodded slowly. "Bobby will want to make a statement. He's been embarrassed. He'll want to show strength."

"So we let him make his statement. And while everyone's watching whatever spectacle he creates, we do something that matters."

"Such as?"

Angie smiled. It was not a warm smile. It was the smile of someone who had been thinking three moves ahead for a very long time.

"We take what he can't afford to lose."

Outside the office, the city hummed with its usual energy.

The El rattled past.

Car horns echoed off buildings.

Somewhere, a saxophone player was attempting jazz and failing in that particular Chicago way that made failure sound almost intentional.

Tony stood at the window and watched it all.

His city.

Or it would be.

Soon.

Bobby Bologna thought this was about territory.

Tony knew it was about something bigger.

It was about the future.

And the future belonged to the people who were willing to take it.

Dinner at Gino's They were halfway through the appetizers when the guy walked in.

Bobby saw him immediately.

Young. Nervous. Wearing a jacket too heavy for the weather, which meant he was carrying.

Bobby took another bite of his calamari.

"We have company," he said quietly.

Sol looked up from his soup. "Where?"

"By the door. Green jacket. Don't stare."

Everyone immediately stared.

"What did I just say?"

The guy in the green jacket walked toward their table.

His hand was in his pocket.

Bobby kept eating.

"You know," Bobby said conversationally, "the calamari here is underrated. Everyone talks about the steak, the chicken parm, but the calamari? Crispy. Tender. Perfect."

Vinny reached for his waistband.

"Don't," Bobby said, still eating. "We're in a restaurant."

"He's got a gun!"

"Probably. But we're in a restaurant. There are rules."

The guy stopped at their table.

"Bobby Bologna?"

"That's me."

"I have a message."

"From who?"

"Mr. Caravelli."

Tony Smiles. Of course.

Bobby gestured to an empty chair. "Sit down."

"I'm not supposed to—"

"Sit. Down."

The guy sat.

Bobby pushed the basket of bread toward him.

"Have some bread. It's good bread."

"I don't—"

"Eat the bread."

The guy took a piece of bread.

He did not eat it.

He held it like he wasn't sure what bread was for.

"What's the message?" Bobby asked.

"Mr. Caravelli wants you to know that your presence in Schaumburg is no longer welcome."

"Schaumburg."

"Yes sir."

"You came here, to my dinner, to tell me about Schaumburg."

"Yes sir."

Bobby set down his fork.

"What's your name, kid?"

"Danny."

"Danny what?"

"Danny Rizzoli."

"Rizzoli. I knew a Rizzoli. Tony Rizzoli. From Bridgeport."

"That's my uncle."

"Tony's your uncle? He's a good guy, Tony. Terrible at cards, but a good guy."

Danny's hand, still in his pocket, relaxed slightly.

"You know my uncle?"

"I know everyone, Danny. That's my job."

Bobby leaned forward.

"Here's what's going to happen. You're going to go back to Mr. Caravelli and tell him that Bobby Bologna received his message. You're also going to tell him that Bobby Bologna is going to finish his dinner, because the steak here is exceptional and I ordered it medium-rare and I'm not letting it get cold. After dinner, I'll think about Schaumburg. Maybe I'll stay out. Maybe I won't. That's for me to decide. Not Tony. Not you. Me."

Danny nodded.

"And Danny?"

"Yes sir?"

"Take the bread. You look hungry."

Danny took the bread.

He stood up.

He walked out of the restaurant.

He did not deliver the message exactly as Bobby said it.

He told Tony Smiles that Bobby Bologna was "really calm" and "offered me bread" and "I think he might be crazy."

Tony Smiles agreed on all counts.

Back at the table, Vinny was vibrating with unused adrenaline.

"You just let him go?"

"What was I supposed to do? Shoot him in a restaurant full of witnesses?"

"Maybe?"

"Vinny. There are children here."

Vinny looked around. There were, in fact, children at a table nearby, eating spaghetti and making a mess.

"Fine."

Sol exhaled slowly. "That was very diplomatic."

"I have my moments."

"What are you going to do about Schaumburg?"

Bobby picked up his fork.

"I'm going to finish my dinner. Then I'm going to think. Then I'm going to do whatever I was going to do anyway."

"Which is?"

"I don't know yet. That's what the thinking is for."

The steak arrived.

It was, as Bobby predicted, exceptional.

He ate every bite.

And when he was done, he tipped thirty percent, because the waiter had handled the armed man at the table with admirable professionalism.

"That waiter should get a raise," Bobby said, as they left.

"A guy pointed a gun at him and he asked if we wanted dessert," Nicky observed.

"That's customer service. That's what this city used to be about."

Sol shook his head. "This city used to be about a lot of things."

"It still is, Sol. You just have to know where to look."

Outside, the night was cold.

Somewhere, Tony Smiles was waiting for a response.

He would keep waiting.

Because Bobby Bologna responded on his own schedule.

And right now, his schedule said it was time for dessert.

"Margie's?" he asked the crew.

"We just ate."

"That was dinner. Dessert is different. Dessert is its own thing."

"That's not how stomachs work, Bobby."

"Maybe that's not how YOUR stomach works."

They went to Margie's.

Bobby got a sundae.

And for one more night, everything was okay.

The Crew Develops a Foolproof Plan

COLD OPEN:

Frankie is on fire.

Not metaphorically. Actually on fire. His left sleeve is burning and he is running in circles in a parking lot while Vinny chases him with a fire extinguisher that is clearly empty.

Nicky is crying.

Sol is on the phone with someone, saying "No, I understand the policy doesn't cover this, I'm asking hypothetically—"

Bobby stands in the middle of it all, covered in what appears to be marinara sauce, holding a single shoe, watching the chaos with the expression of a man who has made a series of decisions he cannot explain.

"This," Bobby says to no one, "is not how I saw today going."

EIGHT HOURS EARLIER

It started, as most disasters did, with Bobby having an idea.

128

"I have an idea," Bobby announced, walking into Frankie's office like he owned it, which he sort of did.

Sol looked up from his calculations. "That's rarely good."

"This one's different. This one's foolproof."

"You said that about the boat."

"The boat was not my fault."

"The boat sank, Bobby."

"It sank slowly. That's different."

The idea was simple.

Tony Smiles had a shipment coming in. Electronics. Legitimate electronics, which made them valuable because legitimate things could be sold to legitimate people for legitimate money that didn't need to be laundered.

Bobby wanted to steal the shipment.

"It's perfect," Bobby explained, drawing on a napkin. "The truck comes down I-90, exits at Cumberland, stops at the warehouse on Montrose. We intercept it before it gets there."

Vinny leaned forward. "How do we intercept it?"

"We block the road."

"With what?"

"A car."

"What car?"

"Your car."

Vinny stared at him. "My car."

"It's the most reliable car we have."

"It's my car."

"Vinny, this is for the crew."

"My. Car."

This argument continued for forty-five minutes.

Sol timed it.

It covered Vinny's emotional attachment to the vehicle, the time he drove it to Wisconsin "for a thing," the fact that he had named it (Maria, after an ex-girlfriend), and a detailed history of every repair he had personally performed.

Nobody asked for the repair history.

Vinny provided it anyway.

"Fine," Bobby said finally. "We use Frankie's car."

Frankie, who had been silent, made a sound like a small animal being stepped on.

"My car?"

"You barely use it."

"I use it every day!"

"For what?"

"For... driving!"

"That's very general, Frankie."

Nicky raised his hand.

"What," Bobby said.

"I have a question about the plan."

"What's the question?"

"What happens after we block the road?"

Silence.

Bobby looked at the napkin. Looked at the crew. Looked back at the napkin.

"We take the stuff."

"How?"

"We... take it."

"From the truck?"

"Yes."

"While the driver is there?"

"We ask him to leave."

"And if he doesn't leave?"

Bobby waved his hand. "We'll figure it out. That's the beauty of a flexible plan."

Sol rubbed his temples. "This is not a plan. This is a series of hopes arranged in sequence."

"That's what all plans are, Sol. Don't be negative."

THE CREW STEALS A TRUCK

The first problem was that Frankie's car wouldn't start.

"I told you it needed work," Frankie said, turning the key for the eighth time.

"You said it was fine!"

"I said it was fine for driving! Not for crime!"

"All driving is potentially crime, Frankie! That's the nature of driving!"

They ended up using Nicky's cousin's van.

Nicky's cousin was named Gerald, and Gerald had questions.

"What do you need the van for?"

"Moving furniture," Nicky said.

"What furniture?"

"A friend's furniture."

"What friend?"

"A friend you don't know."

"I know all your friends, Nicky. You only have like four friends."

"This is a new friend."

Gerald looked at the crew, who were standing behind Nicky trying to look like people who moved furniture and not people who committed felonies.

"Is this about crime?" Gerald asked.

"No."

"Because it looks like crime."

"It's furniture, Gerald."

"Crime furniture?"

"GERALD."

Gerald gave them the van.

He also gave them a lecture about how he wasn't stupid and he knew something was going on and if they damaged his van he would tell Nicky's mother, which was a threat more terrifying than anything Tony Smiles could offer.

The second problem was traffic.

"Why is there traffic?" Bobby demanded, as if traffic was a personal insult.

"It's 5 PM on a Tuesday," Sol said. "This is when traffic happens."

"On I-90?"

"Especially on I-90."

"Since when?"

"Since cars we're invented, Bobby."

They sat in traffic for two hours.

During this time, Vinny and Frankie got into an argument about whether a hot dog was a sandwich.

"It's meat between bread," Frankie said. "That's a sandwich."

"The bread is connected. Sandwich bread is two separate pieces."

"What about a sub? Sub bread is connected."

"A sub is different."

"How is it different?"

"It just is!"

"That's not an argument, Vinny! That's just saying words!"

Bobby turned around from the passenger seat.

"Both of you shut up. A hot dog is not a sandwich. A hot dog is a hot dog. It's its own category. This is not complicated."

"What about a taco?" Nicky asked.

Everyone stared at him.

"What about a taco," Bobby repeated.

"Is a taco a sandwich?"

"Why would a taco be a sandwich?"

"It's meat and stuff in a bread thing."

"A tortilla is not bread."

"What is it then?"

"It's a tortilla!"

"But what is a tortilla?"

Bobby opened his mouth. Closed it. Opened it again.

"Sol. What is a tortilla?"

Sol sighed. "A tortilla is an unleavened flatbread made from corn or wheat flour."

"So it IS bread," Nicky said triumphantly.

"NICKY."

The third problem was that they missed the truck.

By the time they got to the exit, the truck had already passed.

"Where is it?" Bobby demanded, looking around like the truck might be hiding.

"It's probably at the warehouse by now," Sol said, checking his watch.

"We're two hours late."

"So we go to the warehouse."

"The warehouse full of Tony Smiles' people?"

"We'll be subtle."

"Bobby. Nothing about this has been subtle. We're in a van that says "Gerald's Plumbing" on the side."

Everyone looked at the van.

It did, in fact, say "Gerald's Plumbing" on the side.

And also "No Job Too Small!" with a cartoon toilet giving a thumbs up.

"Why does your cousin have a plumbing van?" Bobby asked Nicky.

"He's a plumber."

"Since when?"

"Since always?"

"I thought he sold insurance."

"That's my other cousin."

"How many cousins do you have?"

"Eleven."

"ELEVEN?"

THE CREW GOES TO THE WAREHOUSE

The warehouse was not, as it turned out, full of Tony Smiles' people.

It was full of a different crew entirely.

A crew that nobody recognized.

A crew that seemed very surprised to see a plumbing van pull up.

"Who the hell are you?" the largest man Bobby had ever seen asked.

Bobby, to his credit, did not hesitate.

"Plumbers."

"Plumbers?"

"We got a call. Something about a toilet."

The large man looked at the warehouse. At the van. At Bobby's suit, which was absolutely not plumber attire.

"You're plumbers."

"Specialty plumbers."

"What specialty?"

"High-end toilets. Executive bathrooms. That kind of thing."

Sol was making a sound in the back of the van that might have been a prayer or might have been a stroke.

Frankie had his eyes closed and was mouthing what appeared to be the Lord's Prayer.

Vinny was reaching for a gun he definitely should not have brought.

Nicky was smiling, because Nicky smiled in all situations, appropriate or not.

The large man stared at Bobby for a very long time.

Then he burst out laughing.

"Executive bathrooms! That's good. That's really good." He turned to his colleagues. "You hear that? Executive bathrooms!"

The other men laughed too.

Bobby laughed along, because what else could he do.

"Alright, alright," the large man said, wiping his eyes. "I don't know who you are or what you're actually doing here, but I respect the commitment to the bit. Get out of here before I change my mind."

They got out of there.

Very quickly.

The van's tires squealed in a way that was deeply undignified.

"That went well," Bobby said, as they sped away.

Sol stared at him. "We accomplished nothing."

"We gathered intelligence."

"What intelligence?"

"That wasn't Tony's crew. That was someone else. That's valuable information."

"We almost died!"

"Almost doesn't count."

The fourth problem was that they were being followed.

THE CREW IS FOLLOWED

Vinny saw them first.

"Black sedan. Three cars back. Been there since the warehouse."

Bobby turned to look.

"Don't look!" Vinny hissed.

"How am I supposed to confirm if I don't look?"

"Trust me!"

"I trust you, I just also want to look!"

Bobby looked.

The black sedan was, in fact, three cars back. It had tinted windows and the particular energy of a vehicle that meant business.

"Okay, we're being followed," Bobby confirmed.

"I JUST SAID THAT."

"Who is it?" Frankie asked, his voice climbing toward registers previously unknown to science.

"Could be anyone. Tony's people. The guys from the warehouse. Cops. Angry plumbers."

"Why would angry plumbers be following us?"

"We're driving a plumbing van and we're clearly not plumbers. That might upset real plumbers."

"Is that a thing? Plumber turf wars?"

"Everything is a turf war, Nicky. That's the nature of capitalism."

Sol was doing calculations on a napkin.

"If we take the next exit, we can loop around and—"

"No time for math, Sol! This is a car chase!"

"Car chases benefit from math!"

"NICKY, DRIVE FASTER!"

Nicky drove faster.

This was a mistake, because Nicky was not a good driver under normal circumstances and was an actively dangerous driver under pressure.

He took a turn too hard.

The van tipped slightly.

Everyone screamed.

Somehow, the van did not flip.

This seemed like a miracle but was probably just physics being temporarily generous.

The sedan followed.

It was gaining.

"We need to lose them!" Bobby shouted.

"HOW?" everyone shouted back.

"Do something unexpected!"

Nicky did something unexpected.

He drove directly into a parking lot.

Specifically, the parking lot of a Portillo's.

THE CREW HIDES IN A PORTILLO'S

"Why are we at Portillo's?" Bobby demanded.

"You said do something unexpected!"

"I meant unexpected to THEM, not to ME!"

"This was unexpected to everyone!"

They piled out of the van and ran inside.

The Portillo's was crowded, because it was dinner time, because Portillo's was always crowded at dinner time, because Portillo's was a Chicago institution and institutions didn't care about criminal pursuits.

Bobby led them to a booth in the back.

"Act natural."

"We just ran in here like lunatics!"

"Natural lunatics. Chicago is full of them. We blend in."

A waitress approached.

"What can I get you?"

Bobby looked at the menu like this was a completely normal dinner outing.

"Five Italian beefs. Dipped. Hot giardiniera. And five chocolate cake shakes."

"Anything else?"

"Cheese fries for the table."

"You got it."

She walked away.

Everyone stared at Bobby.

"What? We might be here a while."

The black sedan pulled into the parking lot.

Through the window, they watched two men get out.

The men looked around. Looked at the van. Looked at the Portillo's.

Then they walked inside.

"Don't make eye contact," Bobby whispered.

"Should we run?" Frankie whispered back.

"We just ordered food."

"Bobby, people are trying to kill us!"

"They're not going to do anything in a Portillo's. This is neutral ground."

"Since when is Portillo's neutral ground?"

"Since always. You don't start violence in a Portillo's. It's sacred."

The two men walked past their booth.

Looked at them.

Kept walking.

Sat down at a booth on the other side of the restaurant.

Ordered food.

"They're... eating," Nicky observed.

"Of course they're eating. It's Portillo's. Everyone eats."

"But they were following us."

"And now they're eating. Those things aren't mutually exclusive."

The food arrived.

Both tables ate in silence.

It was the most civilized standoff in Chicago criminal history.

After twenty minutes, one of the men from the sedan walked over to their booth.

"Bobby Bologna?"

Bobby looked up from his beef. "Who's asking?"

"Tony wants to talk."

"He can call me."

"He wants to talk in person."

"Then he can come here. I'm eating."

The man looked at the half-finished meal. At the chocolate cake shakes. At the cheese fries.

"He said you'd say that."

"Then he knows me well."

The man went back to his booth.

Made a phone call.

Came back.

"Tony says okay. He'll meet you here. Tomorrow. Noon."

"I'll be here."

The man nodded.

Then he went back to his booth, finished his food, paid his check, and left.

The crew sat in stunned silence.

"Did we just schedule a meeting through Portillo's?" Sol asked.

"Apparently."

"This is not how business is supposed to work."

"This is exactly how business works in Chicago." Bobby took another bite of his beef. "You want to meet someone, you go where the food is. The food is the neutral territory. The food is the peace."

Nicky raised his hand.

"I have a question."

"What?"

"What happened to the original plan? The truck?"

Everyone looked at each other.

Nobody had an answer.

The truck, wherever it was, had been completely forgotten in the chaos.

"The truck was never the point," Bobby said finally.

"It was literally the entire plan!"

"The plan evolved. That's what good plans do. They evolve."

"Into what? We accomplished nothing!"

"We got a meeting with Tony. That's something."

"We could have gotten a meeting with Tony by calling him!"

"But this way was more interesting."

Sol put his head in his hands.

Frankie was crying quietly.

Vinny was angry, but Vinny was always angry, so this was not notable.

Nicky was eating his third chocolate cake shake.

And Bobby sat back, satisfied, like everything had gone exactly according to plan.

Which, in Bobby's mind, it had.

Because Bobby's plans never worked the way they were supposed to.

They just worked.

Eventually.

In ways nobody could predict.

Including Bobby.

"Alright," Bobby said, finishing his beef. "Same time tomorrow. And Nicky, wash Gerald's van. We're representing."

"Representing what?"

"Chicago, Nicky. We're representing Chicago."

Outside, the sun was setting.

Inside, the crew was exhausted.

And somewhere, a truck full of electronics was arriving at a warehouse, completely untouched, because the people sent to steal it had gotten lost, argued about sandwiches, pretended to be plumbers, gotten chased through the city, and ended up eating dinner instead.

Just another Tuesday in Chicago.

Nicky Peanuts and the Philosophy of Snacks

Nicky Moretti was not stupid.

People thought he was stupid because he asked simple questions and said obvious things and had the kind of face that suggested his thoughts were moving through mud instead of air.

But Nicky wasn't stupid.

He was simple.

There was a difference.

Stupid meant you couldn't understand things. Nicky could understand things. He understood loyalty and friendship and the importance of being there when people needed you. He understood that Bobby was the boss and Sol was the brain and Vinny was the muscle and Frankie was the worrier. He understood his role in the crew, which was to be enthusiastic and present and ready to help with whatever needed helping.

Simple meant you didn't complicate things unnecessarily. Most people spent their lives making easy things difficult—worrying about things they couldn't control, arguing about things that didn't matter, turning every moment into an opportunity for stress.

Nicky didn't do that.

Nicky ate when he was hungry.

Nicky slept when he was tired.

Nicky helped his friends when they needed help.

And when something was bothering him, he ate peanuts, which was how he'd gotten his nickname.

It was a good life.

Maybe not impressive. Maybe not ambitious. But good.

He had gotten into this business almost by accident.

He was twenty-four when his cousin introduced him to a guy who knew a guy who needed someone to do simple tasks—deliveries, mostly, moving things from one place to another without asking questions about what the things were.

Nicky was good at not asking questions.

Not because he was incurious—he was actually very curious about many things, including nature documentaries and professional wrestling and the mechanics of how hot dogs were made—but because he understood that some questions didn't have answers you wanted to hear.

The deliveries led to other tasks.

The other tasks led to meeting Bobby.

Meeting Bobby led to everything else.

That was ten years ago.

Now Nicky was thirty-four, still single, still living in the same apartment he'd rented when he first started working for Bobby. The apartment wasn't fancy—one bedroom, a kitchen that barely fit a single person, a view of a brick wall that had been painted and repainted so many times it looked like geological strata—but it was his.

He had a dog named Meatball, a pit bull mix he'd adopted from a shelter four years ago. Meatball was the best thing in his life, a constant source of unconditional love and enthusiasm that made even the worst days better.

He had a collection of wrestling action figures that he'd been building since childhood, displayed on a shelf in his living room where they could watch over everything. His favorite was Hulk Hogan from 1985, still in decent condition despite decades of handling.

He had a routine that gave his days structure: morning coffee, walking Meatball, checking in with Bobby or Sol or whoever needed him, doing whatever tasks needed doing, evening beer, falling asleep to whatever was on TV.

It wasn't complicated.

It wasn't supposed to be.

People underestimated Nicky.

That was okay.

Being underestimated was useful. When people thought you were stupid, they said things in front of you that they wouldn't say in front of smarter people. They let their guard down. They treated you like furniture, and furniture heard everything.

Nicky heard everything.

He just chose not to share most of it.

The night of the zoo—the bad night, the night that Nicky tried not to think about too much—had changed something in him.

Not a lot. Not in a dramatic way. Just a small shift, like a picture frame that had been straightened.

The lion had looked at him.

That part was true. He hadn't imagined it.

In the middle of everything—the chaos and the fear and the darkness—one of the lions had stopped what it was doing and looked directly at Nicky with eyes that were not dead at all but very, very alive.

It had seen him.

Not just looked at him—seen him.

And in that moment, Nicky had felt something he couldn't quite describe. Recognition, maybe. The sense that the lion understood exactly what was happening and exactly who was responsible and was choosing, for its own reasons, not to make a bigger deal out of it.

Like they had an agreement.

Like they were both predators, of a kind, doing what predators did.

Nicky still went to the zoo sometimes.

Not to that exhibit. Never to that exhibit. But to the other parts. The giraffes, which had always been his favorites. The penguins, who always looked like they were judging you. The gift shop, where he bought Meatball a new toy every time because Meatball deserved nice things.

He told himself he went because he enjoyed it.

But sometimes he wondered if he went because of the lion.

Because of the look.

Because of whatever had passed between them in that moment.

Bobby worried about Nicky after the zoo night. Nicky could tell. Bobby kept checking on him, asking if he was okay, if he needed anything, if he wanted to talk.

Nicky said he was fine.

He was fine.

Or he would be.

The thing about being simple was that you didn't dwell. You experienced something, you processed it, and you moved forward. You didn't get stuck analyzing everything from every angle until the analysis became its own prison.

The lion had looked at him.

He had looked back.

And now it was done.

And Nicky still had peanuts to eat and tasks to complete and a dog waiting at home who would be thrilled to see him regardless of what he'd done or where he'd been.

That was enough.

That was everything.

The Safe House — Location Unknown Every operation needed a safe house.

Somewhere to go when things went wrong. Somewhere to hide when the heat got too hot. Somewhere that existed off the books, unknown to anyone who might be looking.

Bobby's safe house was an apartment in Rogers Park.

The building was unremarkable.

Three stories. Brick. The kind of place that existed in every neighborhood in every city, housing people who were just trying to get by.

The apartment itself was on the second floor. Two bedrooms. One bathroom. A kitchen with appliances from the seventies that still worked because they did not make appliances like they used to.

Bobby had owned it for fifteen years.

Paid cash. Used a fake name. Never told anyone except Sol.

"Why Rogers Park?" Sol had asked, when Bobby first showed him.

"Because nobody looks in Rogers Park. People look in the obvious places. The nice neighborhoods. The connected neighborhoods. Nobody expects anything important to be happening in Rogers Park."

"That's surprisingly strategic."

"I've moments."

The apartment was stocked with everything they might need.

Food that wouldn't expire. Water in jugs along one wall. First aid supplies. A gun in each room because you never knew which room you would be in when trouble arrived.

And cash.

Lots of cash.

Enough to disappear for six months if necessary.

Enough to start over somewhere else if Chicago became impossible.

Bobby came here sometimes when he needed to think.

Not when he was in trouble. Just when he needed space from the constant demands of the life.

He would sit on the couch that smelled like dust and old fabric softener. Stare out the window at the street below. Watch normal people living normal lives and wonder what that was like.

"You know what I realized?" Bobby said to Sol, during one of these visits.

"What?"

"This apartment is the most honest thing I own. No pretense. No performance. Just four walls and a roof and the basic necessities of survival."

"That's depressingly practical."

"Practical is underrated. Everybody wants flashy. Nobody appreciates practical until practical saves their life."

The apartment had a rule.

No business inside these walls.

No meetings. No planning. No discussions of operations or problems or any of the thousand things that normally consumed their days.

This was sanctuary.

This was the one place where Bobby could be something other than Bobby Bologna.

He kept a photo album in the closet.

Old pictures. Family photos. His parents on their wedding day. Bobby as a child, before he understood what the world was and what it would demand of him.

Sometimes he would flip through the album and remember.

What it felt like to be innocent.

What it felt like to believe that the world was fair.

What it felt like before everything got complicated.

"Do you regret it?" Sol asked once. "The path you chose?"

Bobby closed the album.

"Regret is for people who believe they had other options. I never had other options, Sol. This was always who I was going to be. The only question was how I was going to do it."

"And how did you do it?"

"The best I could. Which was sometimes good enough and sometimes not. But always the best I could."

The safe house was still there when Bobby died.

Sol kept paying the rent.

Never told anyone.

Never used it.

Just kept it ready.

In case.

In memory.

In honor of a man who had taught him that sometimes the most important place was the one nobody knew about.

The one where you could be yourself.

Even if yourself was complicated.

Even if yourself was someone the world was not supposed to see.

Ricky The Coat — A Character Study Ricky Mantelli wore the same coat for fifteen years.

Not the same style of coat.

The same actual coat.

Long. Black. Heavy. The kind of coat that suggested its owner took things seriously, possibly too seriously, and definitely owned at least one weapon.

Nobody knew where the coat came from.

Some said it was his father's coat, passed down like an heirloom. Some said he won it in a poker game. Some said he killed a man for it, which was probably an exaggeration but might not have been.

Ricky never explained.

Ricky rarely explained anything.

"Why do you always wear that coat?" Tony Smiles asked him once.

"Because it fits."

"You could buy a new one. Something nicer."

"This one fits."

"That isn't an answer."

"It's the only answer I've."

The coat had seen things.

It had been present at negotiations that went well and negotiations that went badly. It had absorbed smoke from a hundred cigars and rain from a thousand storms. It had been shot at, stabbed at, and set on fire once in an incident nobody talked about anymore.

And still it held together.

Still it fit.

Still it was the first thing Ricky reached for every morning and the last thing he took off every night.

Bobby Bologna respected the coat.

This surprised people.

Bobby and Ricky were on opposite sides. They had tried to hurt each other multiple times. They would probably try again.

But the coat was different.

"You've to admire commitment," Bobby said once. "That man has worn the same coat for longer than most marriages last. That's dedication."

"It's also weird," Sol observed.

"Weird and admirable aren't mutually exclusive."

Ricky The Coat died in 2003.

Heart attack.

They found him in his apartment, still wearing the coat.

Some said that was fitting.

Some said it was sad.

Some said he probably would have wanted it that way.

The coat was buried with him.

Tony Smiles made sure of it.

"He wouldn't have wanted anyone else wearing it," Tony said at the funeral. "It was his. Only his. Some things can't be inherited."

The mourners nodded.

They understood.

Some possessions became part of their owners.

And some owners became part of their possessions.

Ricky The Coat was both.

And now both were gone.

Years later, people still talked about the coat.

How it seemed to have its own presence. Its own weight. Its own way of entering a room before Ricky did.

The coat became legend.

Which Ricky would have hated.

He never wanted attention.

He just wanted to wear his coat in peace.

But legends do not ask permission.

They just happen.

Whether the subjects want them to or not.

The Woman Behind the Smile — Angie Marino Tony Smiles thought he was in charge.

Angie Marino let him think that.

She had been running the North Side operation for three years before Tony even realized it. By the time he caught on, it was too late — she had made herself indispensable.

That was Angie's gift. Making herself essential while remaining invisible.

She watched Bobby Bologna the way a chess player watches an opponent.

Studied his patterns. His weaknesses. His absurd, beautiful, suicidal commitment to living out loud.

Part of her admired him.

Most of her wanted him gone.

"Bobby is predictable," she told Tony. "He will react emotionally. He will escalate. He cannot help himself."

"So we provoke him."

"We give him opportunities to self-destruct. There's a difference."

"What's the difference?"

"Provocation leaves fingerprints. Opportunity looks like coincidence."

Angie had grown up watching her father hit her mother and her mother pretend it wasn't happening. She learned early that visible power

145

was fragile power. She learned to watch. To wait. To let men destroy themselves while she positioned herself to inherit what remained.

When the FAO Schwarz situation escalated, Angie felt something close to satisfaction. Bobby had done exactly what she expected. Reacted with his heart instead of his head. Made himself a target.

The only thing she hadn't anticipated was his death. Not the death itself — the manner. A hot dog. At a basketball game. It was so perfectly, absurdly Bobby Bologna.

When she heard the news, Angie laughed. Not at his death. At the universe. At the cosmic joke of a man who survived decades of violence only to be killed by processed meat.

That night, she poured expensive whiskey and raised it toward the window.

"To Bobby Bologna," she said quietly. "You magnificent idiot."

She drank.

And then she got back to work.

Because the city didn't stop for dead men.

The Delaney File — 1975 Frank Delaney was twelve years old when Bobby Bolognas father killed his brother.

Officially, Patrick Delaney died in a "warehouse incident." Fell from a loading platform. Tragic accident.

But Frank knew. His father knew. Everyone in the neighborhood knew.

Patrick was twenty-two, working for Sal Filoni's operation, doing things the family didn't discuss. He got caught skimming. Not much — a few hundred here and there. But enough.

Sal Filoni believed in lessons.

Patrick Delaney became one.

Franks father drank himself to death over the next decade. His mother moved to Indiana. And Frank stayed. In Chicago. Waiting.

He became a cop because cops could access things civilians couldn't.

Records. Investigations. The official documentation of unofficial crimes.

When Sal Filoni died in 1979 — heart attack, Wrigley Field — Frank felt nothing. The old man was gone. But the son remained. Bobby Bologna. The inheritor of his father's sins.

Frank transferred to Organized Crime in 1992. Spent six years building a case. And then Bobby choked on a hot dog.

The night Frank heard the news, he drove to Resurrection Cemetery. Found Patrick's grave. Stood in darkness.

He had wanted justice. Wanted to look Bobby in the eyes in a courtroom. Wanted the satisfaction of victory.

Instead, the universe gave him a punchline.

"I'm sorry," Frank whispered to his brothers headstone. "I tried."

Patrick didn't answer.

Patrick hadn't answered anything in twenty-three years.

CHAPTER 8.5

The Sit-Down

Carmine's — Rush Street

The restaurant was neutral territory.

This mattered because neutral territory was the only kind where both sides could pretend they weren't measuring each other for coffins.

Tony Smiles had picked the place. Bobby had agreed because saying no would have been weakness, and weakness in this business was the same as bleeding in shark-infested waters.

Bobby arrived first because Bobby always arrived first.

"You're early," Sol observed from the passenger seat.

"Early is on time. On time is late. Late is dead."

"That's very dramatic."

"I'm a dramatic person."

Vinny checked his mirror for the third time in thirty seconds. "We sure about this? Just walking in there?"

"It's a restaurant, Vinny. Not a trap."

"Restaurants can be traps."

"Restaurants with good calamari are rarely traps. The overhead is too high."

Sol rubbed his temples. "That logic is not as sound as you think it is."

"The logic is fine. The calamari is better."

Bobby walked in alone.

This was the protocol. The bosses meet. The crews wait outside.

Everyone pretends they're having a civilized conversation instead of a cold war negotiation.

The maître d' recognized him immediately—not by name, but by type.

You didn't work Rush Street without learning to identify men whose dinner reservations came with implications.

"Mr. Caravelli's table?"

"That's the one."

The walk through the restaurant felt longer than it was. Diners glanced up, then glanced away. The smart ones. The ones who understood that noticing too much in Chicago could become a liability.

Tony Smiles was already seated.

He was smiling.

Of course he was.

Anthony "Tony Smiles" Caravelli was fifty-one years old and looked forty.

This was because he spent money on things like dermatologists and personal trainers, which Bobby found suspicious on principle.

He wore a suit that cost more than Nicky's car. His hair was silver at the temples in a way that suggested he'd paid someone to make it silver at the temples. His teeth were too white. His watch was too gold. Everything about him screamed money, which was the point, because in Tony's world, appearances were ninety percent of the game.

The smile never wavered as Bobby approached.

"Bobby Bologna." The name came out like he was tasting it. "Finally."

"Tony." Bobby slid into the booth across from him. "Nice place. Little fancy for my taste."

"Fancy is the taste, Bobby. That's the whole point."

A waiter materialized with water glasses. Crystal, not regular. Bobby ignored his.

"So," Tony said, still smiling. "We should talk."

"We're talking."

"We should talk about Schaumburg."

Bobby had prepared for this conversation.

Sol had run the numbers. Vinny had run the scenarios. Frankie had run to the bathroom three times because Frankie always ran to the bathroom when stress was involved.

The basic situation was simple: Tony wanted the northwest suburbs.

Bobby wanted the northwest suburbs. The suburbs couldn't support both of them. Something had to give.

"Schaumburg is open territory," Bobby said.

"Schaumburg was open territory. Past tense. I've made arrangements."

"Arrangements can be un-arranged."

Tony's smile flickered—just for a moment, just enough to see something else underneath.

"You know what I like about you, Bobby? You're direct. No games. No politics. Just—" He made a gesture with his hand. "—appetite."

"Is that supposed to be an insult?"

"It's an observation. You want things. You take things. Very simple. Very honest."

"And what do you want, Tony?"

The smile returned, fuller now.

"I want what's best for everyone. Peace. Prosperity. A city where business can happen without... complications."

"Complications meaning me."

"Complications meaning the old ways. The loud ways. The ways that attract attention from people we'd rather not attract attention from."

Bobby leaned forward. "You think I'm loud?"

"I think you beat a tourist for putting ketchup on a hot dog last month. In public. In front of witnesses."

"That was education."

"That was a lawsuit waiting to happen."

"The lawsuit was settled."

"The lawsuit was a symptom." Tony's voice dropped, losing none of its smoothness but gaining an edge. "You're a symptom, Bobby. Of a disease that's killing this business. The cowboys. The hotheads. The guys who think respect comes from volume instead of results."

Bobby felt his jaw tighten. "You want to talk about results? I've been running this territory for fifteen years without a single federal indictment. How many of your guys are in Stateville right now?"

"Employees get arrested. That's part of the cost of doing business."

"Employees get arrested when the boss gets sloppy. When the boss values looking good over being good."

For the first time, Tony's smile showed teeth.

"Be very careful, Bobby."

"Or what?"

The moment stretched.

Two men in a booth, surrounded by civilians eating salmon and discussing theater tickets, having a conversation about territory and power and the very real possibility of violence.

This was Chicago.

This was always Chicago.

"Here's what's going to happen," Tony said finally. "Schaumburg goes to me. Oak Brook goes to me. The northwest corridor, all of it, goes to me. You keep the South Side. You keep your beefs and your bars and your little sports bets. Everyone's happy."

"And if I say no?"

"Then you're saying something much bigger than no. And you should think very carefully about whether you want to say that."

Bobby picked up his water glass. Drank. Set it down.

"Let me tell you something about Chicago, Tony. This city wasn't built by guys in nice suits having polite conversations. It was built by guys who got their hands dirty. Who knew that some fights were worth having even when the odds were bad. Who understood that respect isn't given—it's taken."

"Inspiring. Very inspiring. You should do motivational speaking."

"You know what I think? I think you're scared. I think all this—"

Bobby gestured at the restaurant, at Tony's suit, at everything. "—is armor. Because deep down, you know you can't win a real fight. You can only win if everyone agrees to play by your rules."

Tony's smile vanished.

Just for a second.

But Bobby saw it.

"Schaumburg is mine," Bobby said, standing. "Come and take it."

He walked out without looking back.

In the car, Vinny was vibrating with nervous energy. "What happened? What did he say? Are we at war?"

Bobby stared out the window at the Chicago skyline.

"Not yet."

Sol watched him carefully. "But soon?"

"Soon enough."

"Bobby." Sol's voice was quiet. Serious. "Tony Smiles has three times our manpower. He has connections we don't have. He has resources we can't match. If this goes hot—"

"Then it goes hot."

"That's not a strategy. That's suicide."

Bobby finally turned to look at his oldest friend.

"You know what my grandfather used to say? He said there are two kinds of men in this world. Men who eat, and men who get eaten. Tony

Smiles thinks he's the first kind. But he's wrong. He's the kind of man who hires other people to do his eating for him. And hired teeth aren't the same as real teeth."

"That's a metaphor, Bobby. We need a plan."

Bobby smiled.

"The metaphor is the plan."

Vinny and Nicky exchanged confused looks.

Sol just sighed.

"We're all going to die."

"Eventually," Bobby agreed. "But not today. Today, we eat."

He pointed at a sign up ahead. Portillo's.

"Pull over. I need a beef."

"We just had a life-threatening meeting and you want a beef?"

"Sol. When is a beef ever not appropriate?"

Sol had no answer for that.

Because in Bobby Bologna's world, the answer was never.

INTERLUDE: ANGELA

The Walnut Room — Marshall Field's She was already there when Bobby arrived.

Angela Benedetto—she'd taken back her maiden name after the divorce—sat at a table by the window, looking at the Christmas tree that dominated the center of the restaurant. Forty feet of lights and ornaments and manufactured wonder.

She looked good.

She always looked good.

That was part of the problem.

"Bobby."

"Angela."

He sat down across from her, feeling suddenly self-conscious about his tracksuit. She was wearing something elegant. Something that probably cost more than his car payment.

"You look..."

"Don't." She held up a hand. "Whatever you're about to say, don't. We're not doing that."

"Doing what?"

"The thing where you pretend everything's normal. The thing where you act like we're old friends catching up."

Bobby adjusted his collar. "We ARE old friends."

"We were married, Bobby. For twelve years. That's not friends. That's... something else."

"What's it, then?"

Angela looked at him with those eyes—dark, sharp, seeing everything he tried to hide.

"It's history. Complicated history. The kind you can't simplify no matter how hard you try."

A waiter appeared.

"Coffee," Bobby said.

"Tea," Angela said. "The chamomile."

The waiter disappeared.

"Tea?" Bobby raised an eyebrow. "Since when?"

"Since I decided to stop living like every day was a heart attack waiting to happen."

"That's pointed."

"It's honest. There's a difference."

They sat in silence for a moment.

Around them, the Walnut Room hummed with holiday shoppers.

Families with children. Couples holding hands. Normal people living normal lives.

Bobby had never felt more out of place.

"Why did you want to meet?" he asked finally.

Angela took a breath.

"Because I'm getting remarried. And I wanted you to hear it from me."

The words hit Bobby like a physical blow.

He'd known, on some level. Known that she'd moved on. Known that she was seeing someone—a dentist, Sol had said, from Winnetka. Nice guy. Normal guy. The kind of guy who came home at six and didn't have to check the car for bombs.

But hearing it was different.

Hearing it made it real.

"Congratulations," he managed.

"Don't do that."

"Do what?"

"Pretend you're happy for me. I know you, Bobby. I know what that face means."

"What does it mean?"

"It means you're hurt and you're trying to hide it. You always had the worst poker face."

Bobby almost laughed. "I've been told I have a very good poker face."

"By people who don't know you. I know you."

The drinks arrived.

Bobby wrapped his hands around his coffee cup, needing something to hold.

"The dentist," he said. "What's his name?"

"Richard."

"Richard the dentist from Winnetka."

"Richard the orthodontist, actually. From Wilmette."

"Even better. Richard the orthodontist from Wilmette." Bobby shook his head. "You really upgraded."

"Bobby..."

154

"No, I mean it. An orthodontist. Steady income. Regular hours. Probably has a retirement plan. 401k. The whole thing."

"He does."

"See? Upgrade."

Angela set down her tea.

"You know what Richard doesn't have? He doesn't have men showing up at his door at 2 AM. He doesn't have to check his car for bombs. He doesn't have a life that could end any day for reasons I'd never be allowed to know."

"I never—"

"You never what? Never put me in danger? Never made me wonder if tonight was the night you didn't come home? Never made me feel like a widow every time the phone rang after midnight?"

Bobby was quiet.

"You did all of those things," Angela said. "Every day. For twelve years. And I loved you anyway. That's the tragedy of it. I loved you so much that I stayed longer than I should have. And then I had to leave before the love killed me."

"I would have protected you."

"You couldn't even protect yourself."

"Angela—"

"Do you know what I prayed for? Every night? I prayed that you would choose me. Just once. That you would look at the life we could have and decide that was worth more than the life you had."

"I didn't know how."

"I know. That's why I left."

She reached across the table and took his hand.

Her fingers were warm. Familiar.

"I don't hate you, Bobby. I never hated you. I just couldn't survive you. Some people are too much to love. You're one of them."

Bobby looked at their hands.

Twelve years of marriage. Three years of divorce. And she could still touch him like that.

Like she knew him.

Like she remembered who he was underneath all the noise.

"Are you happy?" he asked.

"Yes."

"Really happy?"

"Really happy. Richard is... simple. In a good way. He comes home. We eat dinner. We watch television. We go to bed. And in the morning, we do it again. It's not exciting. It's not dramatic. But it's steady. And I needed steady."

"I couldn't give you steady."

"No. You couldn't."

They finished their drinks in something that wasn't quite silence but wasn't quite conversation either.

The space between people who had once been everything to each other and were now just... this.

"The wedding's in March," Angela said, standing. "I won't send you an invitation. It would be cruel."

"Thank you."

"But I wanted you to know. From me. Before you heard it from someone else."

Bobby stood too.

"Angela."

"Yes?"

"I'm sorry. For all of it. For everything I couldn't be."

She looked at him for a long moment.

"I know you are. That's what makes it sad."

She kissed him on the cheek—brief, soft, final—and walked away.

Bobby watched her go.

Past the Christmas tree. Past the shoppers. Past the normal people with their normal lives.

Gone.

He sat back down.

Ordered another coffee.

Stared at the Christmas tree until his vision blurred.

"Sir?" The waiter appeared. "Are you alright?"

Bobby wiped his eyes. Allergies. Had to be allergies.

"Fine. I'm fine."

"Can I get you anything else?"

Bobby looked at the menu. At the holiday specials. At all the food he could order that would fill his stomach but not the empty space Angela had left behind.

"No," he said. "I think I've had enough."

He paid the bill.

156

He walked out of Marshall Field's.
And he never told anyone about the meeting.
Some losses were too private to share.
Even for Bobby Bologna.
Especially for Bobby Bologna.

PART THREE

CHRISTMAS WAR ZONE

December 1997

CHAPTER 9

FAO Schwarz — Michigan Avenue

FAO Schwarz looked like Santa Claus had hired a decorator with no concept of restraint.

Lights everywhere.

Garlands on every railing.

Giant nutcrackers guarding the doors like festive soldiers who had seen things.

Inside, it was wall-to-wall parents, kids, tourists, and people who had no idea how close they were to being part of a police report.

Bobby Bologna hated crowds.

He loved Christmas—the food, the traditions, the excuse to wear a nice coat—but crowds made him nervous. Too many people meant too many variables. Too many witnesses. Too many chances for something to go wrong.

"Why are we here?" Frankie whispered, navigating around a child having a meltdown near the stuffed animals.

"Because I have a goddaughter who wants that giant bear." Bobby pointed at a stuffed bear the size of a small refrigerator. "And because Tony Smiles thinks he owns Michigan Avenue now, so I'm here to remind him that I go wherever I want."

Sol pinched the bridge of his nose. "This is not strategic thinking, Bobby. This is provocation."

"Provocation is a strategy."

"It's really not."

The store was chaos.

Christmas music blared from speakers embedded in fake snow-covered columns. A mechanical Santa waved at nobody in particular from a platform above the entrance. Children ran in every direction, their parents trailing behind with the glazed expressions of people who had given up on discipline weeks ago.

Vinny carried a shopping bag. "You said we're here to buy something."

"We are. For my goddaughter. Or my cousin's kid. One of those small people. They all blur together."

"That's concerning."

"What's concerning is how expensive teddy bears are. This is highway robbery with stuffing."

They pushed through the crowds, past displays of toy trains and action figures and that one section that was just board games and somehow still cost three hundred dollars.

Nicky stopped at a display of remote-control cars. "Hey, Bobby. This one goes fast."

"We're not here for cars."

"But it goes really fast."

"Focus, Nicky."

That's when Sol saw the coat.

The same long leather coat.

The same slow, deliberate walk.

Ricky "The Coat" Mantelli, moving through the stuffed animal aisle like winter with a bad attitude.

Behind him: Tony "Smiles" Caravelli, calm as ever, weaving through parents like he belonged there.

Sol grabbed Bobby's sleeve. "We got company."

Bobby squinted. "You gotta be kidding me."

Tony smiled when he saw them. Of course he did.

"Bobby Bologna. You following me now?"

Bobby spread his arms. "I'm buying toys, Tony. You gonna arrest Santa too?"

Parents nearby slowed down, sensing drama but not yet danger. One woman pulled her child closer. A father started videotaping, because that's what fathers did now.

Tony's smile didn't waver. "We tried to handle this reasonable."

Vinny stepped forward. "You brought your boy to a toy store."

Ricky shifted, hand moving toward his coat.

Sol shouted, "DO NOT DO THIS HERE."

Too late.

The first shot hit a display of singing elves.

They died loudly, sparking and squealing and playing half of "Jingle Bells" before finally, mercifully, going silent.

Everything after that was chaos.

Kids screamed.

Parents panicked.

A thousand toys met their maker.

Vinny tackled Bobby behind a shelf of plush bears—the bears provided surprisingly good cover, absorbing bullets with the passive acceptance of things that had no choice in the matter.

Nicky fired wildly and immediately screamed, "I DON'T LIKE THIS."

Frankie ran straight into a carousel of stuffed animals and disappeared under a pile of teddy bears.

Sol dove under the famous floor piano as bullets cracked above him.

Someone stepped on the piano keys. Christmas music started playing.

It was "We Wish You a Merry Christmas."

This felt disrespectful.

Bobby popped up from behind the bears, fired twice, and yelled, "YOU RUINED MY SHOPPING."

A nutcracker exploded.

Somewhere, an alarm started howling.

Mall security—or whatever passed for security in a toy store—rushed in and instantly regretted their life choices.

"EVERYBODY FREEZE," yelled a security guard who was approximately nineteen years old and had definitely not signed up for this.

Nobody froze.

Tony shouted, "END THIS, BOBBY."

Bobby screamed back, "YOU STARTED IT IN SCHAUMBURG."

Angie Marino appeared—she was always appearing—and grabbed Tony. "WE ARE LEAVING. NOW."

Ricky hesitated.

That hesitation saved him.

Cops poured through the doors, guns drawn, uniforms bright against the Christmas displays.

Everyone scattered like roaches in expensive shoes.

Vinny grabbed Frankie out of the bear pile.

Nicky tripped over a toy train and face-planted, then kept running.

Sol crawled out from the piano, hair full of tinsel.

They burst through a side exit into the cold Chicago air and sirens.

Bobby leaned against the wall, breathing hard.

Inside, Christmas music still played.

"I Saw Mommy Kissing Santa Claus."

Like nothing had happened.

Sol stared at him. "This is a war now."

Bobby wiped blood off his knuckle—his own, from a cut on a broken display—and looked at the flashing lights.

"Good," he said. "I hate surprises."

The next morning, every news station led with the same story.

"CHRISTMAS CHAOS: Shootout at Michigan Avenue Toy Store."

Parents we're interviewed. Children were traumatized. The city council called an emergency meeting about public safety during the holidays.

And somewhere in a Lincoln Park bar, Tony Smiles watched the coverage without smiling.

For the first time in years.

INTERLUDE: WHAT BOBBY SAW

Three Days After FAO Schwarz Bobby couldn't stop seeing the kid.

Not anyone from his crew. Not Tony Smiles or Ricky or any of the people who were supposed to be in the line of fire.

A kid. Maybe seven years old. Brown hair. Red sweater. Holding a stuffed elephant.

Standing right in the path of where Vinny's bullet had gone.

The bullet had missed.

Barely.

But Bobby couldn't stop seeing what would have happened if it hadn't.

"You're quiet," Sol observed.

They were at the diner. Donna's place. Bobby was staring at his eggs like they'd personally offended him.

"I'm thinking."

"About what?"

"Nothing."

Sol knew him well enough to know that wasn't true. But Sol also knew him well enough not to push.

The FAO Schwarz incident had been all over the news.

"SHOOTOUT AT TOY STORE." "CHRISTMAS CHAOS."

"MIRACLE NO ONE HURT."

Miracle.

That's what they called it when luck intervened because skill hadn't.

Bobby had been in firefights before. He'd seen violence. He'd done violence. He'd made peace with the fact that his life involved things that normal people only saw in movies.

But never around kids.

Never in a place where children were supposed to be safe.

Never with a stuffed elephant watching.

"Bobby."

Vinny's voice cut through his thoughts.

"What?"

"You been staring at those eggs for ten minutes. They're getting cold."

Bobby looked down. The eggs were, in fact, cold. Congealed.

163

Unappetizing.

"I'm not hungry."

Everyone at the table stopped eating.

Bobby Bologna saying he wasn't hungry was like the sun announcing it wasn't going to rise.

"You sick?" Nicky asked.

"I'm fine."

"You don't look fine."

"I said I'm FINE."

The sharpness in his voice surprised everyone. Including Bobby.

That night, he dreamed about the kid.

Same brown hair. Same red sweater. Same stuffed elephant.

But in the dream, the bullet didn't miss.

In the dream, Bobby watched the kid fall. Watched the elephant tumble from small hands. Watched blood spread across linoleum while Christmas music played and mechanical Santa waved at nobody.

He woke up gasping.

3:47 AM.

The ceiling looked the same as always. The apartment was quiet. The city hummed outside his window.

Everything was fine.

Everything was not fine.

Bobby got out of bed and walked to the bathroom.

Splashed water on his face.

Looked at himself in the mirror.

Who was he?

Fifty-three years old. Never married for long. No children of his own.

A man who had built an empire on loyalty and violence and the understanding that certain things were necessary.

A man who had almost gotten a seven-year-old killed.

The kid's face stared back at him from the mirror. Superimposed. Accusing.

"It wasn't my fault," Bobby told the reflection.

The reflection didn't believe him.

The next day, Bobby did something unusual.

He went to church.

Not for confession—Bobby hadn't been to confession since 1979, and even then he'd left out the important parts. But for... something. He didn't have a word for it.

The church was empty at 10 AM on a Wednesday. Just Bobby and the statues and the particular silence that only churches had. The silence of accumulated prayers. Of centuries of people asking for things they didn't deserve and sometimes receiving them anyway.

Bobby sat in a pew near the back.

"I didn't mean for it to happen," he said to no one. To everyone. To whatever was listening, if anything was. "I didn't know there would be kids. I would never—"

He stopped.

Would never what? Would never have gone to the toy store if he'd known? Would never have provoked Tony Smiles in the first place?

Would never have chosen this life, this path, this version of himself that put children in danger as collateral?

He'd done all of those things.

He'd made all of those choices.

The kid in the red sweater was a consequence of decisions Bobby had made years ago, decades ago, every single day that he woke up and chose to be Bobby Bologna instead of someone else.

"I don't know how to be different," he admitted. "I don't know if I can."

The statues didn't answer.

But Bobby hadn't expected them to.

A week later, something changed.

Bobby was walking past a playground—just walking, not going anywhere in particular—when he heard a kid laugh.

A real laugh. The kind that comes from pure joy. The kind adults forget how to make.

He stopped.

Watched.

A little girl on a swing, maybe six years old, being pushed by her father. Going higher and higher, laughing louder each time, completely unaware of anything except this moment of flight.

Bobby watched until the father noticed him and started to look concerned.

Then he walked away.

"I want to be more careful," Bobby told Sol that night.

"Careful how?"

"With the collateral. With the... the places we do things. The times. I don't want any more situations like FAO Schwarz."

Sol studied him.

"That's new."

"Maybe I'm getting old."

"You've been old for years. This is something else."

Bobby didn't respond.

He didn't have to.

Sol had known him for thirty years. Sol understood things without needing them explained.

"I'll make some changes to how we operate," Sol said. "More careful. More contained."

"Thank you."

"Bobby."

"Yeah?"

"Whatever you're carrying from that day... you don't have to carry it alone."

Bobby looked at his oldest friend.

"Yeah," he said. "I do."

Because that was the weight of being Bobby Bologna.

You carried the things you'd done.

You carried the things you'd almost done.

And you carried them alone, because admitting they mattered meant admitting you weren't as certain as everyone believed.

Some weights couldn't be shared.

Some weights were the price of being who you were.

Bobby paid that price.

Every day.

In the quiet moments.

Where nobody could see.

CHAPTER 10

Marshall Field's — State Street

Marshall Field's was where Chicago went to pretend it was elegant.

Tall ceilings.

Marble floors.

Perfume in the air so thick you could taste it.

And now, thanks to Bobby Bologna and Tony Smiles, it was also where Chicago went to witness the continued deterioration of civil society.

Two days after the FAO Schwarz incident—which the newspapers were already calling "The Toy Store Terror," because newspapers loved alliteration almost as much as they loved making things sound worse than they were—Bobby decided they needed to go shopping again.

"Are you insane?" Sol asked, not for the first time.

"I need gloves."

"There are glove stores that aren't on Michigan Avenue."

"I want gloves from Field's. It's tradition. My mother used to bring me here as a kid."

"Your mother would also want you to not get shot in the cosmetics department."

Bobby adjusted his coat. "She'd understand."

Marshall Field's at Christmas was a spectacle unto itself.

The famous holiday windows drew crowds from across the Midwest—elaborate mechanical displays telling stories about winter and wonder and the magic of the season. Inside, the store was decorated with restraint and taste, which is to say with slightly less restraint than everywhere else on State Street.

The tree in the Walnut Room was legendary.

The shopping was extravagant.

The possibility of violence was, this week, unfortunately elevated.

"I don't see anyone," Vinny reported, scanning the perfume department.

"That doesn't mean they're not here."

"Should we split up?"

"God, no. We stay together. If something happens, we handle it together."

Frankie whispered, "If something happens, I'm going to cry."

"You always cry."

"This time will be special crying. This will be Christmas crying."

They moved through the store in a tight formation—not quite military, but close enough that casual observers might have noticed they were more organized than typical holiday shoppers.

Bobby stopped at a display of leather gloves.

"These are nice."

Sol examined the price tag. "These are three hundred dollars."

"Quality costs money, Sol. That's capitalism."

"That's insanity."

"Same thing, often."

Bobby tried on a pair—black leather, soft as butter, the kind of gloves that made you feel like a slightly classier criminal.

"I'll take these."

The saleswoman smiled. "Excellent choice, sir. Shall I wrap them?"

"Please. They're for me."

"A gift to yourself?"

"The best kind."

That's when Bobby saw the reflection in the display case.

Tony Smiles.

Behind him.

Smiling.

"You really do have terrible taste in shopping destinations," Tony said.

Bobby turned slowly. "And you really do have a stalking problem."

They stood facing each other in the glove department of one of Chicago's finest department stores, surrounded by luxury goods and Christmas cheer and the very real possibility of everything going wrong again.

"You cost me three guys after FAO Schwarz," Tony said, still smiling.

"They got picked up by the cops. My guys are out on bail, but they're not happy."

"Your guys shouldn't have shot up a toy store."

"Your guys shot back."

168

"That's called self-defense. Or reciprocity. Depends who you ask."

Angie Marino appeared beside Tony, because of course she did.

"This needs to stop," she said. "We're attracting too much attention. The cops, the feds, the news. This is bad for everyone."

Bobby laughed. "You don't get to start a fight and then complain about the noise."

"We didn't start anything. We made a business proposal. You responded with territorial aggression."

"Territorial—" Bobby's voice rose. "You were moving into my neighborhoods."

"The suburbs are not your neighborhoods."

"Chicago is my neighborhood. All of it. Every block, every mall, every parking lot. You want to operate here, you talk to me first."

Angie's eyes hardened. "That's not how this works anymore, Bobby. The old rules are dead. The old bosses are dead or in prison. It's a new game now."

"Then I'll learn the new rules by winning."

Ricky "The Coat" Mantelli had been silent until now, lurking near a display of cashmere scarves like a particularly fashionable gargoyle.

He stepped forward.

Vinny stepped forward.

Sol said, very quietly, "Here we go again."

A security guard started walking toward them, drawn by the tension that was probably visible from space.

Bobby looked at the guard. Looked at Ricky. Looked at Tony, still smiling that goddamn smile.

"Not here," Bobby said.

Tony's smile widened. "Where then?"

"Anywhere else. Somewhere without—" Bobby gestured at the store around them. "Without Christmas."

"Christmas is everywhere this time of year."

"Then we wait until January. Give everyone a holiday."

Tony considered this. "That's unexpectedly reasonable."

"I can be reasonable when I want to be."

"That's new."

They stood in silence for a long moment.

Then something happened that nobody expected.

Tony extended his hand.

"Truce," he said. "Until January. Then we figure this out properly."

Bobby looked at the hand like it might bite him.

"You mean that?"

"I mean that I'm tired of spending Christmas in hospitals and police stations. I mean that my wife is threatening to leave me if I come home covered in blood one more time. I mean that even I have limits."

Bobby hesitated.

Then he shook the hand.

"Until January."

"Until January."

They parted ways without further incident.

Bobby bought his gloves. Tony disappeared into the crowd. The security guard stood confused for a while before deciding that whatever had happened was not his problem.

Outside, snow had started falling.

Not the dirty gray snow that accumulated in March.

Real snow. Christmas snow. The kind that made the city look almost magical.

"What just happened?" Frankie asked.

"We bought time," Sol answered. "Not much. But some."

"Is that good?"

"It's not bad. For now."

Bobby looked up at the falling snow, his new gloves warm against his hands.

"Merry Christmas," he said to nobody in particular.

And for a few weeks, at least, it was.

INTERLUDE: ANGIE

Lincoln Park — The Same Night

Angie Marino was the only person in the bar who wasn't pretending to enjoy themselves.

The bar was Tony's. The cocktails had ingredients in them that nobody could pronounce. The clientele was a careful mix of men who had money and men who wanted men who had money to think they had money too. Everyone smiled. Everyone laughed. Everyone watched the door.

Angie sat in the corner booth and watched all of them.

She was forty-one years old. She had been working with Tony for nine of those years, and before that, she had been working with Frank Fratini, who had been a serious man, and before that she had been a paralegal at a firm on LaSalle Street that had taught her two things: how to read a contract, and how to recognize when a contract was being read to her.

She was the only woman in the room who was not waitstaff.

This was no longer remarkable to her. It had been remarkable in 1989. By 1997 it was background.

Her phone — a flip phone, because nobody in this business yet trusted the cell phone — buzzed. A pager number she recognized. Tony, asking where she was. She did not respond.

She was tired tonight in a way she had not been tired before.

The Marshall Field's afternoon had ended in a handshake. Tony had come back to the bar and ordered a kombucha and described the truce in his quiet, smiling way, and Angie had watched him describe it and known three things at once.

The first thing was that Tony believed the truce.

The second thing was that Bobby Bologna also believed the truce.

The third thing was that the truce would not survive January, because Tony was incapable of letting another man be loud and alive in a city he wanted to own.

She knew this because she had been in the room when Tony decided what happened to Mickey Flowers.

She had not been in the room when it happened. Tony was careful about that. Tony was careful about everything. But she had been in the room when the decision was made, and she had watched him decide it the way a man might decide what to order for lunch, and she had thought, at the time: I am working for a person who is wrong on the inside.

She had not done anything about it.

You did not do anything about Tony Smiles. You worked for him until you could leave, and you tried to leave alive.

The kid in the next booth was laughing too loud about something his date had said. Angie watched the date's face. The date was not amused. The date was performing amusement, the way Angie had performed it for years before she stopped.

Angie thought about her mother. Her mother was eighty-three and lived in Elmwood Park in the same house she had lived in for fifty-one years. Her mother thought Angie was an executive at an investment firm.

Her mother was not entirely wrong.

Bobby Bologna would die before the truce broke. Angie did not know this yet. If she had known it, she would have felt mildly relieved, and the relief would have made her ashamed of herself, and the shame would have lasted approximately one drink.

But she did not know it.

She knew only that Tony was smiling somewhere, and that meant something bad was going to happen to somebody, and that her job, when it happened, would be to clean up the parts that money could not.

She paid for her drink in cash.

She left a tip that was generous but not memorable.

She walked out into the snow.

A man on the corner asked her for change. She gave him a twenty, because that was the kind of small mercy you could afford when you were in this business and your conscience was looking for places to land.

She thought, walking to her car: I am going to get out before he kills me.

She also thought: I am going to need to choose my moment carefully.

She was right about both.

Frankie's Cleaner — Two Days Before New Year's Frankie found the card under his windshield wiper at six in the morning.

It was plain white. No logo. No name. Just a phone number and four words in blue ballpoint.

172

WE CAN HELP YOU.

He didn't recognize the handwriting.

He stood in the cold next to his car for a long time, the card pinched between his fingers like it was something contagious. He thought about throwing it out. He thought about burning it. He thought about driving straight to Sol and showing him.

He did none of those things.

He folded the card and put it in his wallet, behind the photo of his wife.

That night at his shop, after his wife had gone to bed, Frankie called Sol about something else entirely. Halfway through the call, casually, like a man who had just thought of it, he said: "Hypothetical."

"Hypothetical what."

"Witness protection. How does that even work."

Sol was quiet for a long beat. "Why are you asking me this, Frankie."

"Trivia. Saw it on a TV show."

"Frankie."

"What."

"Don't *ever* ask me that question again."

Frankie didn't.

The card stayed in his wallet.

The Hospital — After Marshall Field's Nicky took the bullet in his left shoulder.

Which was lucky, if you could call getting shot lucky, because Nicky was right-handed and would still be able to eat normally once he healed.

That was the first thing Bobby thought.

The second thing he thought was: This is my fault.

The hospital waiting room was beige and fluorescent and smelled like industrial cleaner and barely contained despair.

Bobby sat in a plastic chair that was designed to be uncomfortable, as if comfort might encourage people to get shot more often.

Vinny paced.

Sol stared at the wall.

Frankie had already thrown up twice and was working on a third.

"He's going to be fine," Vinny said, for the eighth time. "It's a shoulder. People survive shoulders."

"People die from shoulders," Sol said quietly. "Infection. Blood loss. Complications."

"Don't be negative."

"I'm being realistic."

"Same thing."

Bobby said nothing.

He was thinking about Nicky's face when the bullet hit.

The surprise.

The confusion.

The way he'd looked at Bobby like a child looking at a parent, asking without words: Why did this happen? Why didn't you protect me?

Bobby had no answer.

The doctor came out after two hours.

Young. Tired. The kind of tired that came from seeing too much suffering and not being able to fix all of it.

"He's stable. The bullet went through clean, missed the major vessels. He'll need physical therapy, but he should recover full function."

Vinny exhaled. "See? Shoulders."

"Can we see him?" Bobby asked.

"He's sedated, but yes. One at a time."

Bobby went first.

Because he was the boss.

Because this was his responsibility.

Because if he didn't face what he'd done, he'd never forgive himself.

Nicky looked small in the hospital bed.

He was a big guy — not tall, but solid, built for labor and loyalty — but surrounded by machines and tubes and the institutional bleakness of medical necessity, he looked like a child.

His eyes were closed.

His breathing was steady.

His left shoulder was wrapped in bandages that were already showing spots of red.

Bobby sat in the chair beside the bed.

And for the first time in longer than he could remember, Bobby Bologna cried.

Not the dignified tears of movies.

The ugly crying.

The kind where your face contorts and your nose runs and sounds come out of you that you didn't know you could make.

He cried for Nicky, who had never wanted anything except to be included.

He cried for his father, who had died reaching for food.

He cried for Angela, who had deserved better than he could give.

He cried for himself, for the man he'd become, for the choices that had led to this room, this bed, this innocent person bleeding because Bobby had to prove something to people who didn't matter.

Nicky's eyes opened.

Groggy. Confused. But present.

"Bobby?" he whispered.

Bobby wiped his face quickly. "Yeah. Yeah, I'm here."

"Did we win?"

"Did we what?"

"The fight. At the store. Did we win?"

Bobby almost laughed. Almost.

"Nobody won, Nicky."

"Oh." Nicky seemed to think about this. "That's okay. Winning isn't everything."

"What is everything?"

"Being together. With the crew. With you." Nicky smiled weakly. "I'd take a bullet for you, Bobby. I mean, I did. But I would again."

Bobby reached out and took Nicky's hand.

Held it.

Didn't let go.

"You're not taking any more bullets. That's an order."

"Okay, Bobby."

"Promise me."

"I promise."

Nicky fell back asleep.

Bobby stayed until the nurses made him leave.

And something changed in him that night.

Not everything.

He was still Bobby Bologna.

He was still going to make terrible decisions and live too loud and eat too much and probably die in some ridiculous way that people would talk about for years.

But something was different.

Something was softer.

175

Something had cracked open that might never close again.

Maybe that was growth.

Maybe that was just exhaustion.

Bobby didn't know.

He just knew that Nicky was alive.

And that he would do anything to keep it that way.

Even if anything meant changing.

Even if anything meant becoming someone different.

Even if anything meant admitting that he'd been wrong.

That was the hardest part.

Admitting you're wrong.

Bobby had never been good at it.

But sitting in that hospital, holding Nicky's hand, watching his friend breathe— He was starting to learn.

CHAPTER 10.5

The Scheme

Bobby's Apartment — The Planning Meeting

"Okay," Bobby said, standing in front of a whiteboard he'd bought specifically for this meeting. "Here's the plan."

The whiteboard was blank.

"There's nothing on the board," Nicky observed.

"The plan is in my head. The board is for emphasis."

"Emphasis of what?"

"Of the plan. Which is in my head."

Sol closed his eyes. "We're all going to prison."

THE PLAN (as explained by Bobby over the next forty-five minutes, with frequent interruptions): Tony Smiles was moving product through a warehouse in Cicero.

The warehouse was protected, but not heavily. Tony thought nobody knew about it. Bobby knew about it because Bobby paid attention to things that Tony thought nobody was paying attention to.

The plan was simple: hit the warehouse, take the product, send a message.

"What kind of message?" Frankie asked.

"The kind that says 'don't mess with Bobby Bologna.'"

"That's not very specific."

"It doesn't need to be specific. It needs to be loud."

"I thought you said earlier that volume wasn't respect."

"That was different."

"How?"

"Because I said so."

THE ARGUMENT ABOUT LOGISTICS:

"We need a getaway vehicle," Vinny said.

"We have cars."

"We need a different car. One that can't be traced back to us."

"Where are we going to get a car that can't be traced?"

"We steal one."

"That's a separate crime."

"It's a related crime. Crime adjacent."

"'Crime adjacent' isn't a legal term," Sol observed.

"Everything we do isn't a legal term. That's the whole point."

Bobby held up his hands. "Okay. Vinny, you handle the car. Make sure it's fast, reliable, and not too flashy."

"What's too flashy?"

"No red. No yellow. Nothing that screams 'look at me, I'm committing crimes.'"

Vinny nodded. "Got it. Subtle crimes."

"Exactly."

THE ARGUMENT ABOUT TIMING:

"When do we hit the warehouse?" Nicky asked.

"Tuesday night."

"Why Tuesday?"

"Because Tony's guys take Tuesdays off. Something about bowling."

"Bowling?"

"They have a league."

"Criminals have bowling leagues?"

"Apparently."

Frankie raised his hand. "What if they cancel bowling?"

"Why would they cancel bowling?"

"I don't know. Weather. Sickness. Personal conflicts within the bowling league."

"Do you have personal conflicts within bowling leagues?"

"I don't bowl."

"Then why are you bringing up personal conflicts within bowling leagues?"

"I'm trying to anticipate problems!"

"Anticipate different problems! Problems that might actually happen!"

THE ARGUMENT ABOUT WEAPONS:

"What do we bring?" Nicky asked. "Guns?"

"No guns."

Everyone stared at Bobby.

"No guns?"

"Guns are loud. Guns attract attention. Guns turn a robbery into a different kind of thing. We go in with bats. Maybe some pipes. Persuasion tools."

"'Persuasion tools.'"

"That's what I said."

Vinny looked uncomfortable. "Bobby, what if they have guns?"

"They won't have guns."

"How do you know?"

"Because it's a warehouse, Vinny. Nobody guards a warehouse with guns. They guard it with locks and maybe a guy."

"What kind of guy?"

"The kind who opens locks and then goes home because he doesn't get paid enough to fight."

"What if he does fight?"

"Then we persuade him not to."

"With the persuasion tools."

"Now you're getting it."

THE ARGUMENT ABOUT SNACKS:

"I'm bringing sandwiches," Nicky announced.

"What?"

"For the stakeout. We might be there a while. I don't want to get hungry."

"This isn't a picnic, Nicky."

"Picnics and stakeouts both involve waiting. Waiting makes me hungry."

"Everything makes you hungry."

"That's why I'm bringing sandwiches."

Sol looked at Bobby. "He has a point."

"He does not have a point."

"Hunger affects performance. If Nicky gets hungry, he gets distracted. If he gets distracted, he makes mistakes. Mistakes get us caught."

"So your professional advice is that we should bring snacks to our crime?"

"My professional advice is that we should account for all variables. Hunger is a variable."

Bobby stared at his accountant.

"Fine. Nicky brings sandwiches. But if I hear crinkling at a critical moment, I'm throwing the sandwiches out the window."

179

"That would be littering," Frankie pointed out.

"LITTERING IS NOT OUR BIGGEST CONCERN RIGHT NOW, FRANKIE."

THE ACTUAL HEIST (Tuesday night, 11:47 PM): They arrived at the warehouse in a stolen Honda Civic that Vinny had acquired through means nobody asked about.

"This is the subtle crime car?" Bobby asked, looking at it.

"It's a Civic. Civics are everywhere. We'll blend in."

"It's bright orange, Vinny."

"That's the only one that was available."

"When I said no red and no yellow, orange was implied."

"You should have been more specific."

The warehouse was quiet.

Too quiet.

"Why is it so quiet?" Nicky whispered.

"Because nobody's here. That's the point."

"It feels wrong."

"It feels like an empty warehouse, which is what it is."

They approached the side door.

Vinny pulled out a lockpick set that he claimed to have learned from a mail-order VHS tape, which did not inspire confidence.

"You know how to use those?" Bobby asked.

"I've practiced."

"On what?"

"My own door."

"That's not the same kind of lock."

"Locks are locks."

"That is absolutely not true."

Vinny tried the lock for seven minutes.

Then Nicky tried.

Then Frankie tried, though his hands were shaking so badly he dropped the picks twice.

Then Sol walked over and kicked the door in.

Everyone stared at him.

"It was unlocked," Sol said. "The whole time. It was unlocked."

"Why didn't you say something?"

"I assumed one of you would check."

180

"We're professional criminals! We don't check if doors are unlocked! We pick them!"

"Apparently not well."

Inside the warehouse, they found:

Sixteen pallets of what appeared to be counterfeit designer handbags.

A card table with three chairs and a half-eaten pizza.

One very confused cat.

No drugs.

No money.

No product of any kind that they could actually use.

"This is... not what I expected," Bobby said.

"Handbags?" Vinny held one up. "Tony Smiles is running a fake handbag operation?"

"Designer handbags are very profitable," Sol said, examining one. "The markup is substantial. Low risk, high reward."

"But they're handbags."

"Crime doesn't have to be glamorous, Vinny. Crime has to be profitable."

Nicky was petting the cat. "Can we keep him?"

"We are not keeping a crime cat, Nicky."

"He seems nice."

"All cats seem nice until they scratch you."

"That's a metaphor for something."

"It's not a metaphor. It's a statement about cats."

THE REVISED PLAN (developed in the warehouse, surrounded by fake Louis Vuitton): "Okay," Bobby said. "New plan. We take the handbags."

"Why?"

"Because we're here. Because we can't leave empty-handed. Because taking Tony's handbags sends the same message as taking anything else."

"The message being 'we took your handbags'?"

"The message being 'we can get to you. We know where you operate. Your bowling night security isn't as tight as you think.'"

Frankie raised his hand again. "What are we going to do with sixteen pallets of fake handbags?"

"We'll figure that out later."

"That's not a plan."

"It's a plan adjacent. Like the crime adjacent. Plans evolve."

They loaded the handbags into the orange Honda Civic.

This took longer than expected because a Honda Civic is not designed to hold sixteen pallets of anything.

In the end, they fit approximately eight percent of the handbags in the car and had to leave the rest.

"This is humiliating," Vinny said.

"It's a strategic partial victory."

"It's eight percent. That's not even a tenth."

"It's almost a tenth. And it's the principle."

The cat had climbed into the car and refused to leave.

"We're keeping the cat," Nicky announced.

"We are not—" Bobby stopped. Sighed. "Fine. We're keeping the cat. What's his name?"

"I'm naming him Tony."

"You're naming the cat after Tony Smiles?"

"So every time we call him, we're calling Tony Smiles."

Bobby considered this.

"That's actually not bad."

"I have my moments."

THE AFTERMATH:

Tony Smiles found out about the raid by Thursday.

He was not happy.

But he was also not sure what to do, because explaining that someone had stolen his counterfeit handbags meant admitting he was running a counterfeit handbag operation, which was not the image he was trying to cultivate.

So he did nothing.

And Bobby won.

Sort of.

"That was a disaster," Sol said, at the post-operation debriefing (which was just them eating Italian beef at Al's).

"That was a success."

"We got eight percent of fake handbags and a cat."

"We got a message delivered. The handbags were a bonus."

"What are we going to do with the handbags?"

Bobby looked at them, stacked in the corner of the restaurant where Counter Marco was pretending not to notice.

"I know a guy."

"What guy?"

"A guy who knows things about handbags."

"That's not an answer."

"It's the only answer you're getting."

The cat—Tony—jumped onto the table and began eating Nicky's sandwich.

"He's eating my sandwich," Nicky observed, making no move to stop it.

"That's what you get for naming him after a mob boss."

"I thought it was a good name."

"It is a good name. Good names come with good appetites."

Bobby watched the cat eat.

Sol watched Bobby.

And somewhere across the city, Tony Smiles was trying to explain to his insurance company why sixteen pallets of "decorative accessories" had gone missing without technically admitting what they were.

It wasn't a clean victory.

But in Chicago, clean victories were rare.

You took what you could get.

And sometimes, what you got was a cat named Tony and eight percent of a counterfeit handbag operation.

Which, all things considered, wasn't bad for a Tuesday.

INTERLUDE: FIVE MEN, ONE QUESTION

Bobby's Apartment — 2 AM The phone call had come an hour ago.

Tony Smiles had made a move. A real move. Not the posturing and positioning of the past few months, but an actual, concrete action that demanded a response.

He had taken the Roseland route.

Not violently—that wasn't Tony's style. He had simply... absorbed it.

Talked to the right people. Made the right offers. And now what had been Bobby's for fifteen years was Tony's without a single punch thrown.

Bobby had called an emergency meeting.

Now they sat in his living room—Bobby, Sol, Vinny, Nicky, and Frankie—and nobody knew what to say.

Bobby spoke first. Because Bobby always spoke first.

"We hit back. Tonight. We take something of his—something bigger than Roseland—and we make sure everyone knows we're not going to roll over."

This was Bobby's answer to everything. Direct action. Immediate response. The philosophy of a man who believed that hesitation was death.

Sol spoke second. Because Sol always calculated.

"That's exactly what he wants. He takes Roseland knowing you'll overreact. You overreact, you make a mistake. You make a mistake, he uses it against you. This is chess, Bobby. He's three moves ahead."

"So what do you suggest? We do nothing?"

"I suggest we do something smart instead of something loud. There's a difference."

Vinny stood up. He couldn't sit still when he was angry, and Vinny was always angry.

"I say we find whoever talked to Tony. Whoever gave him the in. We find them and we make an example."

"That's not a strategy," Sol said. "That's revenge."

"So? Revenge is a strategy. Revenge tells people what happens when they cross us."

"Revenge tells people we're emotional and reactive. Which is exactly what Tony wants everyone to think."

Vinny's jaw tightened. "You calling me emotional?"

"I'm calling the situation emotional. There's a—"

"If you say 'there's a difference' one more time, Sol, I swear to God."

Frankie raised his hand.

He always raised his hand, even in meetings where hand-raising wasn't required. It was a habit from childhood, from being the kid who followed rules because rules felt safe.

"What if... what if we don't do anything?"

Everyone looked at him.

"I mean, not nothing nothing. But what if we just... wait? See what Tony does next? Maybe he'll make a mistake. Maybe this is all he wanted and he'll stop now."

Vinny laughed. It wasn't a kind laugh.

"Frankie. Tony Smiles doesn't stop. Tony Smiles keeps going until there's nothing left to take. You think he took Roseland because he wanted Roseland? He took Roseland because it's the first step. Next month it'll be Pullman. Month after that, Hegewisch. Month after that, we're working for him instead of with Bobby."

"So what do we do?"

"We fight. That's what we do. That's what we've always done."

"Fighting hasn't been working great lately, Vinny."

"Then we fight BETTER."

Nicky had been quiet.

This was unusual. Nicky was usually eating something, or asking about eating something, or thinking about what he would eat next. But tonight he just sat there, looking at his hands.

"Nicky?" Bobby finally said. "You got thoughts?"

Nicky looked up.

"I don't understand why people can't just... get along."

Silence.

"Like, there's enough for everyone, right? Tony has his thing. We have our thing. Why does he need our thing too? Why can't people just be happy with what they have?"

Vinny opened his mouth to say something cutting, but Bobby held up a hand.

"Go on, Nicky."

"I'm just saying... my mom always told me that fighting never solves anything. It just makes more fighting. And she was right. Every time we fight Tony, he fights back. Every time he fights us, we fight back. It never ends. Maybe the answer is... not fighting?"

"That's naive," Sol said, but gently.

"Maybe. But being smart hasn't stopped him either. Being tough hasn't stopped him either. Maybe naive is all we got left."

The room was quiet.

Five men. Five perspectives. Five different ways of seeing the same problem.

Bobby: Hit back hard and fast.

Sol: Think three moves ahead.

Vinny: Make an example.

Frankie: Wait and hope.

Nicky: Wonder why people couldn't just get along.

None of them were entirely wrong.

None of them were entirely right.

That was the thing about being in a crew. You had to find the answer that worked for everyone, even when everyone wanted something different.

"Here's what we're going to do," Bobby said finally.

Everyone leaned in.

"Sol—you're going to find out exactly how Tony took Roseland. Who talked. What was offered. I want to understand his method."

Sol nodded.

"Vinny—you're going to reach out to our people. Not to threaten. Not to punish. Just to remind them who their friends are. Make sure they know we're still here, still strong, still watching."

Vinny's jaw unclenched slightly.

"Frankie—you're going to keep your ears open. The dry cleaning business hears everything. People talk when they're picking up shirts. I want to know what the street is saying."

Frankie nodded nervously.

"Nicky—" Bobby paused. "You're going to be Nicky. You're going to remind us that there are human beings on all sides of this. That's your job. Don't let us forget."

Nicky smiled slightly.

"What about you?" Sol asked.

Bobby looked at his crew. His family. The men who had stood beside him through everything.

"I'm going to think. Really think. About what we're fighting for and whether it's worth the fight."

"That doesn't sound like you," Vinny said.

"Maybe that's the point."

They left at 3 AM.

Sol was already making calls.

Vinny was already making lists.

Frankie was already worrying.

Nicky was already hungry.

And Bobby was already staring out the window at the city he loved, wondering if loving something meant you had to destroy yourself to keep it.

He didn't have an answer.

But asking the question felt like progress.

CHAPTER 11

Gino Giorgetti's — The Holidays

The Christmas truce lasted exactly seventeen days.

Which, for Bobby Bologna, was actually pretty good.

They gathered at Gino Giorgetti's on the night after New Year's, when the decorations were coming down and the city was settling into that gray January malaise that would last until April at least.

Bobby sat in the back booth, surrounded by what remained of his crew.

Vinny, who was nursing a drink and a grudge.

Frankie, who was nursing anxiety and a menu.

Nicky, who was nursing a bowl of breadsticks.

And Sol, who was nursing concerns about absolutely everything.

"The truce is over," Sol said, stating the obvious.

"I'm aware."

"Tony's going to move fast. He's been waiting. Building up. Getting ready."

Bobby sipped his wine. "So have we."

"Have we though? Have we really? Because from where I'm sitting, we've spent the last two weeks eating and watching football."

"That's called strategic rest, Sol. Sun Tzu wrote about it."

"Sun Tzu did not write about Italian beef."

"He would have if he'd known about it."

The truth was, Bobby was tired.

Not the kind of tired you fix with sleep. The deeper kind. The kind that accumulated over years of always watching your back, always planning the next move, always wondering if today was the day everything fell apart.

He was forty-three years old.

He'd been doing this since he was twenty.

Twenty-three years of deals and threats and occasional violence and constant vigilance.

And now there was Tony Smiles, younger and hungrier and backed by people with more money and fewer morals.

"What do we actually have?" Bobby asked.

Sol pulled out his notebook. "In terms of assets? We have the unions on the West Side, but they're getting pressure from Tony's people. We have the construction interests in Cicero, but the mayor there is making noise about reform. We have the restaurants and clubs, but those are cash businesses that depend on relationships, and relationships are fraying."

"That's not encouraging."

"It's reality. Which is rarely encouraging."

Vinny slammed his hand on the table. "So we hit them. Hit them hard, hit them first, show them we're serious."

Sol shook his head. "That's what they want. They want us to overreact. They want an excuse to come down on us with everything they've got."

"Then what? We just wait for them to destroy us slowly?"

"We don't wait. We maneuver. We find allies. We make Tony's position untenable through other means."

Bobby looked at his accountant. "You have something specific in mind."

Sol nodded slowly. "Tony has political protection. City hall, aldermen, the kind of people who can make problems appear and disappear. But those people are mercenary. They protect whoever pays them."

"So we outbid him?"

"We make it dangerous to take his money. We shine a light on the relationships. We let the press know where the bodies are buried, metaphorically speaking."

Vinny frowned. "That's rat behavior."

"It's survival behavior. There's a difference."

Bobby considered this.

He'd been raised in a world where problems were solved with loyalty and violence, where you protected your own and destroyed your enemies and everything was clear and simple.

That world was dying.

Maybe already dead.

The new world was politicians and lawyers and public relations. The new world was playing nice while planning betrayals. The new world was making sure you looked like the good guy even when you weren't.

Bobby wasn't sure he knew how to operate in that world.

"What about Johnny No Thumbs?" Frankie asked. "He's got pull on the South Side. Could we bring him in?"

Sol shook his head. "Johnny's been quiet since the zoo thing. He doesn't want any part of what's happening."

"The zoo thing worked though."

"The zoo thing almost got us arrested. And it put heat on everyone."

Nicky looked up from his breadsticks. "What about just... not doing this anymore?"

Everyone stared at him.

"What do you mean?" Bobby asked.

"I mean... we could just stop. Get real jobs. Move somewhere warm. Florida, maybe."

Silence.

Then Vinny laughed. "Florida? Are you serious?"

"They have beaches."

"They have humidity and old people."

"Old people have wisdom."

"Old people have opinions about early bird specials."

Bobby raised his hand for silence.

"We're not moving to Florida."

"I was just suggesting—"

"Florida is where dreams go to die, Nicky. We're not dying in Florida."

"People die everywhere."

"Not like they die in Florida. Not with the heat and the hurricanes and the news stories about men doing weird things with animals."

Sol sighed. "This is not a productive conversation."

"It's also not wrong. Florida is cursed."

The waiter arrived with more wine and the kind of steak that costs more than most people's car payments.

They ate in relative silence, the weight of the situation settling over them like the Chicago weather.

Bobby thought about his grandfather, who had come to this city with nothing and built something.

He thought about his father, who had taken that something and squandered it.

He thought about himself, who had rebuilt from the ashes and was now watching those ashes gather around his feet again.

"Here's what we're going to do," Bobby said finally.

Everyone leaned in.

"We're going to make this personal. Not violent—Sol's right about that. Personal. Tony cares about his image. He cares about looking legitimate. He cares about being taken seriously by people who think they're better than him."

Sol nodded slowly. "Go on."

"We find the places where his mask slips. The things he's done that he doesn't want people to know. The deals that look bad. The relationships that look worse. And we make sure the right people find out about them."

"That's going to take time."

"Then we take time. We play the long game."

Vinny frowned. "I'm not good at long games."

"Then you'll learn."

They finished their meal and paid in cash and walked out into the January night.

The city was cold and dark and exactly as indifferent as it always was.

Bobby stood on the sidewalk and looked up at the buildings, the lights, the endless vertical reach of a place that had been built on ambition and stubbornness.

"We're going to survive this," he said, to nobody in particular.

Sol stood beside him. "You sure about that?"

"No. But I'm going to act like I am. That's half the battle."

"Which half?"

Bobby smiled. "The half that people can see."

They got in the car and drove away, leaving behind the restaurant and the conversations and the plans that might or might not work.

January stretched ahead of them, cold and uncertain.

The truce was over.

Whatever came next would define everything.

PART FOUR

BULLS FEVER

Spring 1998

CHAPTER 11.5

The Restaurant Situation

"Bobby Bologna Saves Gino's"

Thursday, 11:30 AM Gino's East was in trouble.

Not mob trouble. Not money trouble.

Health inspector trouble.

"What do you mean, shut down?" Bobby stared at Counter Gino like he'd announced the death of a family member.

"The health inspector. She found violations."

"What violations?"

"I don't know. She used words. There was a clipboard. She seemed angry about the refrigerator."

"The refrigerator is fine."

"She said there was something growing in it."

"There's CHEESE growing in it. That's what refrigerators are FOR."

"I don't think that's what she meant."

THE PROBLEM:

Gino's East had been serving deep dish pizza since 1966. It had survived disco, recessions, the Cubs being terrible, and the great pizza wars of the 1980s when three different restaurants claimed to have invented deep dish and everyone picked sides like it was a holy war.

It could not survive a health code violation.

Not because the violation was serious—it wasn't—but because the inspector, one Margaret Chen, had a vendetta.

"She's been out to get us for years," Gino explained. "Ever since we refused to let her brother-in-law host his birthday party here."

"Why'd you refuse?"

"He wanted to bring his own cake. TO A PIZZA RESTAURANT. That's disrespectful."

Bobby nodded solemnly. "That IS disrespectful."

"So now she inspects us every month. And every month she finds something."

THE PLAN (as conceived in the back booth): "We gotta do something," Bobby announced.

"Like what?" Sol asked. "She's a city employee. We can't exactly make her disappear."

"Who said anything about disappearing? We're gonna CHARM her."

Everyone stared.

"Charm," Vinny repeated.

"Charm."

"Bobby, you once threatened a man for putting ice in his wine."

"That was education, not threatening. And ice in wine is a crime against God."

"My point is that 'charm' might not be your strongest skill."

Bobby considered this.

"Fine. Then we'll convince her. Through persuasion."

"What kind of persuasion?"

"The kind where we explain that Gino's is a Chicago institution and shutting it down would be a crime against the city."

Sol sighed. "That's not how health codes work."

"Then we'll MAKE it how health codes work."

STEP ONE: THE APPROACH

Margaret Chen was having lunch at a diner on Division Street when Bobby Bologna sat down across from her.

"Ms. Chen."

She looked up from her salad. "Who are you?"

"A concerned citizen."

"Concerned about what?"

"About Gino's East. I hear you're trying to shut them down."

Margaret's eyes narrowed. "I'm not trying to shut anyone down. I'm enforcing health codes. There's a difference."

"Is there?"

"Yes. One is personal. The other is professional."

"And which is this?"

Margaret set down her fork.

"Sir, I don't know who you are, but I don't appreciate being ambushed at lunch."

"This isn't an ambush. This is a conversation."

"Conversations don't usually involve strange men appearing at your table uninvited."

Bobby smiled his most charming smile.

It was not, historically, a very charming smile.

"Let me buy you lunch."

"I already have lunch."

"Let me buy you better lunch."

"Are you trying to bribe a city official?"

"I'm trying to buy you lunch. There's a difference."

"Is there?"

STEP ONE GOES POORLY:

Margaret Chen stood up, took out her phone, and made a call.

"Yes, I'd like to report an attempted bribery. Division Street. Fat man in a tracksuit. Yes, I'll hold."

Bobby left before the police arrived.

STEP TWO: THE ALTERNATIVE APPROACH

"That went well," Sol observed.

"She's unreasonable."

"She's doing her job."

"Her job is unreasonable."

They were back at Gino's, in the back booth, strategizing.

"Maybe we go over her head," Vinny suggested. "Talk to her boss."

"Who's her boss?"

"I don't know. Whoever's in charge of health inspectors."

"That's the Department of Public Health."

"So we go there."

"And say what? 'Please tell your employee to stop doing her job'?"

"We say it more politely than that."

STEP TWO: THE DEPARTMENT OF PUBLIC HEALTH

The Department of Public Health was in a building that looked like it had been designed by someone who hated both health and the public.

Bobby, Vinny, Sol, and Nicky walked in like they owned the place. They did not own the place.

"We need to speak to whoever's in charge of health inspectors," Bobby announced to the receptionist.

"Do you have an appointment?"

"I don't need an appointment. I'm a concerned citizen."

"Concerned citizens still need appointments."

"Since when?"

"Since always. That's how appointments work."

Bobby leaned on the counter.

"Listen. Gino's East is a Chicago institution. It's been serving pizza for over thirty years. Your inspector is trying to shut it down over a refrigerator. A REFRIGERATOR. Do you understand what that means for the city? For the culture? For PIZZA?"

The receptionist blinked.

"Sir, I just answer phones."

"Then answer THIS: how do I get an appointment?"

"You call the main number and schedule one. There's usually a three-week wait."

"THREE WEEKS?"

"It's a busy department."

Bobby's eye twitched.

STEP TWO ALSO GOES POORLY:

Bobby did not wait three weeks.

Bobby attempted to walk past the receptionist toward the offices.

This triggered a silent alarm.

Building security arrived.

There was a... discussion.

Later, outside the building: "We're banned," Sol reported. "Officially banned from the Department of Public Health."

"How can they ban us? It's a public building."

"Apparently they can ban anyone who 'threatens the orderly function of city services.'"

"I didn't threaten anything."

"You told the security guard you'd 'remember his face.'"

"That's not a threat. That's a statement of fact. I have a good memory for faces."

"Bobby. In context, that's a threat."

STEP THREE: THE NUCLEAR OPTION

"We go to the alderman," Bobby decided.

"Which alderman?"

"Whichever one handles this district."

"That's Alderman Kowalski."

"Then we go to Kowalski."

Sol hesitated. "Bobby... Kowalski doesn't like you."

"What? Why?"

"Because of the thing."

"What thing?"

"The thing at his daughter's wedding."

Bobby searched his memory. "I don't remember any thing."

"You told his daughter her dress made her look like a 'haunted napkin.'"

"That was a COMPLIMENT. Haunted napkins are very in right now."

"They are absolutely not in right now."

"They're in with the right people."

"BOBBY."

STEP THREE: ALDERMAN KOWALSKI

Alderman Kowalski's office was on the third floor of a building that had seen better days, worse days, and days that defied classification entirely.

Bobby walked in without an appointment.

"Mr. Bologna." Kowalski's voice could have frozen Lake Michigan.

"What a surprise."

"Alderman. I need your help."

"Do you."

"Gino's East is being targeted by a health inspector. Unfairly targeted. I need you to make some calls."

Kowalski leaned back in his chair.

"You want me to interfere with a health inspection."

"I want you to ensure FAIR treatment for a Chicago institution."

"That's the same thing."

"It's the same thing said differently. Politics is all about saying the same thing differently."

Kowalski almost smiled. Almost.

"You called my daughter a haunted napkin."

"I stand by that assessment."

"Get out of my office."

STEP THREE GOES CATASTROPHICALLY:

Bobby did not get out of Kowalski's office.

Bobby continued to argue.

Kowalski called security.

A different security team than the one at the Department of Public Health, but with similar dispositions.

There was another... discussion.

That evening, Gino's East: "So to summarize," Sol said, reading from his notes. "We are now banned from the Department of Public Health, banned from Alderman Kowalski's office, and Margaret Chen has filed a restraining order."

"A restraining order seems excessive."

"You showed up at her lunch, Bobby."

"I was being FRIENDLY."

"You sat at her table uninvited and offered to buy her 'better lunch.' That's not friendly. That's alarming."

Gino appeared with a pizza. "So what happens now?"

Everyone looked at the pizza.

Nobody had an answer.

THE RESOLUTION:

Gino's East was shut down for two weeks while they addressed the health code violations.

The violations, it turned out, were minor. A refrigerator seal that needed replacing. A handwashing sign that had faded. A storage area that needed reorganizing.

Total cost of repairs: $340.

Total cost of Bobby's "help":

One restraining order.

Two building bans.

One alderman who now actively hated him (instead of passively).

Gino's reputation as "that place where the mob guy tried to bribe the health inspector" (unproven but widely believed).

"You made it worse," Sol observed, when Gino's finally reopened.

"I made it VISIBLE. There's a difference."

"It was a refrigerator seal, Bobby. They would have fixed it in a day."

"But now everyone knows that Gino's has POWERFUL FRIENDS."

"Everyone knows that Gino's has INSANE friends. That's not the same thing."

Bobby took a bite of pizza.

"This pizza is worth fighting for."

"Nobody's arguing about the pizza."

"Then what are we arguing about?"

"Your METHODS, Bobby. Your methods are the problem."

Bobby chewed thoughtfully.

"My methods got results."

"Your methods got a restraining order."

"That's a kind of result."

Sol gave up.

Some battles couldn't be won.

Some battles shouldn't be fought.

And some battles were about refrigerator seals and ended with everyone worse off than when they started.

This was, unfortunately, most of them.

CHAPTER 12

Sports Radio and Other Forms of Religion

Chicago in the spring of 1998 was not a city.

It was a cult.

And the Bulls were its gods.

The playoff run had consumed everything. Every bar, every barbershop, every conversation that lasted longer than thirty seconds eventually turned to basketball. People who had never watched a game in their lives suddenly had opinions about Scottie Pippen's back and Steve Kerr's shooting percentage and whether this would be the last season, the last run, the last time they'd see something this beautiful.

Bobby Bologna was no exception.

In fact, Bobby might have been worse than most.

"We need to talk about the Pacers series," he announced at the morning meeting, which was supposed to be about territory and money and the ongoing cold war with Tony Smiles.

Sol looked up from his ledger. "We're not talking about basketball. We're talking about the Cicero situation."

"The Cicero situation can wait. The Pacers situation cannot."

"The Pacers are a basketball team."

"The Pacers are a threat, Sol. A genuine threat. Reggie Miller alone—"

"Bobby. Please."

It had started in April, when the playoffs began and Bobby's superstitions kicked in.

Every serious sports fan has rituals. Lucky shirts. Specific seats.

Foods that must be consumed at specific times. These rituals are irrational and everyone knows they're irrational, but everyone does them anyway because sports exist in a realm where rationality has no power.

Bobby's rituals were... extensive.

He had to eat Italian beef during the first quarter. Specifically from Al's, and specifically dipped with hot giardiniera. Any deviation from this pattern would, in Bobby's mind, cause the Bulls to lose.

He had to sit in the same chair. Not just the same type of chair—the same actual physical chair, which meant that for away games he had to watch from the same barstool at Rosie's on Division Street.

He could not speak during free throws. This was common, but Bobby took it further: he could not move during free throws. He would freeze mid-bite, mid-drink, mid-sentence, remaining perfectly still until the ball went through the hoop or the opportunity was lost.

And he wore the same jersey—a red number 23, faded from years of washing—to every single game.

"That jersey smells," Vinny observed.

"It smells like winning."

"It smells like you haven't washed it since March."

"Exactly. Winning."

The crew had learned to work around these superstitions, because arguing with them was pointless and Bobby would just get more intense.

Sol scheduled meetings for non-game days.

Frankie made sure to have Al's on standby.

Vinny learned to stop talking during the fourth quarter entirely.

And Nicky—Nicky had somehow become Bobby's ritual partner, which meant he had to mirror Bobby's behaviors even though he didn't fully understand them.

"Why can't I eat during the third quarter?" Nicky asked.

"Because that's when momentum shifts."

"What does momentum have to do with eating?"

"Everything is connected, Nicky. The universe is watching."

"The universe watches basketball?"

"The universe watches Chicago. And Chicago watches basketball."

The thing was, Bobby genuinely believed it.

Not in a casual, half-joking way. In a deep, sincere, almost religious way. The Bulls winning was not just entertainment—it was meaning. It was purpose. It was proof that good things could happen to a city that had suffered enough.

Chicago had spent decades being the second city. Second to New York, second to LA, second in attention and respect and cultural relevance.

But the Bulls had changed that. Jordan had changed that. Six championships in eight years had changed that.

And Bobby had been there for all of it.

He'd watched the first three-peat happen. He'd suffered through the baseball years, when Jordan had abandoned them to chase a dream nobody understood. He'd celebrated the return, the comeback, the dynasty reborn.

This might be the last one.

Jordan was getting older. Pippen was getting injured. Phil Jackson was getting tired of the politics.

This might be the last chance to see something magical.

And Bobby was not going to let superstition-related negligence ruin it.

"The point is," Bobby said, returning to his original topic, "the Pacers have home court advantage if they win tonight."

Sol sighed. "And what do you propose we do about that?"

"I propose we watch the game correctly. I propose we follow the protocols. I propose we take this seriously."

"It's a basketball game."

"It's a basketball game that determines whether we have destiny on our side."

Vinny looked confused. "Does destiny apply to basketball?"

"Destiny applies to everything, Vinny. Chicago's destiny and my destiny are linked. When the Bulls win, I win. When the Bulls lose, everyone loses."

Frankie whispered, "That's not how causality works."

"Causality works however I say it works. I'm the boss."

Sol closed his ledger and looked at Bobby with something approaching concern.

"Bobby. I need to ask you something, and I need you to be honest with me."

"Go ahead."

"Are you using the Bulls to avoid thinking about our actual problems?"

Silence.

Bobby stared at his accountant for a long moment.

Then he smiled.

"Obviously."

"That's not healthy."

"Neither is our line of work. At least basketball doesn't shoot back."

Sol couldn't argue with that.

The game that night went to overtime.

Bobby nearly had a heart attack.

Reggie Miller hit a three that cut the lead to two.

Bobby stopped breathing.

Jordan got the ball with fifteen seconds left.

Bobby started praying to saints he didn't believe in.

The Bulls won by three.

And Bobby, standing in Rosie's bar surrounded by screaming fans and empty glasses, felt something he rarely felt anymore: Hope.

Pure, irrational, basketball-shaped hope.

The kind that made everything else seem manageable.

Even Tony Smiles.

Even the Cicero situation.

Even the slow, grinding reality of a life spent always watching his back.

For ninety minutes, twice a week, Bobby got to be something other than a mob boss.

He got to be a fan.

And that was worth protecting.

Whatever it took.

Bulls Fever April in Chicago was supposed to be about baseball.

But in 1998, April was about basketball.

Because the Bulls were making another run.

And Bobby Bologna was losing his mind.

"You changed seats," Bobby said, horrified.

Vinny looked up. "I got here first."

"That's not your seat."

"There are no assigned seats."

"EVERY SEAT IS ASSIGNED."

Sol had watched Bobby's superstitions evolve.

Same jersey. Same seat. Same snacks.

But as wins accumulated, rituals multiplied.

Rules about when to stand. Rules about what could be said during free throws. Rules about the order food items had to be consumed.

The rules had rules.

"I have a theory," Nicky said during a commercial.

"Please don't share it," Sol replied.

"I think the Bulls can feel us. Psychically. When we do the rituals correctly, they play better."

"That's not how physics works."

"Have you tested it? With basketball?"

Sol stared at him.

Bobby returned with nachos arranged in a specific configuration.

"These need to be eaten outside in. Clockwise."

Frankie looked at them with despair. "They're just chips."

"Nothing is just anything. Everything matters. Every choice. Every chip."

"That's not healthy."

"Healthy is for people who don't care about championships."

The Bulls won.

They always seemed to win when Bobby did the rituals correctly.

Which either meant the rituals worked, or Bobby had confused correlation with causation, or the universe was playing an elaborate joke.

Sol suspected the third option.

"Three-nothing," Bobby announced. "One more win and we advance."

"The rituals are working," Nicky said.

"The Bulls are winning because they're talented," Sol said.

"That's what someone who doesn't believe would say."

Bobby turned to Vinny. "Same time tomorrow. Same seats. SAME. SEATS."

Vinny nodded wearily.

Later, Sol made a note in his journal: "Bobby's superstitions are getting worse. A man who thinks he can control fate through nachos is a man who will be devastated when fate does what fate does."

He closed the journal.

Somewhere, Bobby was arranging tomorrow's snacks.

Somewhere, the Bulls were sleeping, unaware that a man in a tracksuit believed their destiny was linked to his chip consumption.

Somewhere, the universe was laughing.

But they would keep playing anyway.

Because in Chicago, hope was the cruelest sport of all.

CHAPTER 13

Bad Hit During a Big Game

The job was simple.

They we're all supposed to be simple.

A meeting with a guy who owed money. A conversation about timelines. Maybe some light intimidation to ensure the timeline was respected.

Nothing that should have taken more than an hour.

Nothing that should have involved guns.

Nothing that should have happened during Game 5 of the Eastern Conference Finals.

"This is bad timing," Bobby said, for the third time, as they drove toward the warehouse on the West Side.

Sol was in the passenger seat, reviewing notes. "It's the only time Deluca's available. He's got something going on every other night this week."

"So we reschedule."

"We've rescheduled twice. A third time makes us look weak."

"Missing the game makes me look absent."

Vinny, behind the wheel, glanced in the rearview. "We can be quick. In and out. We'll catch the second half."

"The second half is crucial. That's when Jordan takes over."

"Then we'll be really quick."

The warehouse was one of those places that used to be something important—a manufacturing facility, maybe, or a distribution center—and was now just another empty shell waiting to be turned into condos or art galleries or whatever empty shells became in the new Chicago.

Deluca was waiting inside with two of his guys.

He was the same Deluca from before—the mechanic who had owed money and made threats and generally been a problem that kept not going away.

He looked nervous.

He should have.

"You owe thirty-four hundred now," Sol said, consulting his notebook.

"The original thirty-two, plus interest."

Deluca spread his hands. "I got it. I got most of it."

"Most of it isn't all of it."

"I need another week."

Bobby stepped forward. "You've had six months of weeks, Deluca. At some point, weeks stop being weeks and start being lies."

"I'm not lying. Business has been slow."

"Business is slow for everyone. That's not an excuse. That's weather."

Bobby was distracted.

He kept checking his watch.

Kept thinking about the game that was starting right now, without him, in a bar where he should have been sitting.

He could feel the basketball happening, somewhere across the city.

He could feel Jordan warming up, getting ready to do Jordan things.

And he was here, in a warehouse, having the same conversation he'd had a hundred times before.

"Look," Bobby said, "here's what's going to happen. You're going to give us what you have now—whatever that is—and you're going to have the rest by Friday. Not next Friday. This Friday. Three days."

Deluca nodded eagerly. "Yeah, okay, I can do that."

"And if you don't—"

"I will. I swear."

"—then we're going to have a different kind of conversation. The kind without words."

Deluca swallowed. "I understand."

It should have ended there.

It would have ended there, if one of Deluca's guys hadn't made a stupid decision.

The guy—young, nervous, clearly new to whatever this was—reached for something in his jacket.

Maybe it was a weapon.

Maybe it was just his phone.

Maybe he was scratching an itch.

Nobody would ever know, because Vinny shot him.

Everything after that was chaos.

The other guy pulled an actual gun.

Frankie dove behind a stack of pallets.

Nicky froze, which was becoming his signature move in crisis situations.

Sol grabbed Bobby and pulled him down.

Shots echoed off the concrete walls, impossibly loud in the enclosed space.

Deluca was screaming something—apologies, probably, or denials, or just pure fear.

Bobby couldn't hear over the gunfire.

When it was over, two people were dead.

Deluca's two guys.

One shot by Vinny (arguably justified, given the reaching).

One shot by Frankie (definitely justified, given the shooting back).

Deluca himself was alive, cowering behind a forklift, begging for his life.

Bobby stood over him, breathing hard, ears ringing.

"This," he said slowly, "was not the plan."

"I'm sorry, I'm sorry, they weren't supposed to—"

"They weren't supposed to do a lot of things. And now they're dead."

They left Deluca alive, because killing him would create more problems than it solved.

They left the warehouse quickly, because the gunfire had definitely attracted attention.

They drove back toward the city in silence, the weight of what had happened settling over them.

Bobby checked his watch.

Halftime.

He'd missed the entire first half.

"That was bad," Sol said, when they were far enough away to think clearly.

"No kidding."

"Two bodies, Bobby. Two bodies that belong to someone. People are going to have questions."

"Deluca's people?"

"Deluca doesn't have people. He's a mechanic who got in over his head. Those guys were probably freelance."

"Then who's going to ask questions?"

Sol was quiet for a moment.

"Everyone. When people turn up dead, everyone asks questions. Cops. Competitors. People who want to know if we're vulnerable."

Bobby stared out the window at the city passing by.

"We're not vulnerable."

"We made mistakes tonight. Mistakes make us look vulnerable. That's not the same as being vulnerable, but in this business, perception matters more than reality."

They stopped at a bar on the West Side—not Rosie's, nowhere regular—and caught the last quarter of the game.

The Bulls were up by twelve.

They'd win by fifteen.

Jordan had thirty-two points.

Bobby watched without seeing, his mind still back in that warehouse, still hearing the gunfire, still processing the sudden violence of a simple job gone wrong.

"We'll handle the cleanup tomorrow," Sol said quietly.

"Yeah."

"And we need to think about what this means for the Tony situation."

"Yeah."

"Bobby. Are you listening?"

Bobby turned to look at his accountant, his oldest friend, his voice of reason in a world that had very little of it.

"I'm listening," he said. "I'm just not sure what I'm hearing anymore."

Sol nodded slowly.

"That's the problem with this life. Eventually, you stop being able to hear the things that matter."

On the TV, the Bulls celebrated their victory.

Bobby didn't celebrate.

He just watched, and thought, and wondered when everything had started feeling so heavy.

CHAPTER 14

Bobby's Big Flex

Two weeks later, Bobby announced his plan.

"Courtside tickets," he said, dropping the words like bombs. "Game Six. Salt Lake City."

Sol's face went through several expressions in rapid succession: confusion, disbelief, horror, and finally a kind of resigned despair that suggested he had been expecting something like this and was somehow still disappointed.

"You want to fly to Utah," Sol said slowly.

"I want to witness history."

"You want to be extremely visible in another state during an extremely public event while we're in the middle of an extremely delicate situation."

"I want to see Jordan win his sixth championship."

"Those are the same thing, Bobby."

They we're in Frankie's office—which had become the de facto headquarters since Bobby's actual office had developed a rat problem that nobody wanted to discuss—and the mood was tense.

The situation with Tony Smiles had escalated.

The cleanup from the warehouse job had been messier than expected.

Rumors were circulating about Bobby's crew, about their competence, about whether the old ways were still working.

And now Bobby wanted to go to Utah.

"How did you even get courtside tickets?" Vinny asked.

"I know a guy who knows a guy who knows someone at the arena."

"That's a lot of guys."

"That's how things work."

Sol shook his head. "This is a terrible idea. You'll be on television. Everyone will see you."

"Everyone will see me witnessing history. Everyone will see me at the biggest game of the decade. Everyone will see that Bobby Bologna goes where he wants, when he wants, and nothing can stop him."

"Everyone will see a target."

"Everyone will see a boss."

The truth was, the tickets had cost Bobby more than money.

They had cost favors. Real ones. The kind that would come due eventually, probably at the worst possible time.

He'd called in markers from people he'd been saving for emergencies.

He'd made promises he wasn't sure he could keep.

He'd traded future leverage for present glory.

But the Bulls we're going to win their sixth championship—he could feel it, the way he could feel weather changes in his knees—and he was going to be there when it happened.

Some things were worth more than strategic thinking.

Some things were worth being stupid for.

"Who's going?" Frankie asked, trying to sound casual and failing.

"Me. Sol. Vinny. Nicky." Bobby paused. "You too, if you want."

"I don't think I should be on an airplane."

"Why not?"

"I have a thing about enclosed spaces."

"It's a commercial flight, not a submarine."

"Planes are basically submarines that fly. That's worse."

Sol made one more attempt at reason.

"Bobby. Please listen to me. We are in a precarious position right now. Tony Smiles is waiting for us to make a mistake. The police are watching everything after the warehouse incident. The community is nervous about leadership."

"I know all of this."

"Then why are you doing something so public?"

Bobby leaned back in his chair.

"Because sometimes you have to remind people who you are. Not through violence. Not through business. But through presence. Through confidence. Through showing up at the biggest stage and saying 'I belong here.'"

"That's very philosophical."

"I've been reading."

"Reading what?"

"Mostly sports biographies. But also some philosophy. Nicky got me a book about Stoicism."

Sol looked at Nicky. "You can read?"

Nicky beamed. "I'm learning."

The flight was booked.

The hotel was arranged.

The suits were prepared.

Bobby Bologna was going to Utah, and nothing was going to stop him.

Not common sense.

Not strategic thinking.

Not the growing certainty in Sol's gut that something was about to go very, very wrong.

Because Bobby was right about one thing: the Bulls we're going to win.

He could feel it.

The way he could feel Chicago in his bones.

The way he could feel destiny calling.

And when destiny called, Bobby Bologna always answered.

Even if the call was coming from Salt Lake City.

Even if the answer might cost him everything.

INTERLUDE: 3 AM — BOBBY ALONE

3 AM — Bobby Alone Some nights, Bobby couldn't sleep.

Not because of guilt. He had made peace with the things he had done, or at least convinced himself he had.

Not because of fear. He wasn't afraid of Tony Smiles or cops or even death. Death was just an ending, and endings came for everyone.

It was something else.

Something quieter.

He sat in his kitchen at three in the morning, drinking coffee he didn't want, staring at the darkness outside his window.

The city was quiet.

The city was never quiet.

But at three in the morning, if you listened carefully, you could almost believe it was.

He thought about his father.

About Wrigley Field.

About the hot dog his father never got to eat.

He thought about Angela.

About the look on her face when she finally understood that she would never be enough. That Chicago would always come first. That he had chosen a city over a person, and he would make that choice again if he had to.

He thought about the crew.

About Sol, who was smarter than all of them and stayed anyway.

About Vinny, who was broken in ways that couldn't be fixed.

About Nicky, who trusted him completely and didn't understand that trust was dangerous.

About Frankie, who wanted out but was too scared to leave.

He thought about what he had built.

And he wondered if any of it mattered.

The question came in the dark, as it always did: What are you doing?

Not what are you doing tomorrow. Not what are you doing with Tony Smiles.

What are you doing with your life.

Bobby was forty-three years old.

He had no wife. No children. No legacy except a nickname and a reputation.

He would die eventually—everyone died eventually—and what would be left?

Stories. Maybe.

Funny stories about a guy who ate too much and talked too loud and thought he was more important than he was.

Was that enough?

Was that a life?

Bobby finished his coffee.

Rinsed the cup.

Went back to bed.

He wouldn't find any answers tonight.

He never found answers at three in the morning.

Just questions.

And the questions were always the same.

The next morning, he woke up late.

Made breakfast.

Called Sol about business.

Became Bobby Bologna again.

The doubts went back into whatever drawer he kept them in.

Locked.

Hidden.

Waiting for the next night when sleep wouldn't come.

That was the thing about doubt.

It never went away.

It just learned to be patient.

The Diner — Angela

Bobby's ex-wife agreed to meet him at a diner in Naperville.

Neutral territory.

Her territory, really — she lived out here now, in the suburbs, in a house with a two-car garage and a husband named Richard who sold insurance and had never, as far as Bobby knew, punched anyone in his entire life.

Bobby hated everything about Naperville.

But he came anyway.

Because Angela had asked.

And Bobby had never been able to say no to Angela.

She was already there when he arrived.

Still beautiful. Different, but beautiful. The hard edges she'd developed during their marriage had softened. The tension she'd carried like armor had melted away.

She looked happy.

Bobby didn't know if that made him feel better or worse.

"You look good," he said, sliding into the booth across from her.

"You look tired."

"That's my brand."

She almost smiled. "Still making jokes."

"Still breathing. Same thing."

They ordered coffee. Neither of them was hungry.

The silence stretched between them, filled with all the things they'd said and all the things they hadn't.

Finally, Angela spoke.

"I heard about the trouble. The Christmas stuff. The news."

"News exaggerates."

"Does it?"

Bobby looked at his coffee. "Sometimes."

"I wanted to see you," Angela said, "because I'm worried. And because I realized I never actually said goodbye."

"You said goodbye. When you left."

"That was angry goodbye. That was throwing things goodbye. I never said the real one."

"What's the real one?"

Angela looked at him with eyes that had once looked at him with love, then with hatred, and now with something in between.

"Goodbye, Bobby. I hope you find whatever you're looking for. I hope Chicago gives you what I couldn't."

Bobby felt something crack inside him.

Not break. He'd been broken before. This was different.

This was the hairline fracture that happens when someone you loved finally let's you go.

"Angela—"

"Don't." She held up her hand. "Don't apologize. Don't explain. I don't need it anymore. I just needed to say this."

"Say what?"

"That I understand now. I didn't then, but I do now." She paused.

214

"You loved Chicago more than you ever loved me. You loved that city more than anything. The food and the teams and the neighborhoods and the chaos of it all."

"That's not—"

"It's true. And I'm not angry anymore. I used to be. I used to hate you for it. But now I just feel sad. Sad that you had so much love in you and you gave it all to a place instead of a person."

Bobby didn't know what to say.

Because she was right.

And he'd never been able to admit it.

"I did love you," he said finally. "In my way."

"I know. Your way just wasn't enough."

"No. I guess it wasn't."

Angela reached across the table and took his hand.

Just for a moment.

Just long enough to remember what they'd been before they became what they became.

"Take care of yourself, Bobby. And for God's sake, stop making the news."

"I'll try."

"You won't."

"No. Probably not."

She left first.

Bobby sat in the booth for another hour, drinking cold coffee, thinking about all the choices he'd made and all the choices he hadn't.

The waitress asked if he was okay.

He said yes.

He was lying.

Outside, Naperville continued being Naperville.

Clean streets. Nice lawns. People who slept soundly because their lives were predictable.

Bobby got in his car and drove back to Chicago.

Back to the city that had won.

Back to the love that had cost him everything else.

Angela was right.

He had loved Chicago more than her.

More than anyone.

He hoped it was worth it.

Some days, he wasn't sure.

But it was too late to choose differently now.

The only direction was forward.

Toward whatever was coming.

Which was Utah.

And then nothing.

But he didn't know that yet.

He just knew he was sad.

And hungry.

Always hungry.

Sofia — Bobby's Heart Sofia Marchetti was seven years old and completely unaware that her godfather was a criminal.

To her, Uncle Bobby was just the man who brought cannoli and told funny stories and always, always remembered her birthday.

Bobby visited every Sunday.

This was non-negotiable. Wars could wait. Business could wait. Even food could wait, though rarely.

But Sunday dinner with Sofia and her parents was sacred.

Sofia's mother, Maria, was Bobby's cousin. Her father, Dominic, was a plumber who had no idea what Bobby actually did and had been carefully instructed never to ask.

They lived in a small house in Edison Park with a yard that Dominic maintained with obsessive precision and a kitchen that Maria ruled with absolute authority.

Bobby loved that house.

It was the closest thing to normal he had ever known.

"Uncle Bobby!" Sofia screamed, running to the door the moment she heard his car.

Bobby scooped her up, lifting her high. "There she is. The smartest kid in Chicago."

"Ms. Patterson says I'm the second smartest."

"Ms. Patterson doesn't know what she's talking about."

Sofia giggled. "She's my teacher."

"Teachers can be wrong. Trust me. I made a lot of teachers very wrong."

Dinner was pasta and meatballs and the kind of bread that only existed in homes where grandmothers had passed down recipes through generations of love and mild disapproval.

Bobby ate three helpings.

Sofia ate one helping and spent the rest of dinner asking questions.

"Uncle Bobby, why do you always wear fancy clothes?"

"Because looking good makes you feel good."

"Uncle Bobby, why do you always bring food when there's already food?"

"Because you can never have too much food."

"Uncle Bobby, why don't you have kids?"

The table went quiet.

Bobby set down his fork.

"Because," he said carefully, "some people are meant to be parents, and some people are meant to be the fun uncle who spoils other people's kids."

"Is that why you spoil me?"

"I don't spoil you. I invest in you. There's a difference."

Sofia considered this with the gravity of a seven-year-old philosopher.

"Okay," she said. "Can I have more bread?"

"See? Smart. The smartest."

After dinner, Bobby sat with Sofia on the porch while she showed him her drawings.

She was good. Really good. The kind of good that suggested actual talent, not just parental optimism.

"This is you," she said, holding up a portrait that was surprisingly accurate. Bobby's face, his suit, his posture of someone who owned every room he entered.

"You made me look handsome."

"You are handsome."

"Your mother tell you to say that?"

"No. I have eyes."

Bobby laughed — a real laugh, the kind that only Sofia could draw from him.

"Keep drawing, kid. Keep being exactly who you are. Promise me."

"I promise." Sofia hugged him. "Will you come to my recital?"

"When is it?"

"June 20th."

Six days after the Bulls game in Utah.

Bobby smiled. "I'll be there. Wouldn't miss it."

He missed it.

He was dead by then.

Sofia waited in her costume, watching the door, asking her mother when Uncle Bobby was coming.

Maria didn't know how to explain that Uncle Bobby was never coming again.

So she just held her daughter and said he was watching from somewhere else.

Somewhere with good food and basketball and all the things he loved.

Years later, Sofia Marchetti would become an artist.

A real one.

Her first gallery show was called "Sunday Dinners" — a series of paintings about family, food, and the people we lose.

The centerpiece was a portrait of a man in a suit, eating pasta, laughing at something outside the frame.

The title was simple: "Uncle Bobby."

It sold for forty thousand dollars.

Sofia donated the money to a children's art program in Chicago.

Because that's what Uncle Bobby would have wanted.

Investment in the future.

Not spoiling.

Investment.

The Great Beef Debate It started because Nicky said something stupid.

This was not unusual. Nicky said stupid things constantly. But this particular stupid thing had consequences.

"I think Al's is overrated."

The table went silent.

Bobby set down his fork.

Vinny's eye twitched.

Sol quietly closed his notebook, as if preparing to document a murder.

Frankie made the sign of the cross.

"What did you say?" Bobby asked, his voice dangerously calm.

"I said I think Al's is overrated. The beef is good but it's not the best. Johnnie's is better."

The silence that followed was the kind usually reserved for funerals and tax audits.

"Johnnie's," Bobby repeated.

"Yeah. The bread is better. The ratio is better. The giardiniera is—"

"The giardiniera is WHAT, Nicky?"

"...spicier?"

Bobby stood up.

This was not a good sign.

Bobby standing up during a meal meant someone had committed an offense *so grievous* that food could no longer be consumed in their presence.

"I have eaten at Al's since I was six years old. My father ate at Al's. My grandfather ate at Al's. Al's is the foundation of Italian beef in this city."

"I'm just saying—"

"You're just saying HERESY, Nicky. You're just saying words that should not be said in polite company."

"It's just beef!"

Bobby recoiled like he'd been slapped.

"Just beef. Just. Beef." He turned to the others. "You hear this? Just beef."

Vinny, who agreed with Bobby on almost nothing, agreed with him on this.

"Nicky, you can't say that. It's disrespectful."

"To who?"

"To everyone! To the tradition! To Al himself!"

"Al is dead!"

"That makes it worse!"

Sol intervened, because Sol always intervened, because Sol was the only one with any sense.

"Perhaps we could acknowledge that beef preference is subjective."

Everyone turned to look at him with matching expressions of horror.

"Subjective," Bobby said, like the word was poison.

"Different people prefer different—"

"SOL. There are opinions, and there are facts. Al's being the best is a fact. Johnnie's being second is a fact. Mr. Beef is third. These are not debatable positions. They are reality."

"What about Portillo's?" Nicky asked.

Bobby's face went through several emotions, none of them good.

"Portillo's is fast food."

"It's still beef!"

"It's a different category! You don't compare Portillo's to Al's! That's like comparing—" Bobby struggled for an analogy. "That's like comparing a Honda to a Ferrari!"

"A Honda is reliable."

"NICKY."

This argument continued for three hours.

It covered the history of Italian beef in Chicago.

The proper ratio of meat to bread.

The acceptable moisture level of a properly dipped sandwich.

The ethics of asking for ketchup (summary: there are no ethics, only sin).

And somehow, the Bulls, even though the Bulls had nothing to do with beef.

"Jordan would eat at Al's," Bobby declared.

"You don't know that."

"Jordan is a winner. Winners eat at Al's. That's just science."

"That's not science, Bobby. That's not even close to science."

"It's food science."

"Food science is a different thing!"

By the end of the evening, Nicky had agreed to eat at Al's three times a week for a month as "re-education."

Vinny had punched a wall.

Sol had written seventeen pages of notes that would never be useful for anything.

And Frankie had stress-eaten an entire pizza, which only confused the debate further.

"Can we talk about actual business now?" Sol asked, as the sun came up.

"This was actual business," Bobby said. "This was the most important business."

"We have a meeting with Tony tomorrow."

"Today."

"What?"

"It's 6 AM. The meeting is in six hours."

Everyone looked at each other.

They had argued about beef all night.

They had a meeting with their rival in six hours.

Nobody had prepared anything.

"We should probably sleep," Sol said.

"No time for sleep," Bobby said. "We need to eat first."

"We've been eating all night!"

"That was arguing. This is breakfast. Different stomach."

And somehow, impossibly, they went to get breakfast.

Because that was the crew.

Five men who would rather eat than sleep.

Five men who would argue about beef until dawn.

Five men who had absolutely no idea what they were doing but did it with confidence anyway.

Bobby Bologna's crew.

God help them all.

The Night Before Utah June 13, 1998 Bobby told the crew he was going to bed early.

He lied.

Instead, he drove to Resurrection Cemetery. Parked outside the gates.

Waited for the security guard to finish his rounds. Then climbed the fence like he was nineteen again.

His father's grave was near the back. The headstone was simple:

SALVATORE FILONI

1927 - 1979

BELOVED HUSBAND AND FATHER

Bobby sat in the grass beside the grave. The night was warm.

"Hey, Pop."

The headstone said nothing.

"The Bulls are about to win again. Number six. Can you believe it? Jordan is incredible. You would have loved him."

Bobby pulled a flask from his jacket. Poured some on the ground.

Drank the rest.

"I keep thinking about that day at Wrigley. The day you died. How you were just going to get a hot dog. How I said I was good. How I let you go."

Bobby's voice cracked. He hadn't cried at his father's funeral. Too angry. Too numb. But now, nineteen years later, the tears came.

"I should have gone with you. I should have said I wanted the hot dog too. I've spent my whole life trying to make up for that moment. Eating everything. Saying yes to everything. Never letting a chance go by."

He stood up. Looked at the headstone one more time.

"I'm going to watch Jordan win tomorrow. And I'm going to eat a hot dog for you. The biggest hot dog they have. And I'm going to enjoy every bite, because that's what you would have wanted. Looking for joy. Looking for something delicious."

Bobby kissed his fingers and touched the headstone.

"I love you, Pop. I'll see you when I see you."

He walked back to his car. Drove home.

He didn't know he had just said goodbye.

He didn't know that in thirty-six hours, he would be buried not far from where his father lay.

He didn't know that the hot dog he promised would be the last thing he ever ate.

Either way, Bobby went home. Packed his bag. Slept better than he had in years.

And in the morning, he flew to Utah.

To watch Michael Jordan.

To eat a hot dog.

To become legend.

The Last Chicago Morning The morning before the flight to Utah, Bobby ate breakfast at Lou Mitchell.

This was tradition.

Lou Mitchell had been serving breakfast since 1923. Three-quarters of a century of eggs and pancakes and the particular chaos of a diner that knew exactly what it was and made no apologies.

Bobby came here before important things.

Before big meetings. Before difficult decisions. Before moments when he needed the strength that only a proper Chicago breakfast could provide.

He ordered the usual.

Double order of bacon. Eggs over easy. Hash browns. Toast. Coffee.

The waitress knew him by name.

"Big day, Bobby?"

"The biggest. Flying to Utah. Bulls game."

"You think they gonna win?"

"I know they gonna win. Jordan doesn't lose when it matters."

"Well, you've a safe trip. And eat up. You're going to need your strength."

She didn't know how right she was.

Nobody did.

The crew joined him one by one.

Sol first, because Sol was always first. Ordered coffee. Picked at toast.

Didn't seem hungry but showed up anyway because that was what crew did.

Vinny next, already talking about something that had happened the night before, something that involved a parking spot and a disagreement and the particular satisfaction of being right.

Nicky last, looking at the menu like it might have changed since the last time he was here, which was three days ago.

Frankie didn't come. Frankie was afraid of flying and had said his goodbyes the night before, along with extensive instructions for what should happen to his dry cleaning business if the plane crashed.

"This is it," Bobby said, looking at his crew. "Championship number six. The last one."

"You don't know it's the last one," Sol said.

"I know. Jordan is tired. Pippen is hurt. Phil is leaving. This is the end of something. Maybe the end of everything."

"You're being dramatic."

"I'm being realistic. Which is unusual for me, so pay attention."

They ate in silence for a while.

The particular silence of men who had said everything already and we're just enjoying each other's presence.

Then Bobby raised his coffee cup.

"To Chicago," he said.

"To Chicago," the crew echoed.

"To the Bulls."

"To the Bulls."

"And to whatever comes next."

Nobody repeated that one.

Because nobody knew what came next.

And not knowing was part of what made it exciting.

And terrifying.

And worth doing anyway.

Bobby finished his breakfast.

Paid the check.

Tipped generously, as always.

Walked out into the Chicago morning.

The sun was shining.

The city was alive.

And somewhere, in Utah, destiny was waiting.

He did not look back.

Bobby never looked back.

That was not his style.

But if he had, he would have seen the waitress watching him through the window.

Smiling.

Waving.

Not knowing she was saying goodbye for the last time.

Not knowing that in two days, she would hear the news and cry into her apron.

Not knowing that she was part of the last normal morning Bobby Bologna would ever have.

"You ready?" Sol asked, at the car.

Bobby took one more breath of Chicago air.

"Yeah," he said. "I'm ready."

They got in the car.

Drove to the airport.

And flew toward the ending nobody expected.

But maybe everybody should have.

United Center — Before Utah Before they went to Utah, they watched Game Five in Chicago.

At the United Center.

Which was not courtside because Bobby had saved those tickets for the clinching game. But it was still the United Center. Still the house that Jordan built. Still the closest thing to a church that Bobby Bologna would ever voluntarily enter.

The arena was packed.

Twenty-three thousand people, all of them believing. All of them certain that this was the year, this was the moment, this was the night when history would be made.

They were right.

Just not the way they expected.

Bobby stood in the concourse before the game, looking at the championship banners hanging from the rafters.

Five of them.

Soon to be six.

Each one representing a season of perfection. A year when Chicago was the center of the basketball universe. A time when being a Bulls fan meant being part of something larger than yourself.

"You know what I love about those banners?" Bobby asked Sol.

"Their historical significance?"

"No. The fact that they're always there. No matter what else changes, those banners stay. Permanent. Undeniable. Nobody can take them down. Nobody can pretend they didn't happen. They just hang there, reminding everyone what we accomplished."

They found their seats.

Good seats. Not courtside, but close enough to see faces. Close enough to hear players talking. Close enough to feel like participants instead of spectators.

Nicky was vibrating with excitement.

"I can't believe we're here. I can't believe this is happening."

"Believe it," Bobby said. "And pay attention. Moments like this don't come often."

The game started badly.

The Jazz came out hot. The Bulls came out cold. The first quarter was a disaster of missed shots and sloppy turnovers.

The crowd got nervous.

Bobby didn't.

"Relax," he told the crew. "This is how it always goes. They start slow. They adjust. They win. That's the pattern."

"Patterns can be broken," Sol said.

"Not this pattern. Not these Bulls. Not with Jordan."

He was right.

The second quarter was better. The third was dominant. By the fourth, the Bulls were pulling away, and the arena was so loud you could feel it in your bones.

Bobby stood for the entire fourth quarter.

Screaming. Cheering. Living every possession like it was the only thing that mattered.

Because in that moment, it was.

The Bulls won.

Series lead: 3-2.

One more win and it was over.

One more win and the dynasty was complete.

One more win and Bobby Bologna would be able to say he had watched all six championships happen in real time.

After the game, they walked through the parking lot in a daze.

The kind of daze that comes from witnessing something beautiful.

From being present at history. From understanding that you've just been part of something that will be talked about for decades.

"Utah," Bobby said. "Game Six. We're going."

"Are you sure?" Sol asked. "Those tickets cost a fortune."

"Some things are worth more than money. Some things are worth everything you've."

They drove home through Chicago streets that were alive with celebration.

Honking horns. Cheering fans. The particular joy of a city that had found something to believe in.

Bobby rolled down the window and breathed it in.

This was his city.

This was his moment.

And nothing could take it away.

He did not know, of course, that this was his last Bulls game in Chicago.

He did not know that the Utah trip would be a one-way journey.

He did not know that he was living his final week on earth.

But maybe it was better that way.

Maybe it was better to go out believing.

Better to go out hopeful.

Better to go out like Bobby Bologna.

Full speed ahead.

No regrets.

The Chicago way.

INTERLUDE: GAME NIGHT

Rosie's Bar — Chicago — May 1998 The Bulls were playing Indiana.

This mattered because everything about the Bulls mattered in 1998.

This was the last dance. Everyone knew it. Jordan was hinting. Pippen was injured. Phil Jackson was floating away on his Zen cloud toward destinations unknown.

Every game might be the last game.

And Bobby Bologna did not miss games.

Rosie's Bar was not a sports bar.

It was a neighborhood bar that happened to have a television and an owner named Rosie who had learned long ago that fighting against Bulls fever was pointless. You either put the game on or you lost every customer for three months.

So the game was on.

And Bobby's crew was there.

All of them. Together. Arranged in their usual spots with their usual drinks and their usual superstitions.

Bobby in the center, of course. Where the view was best. Where he could see both the television and the door, because old habits died harder than point guards.

Sol to his left, pretending to read a newspaper while actually watching the game with an intensity that would have surprised anyone who thought he didn't care about sports.

Vinny to his right, already arguing with someone about something.

Vinny was always arguing. The content changed; the arguing was constant.

Nicky at the end, surrounded by enough food to feed a small family, working his way through it with the focused determination of a man who had never met a meal he didn't want to finish.

And Frankie, wherever Frankie was, probably in the bathroom, probably worried about something, probably convinced that the feds were going to burst through the doors any minute even though the feds didn't bust people at bars for watching basketball.

This was the crew.

This was family.

This was what mattered.

"They're playing soft," Vinny announced during a timeout.

"They're managing the clock," Bobby corrected.

"Managing the clock is what you say when you're playing soft but don't want to admit it."

"Managing the clock is strategy."

"Strategy is what you call it when you're—"

"VINNY. I swear to God."

Sol turned a page in his newspaper. "Statistically, arguing during timeouts has no effect on game outcomes."

"I'm not arguing to affect the outcome. I'm arguing because I'm right."

"You're arguing because you can't not argue. It's pathological."

"That's a big word."

"I know many big words. Would you like me to use more of them?"

"I would like you to admit that they're playing soft."

"They're up by seven."

"They're up by seven softly."

Nicky raised his hand.

Nobody acknowledged him.

He kept it raised.

"What, Nicky?" Bobby finally asked.

"I think Reggie Miller looks tired."

"Okay."

"I'm just saying. He looks tired. His legs are heavy. When your legs are heavy, you miss shots."

"Thank you for the analysis."

"I'm welcome." Nicky returned to his food. "Also, I think we should get more nachos."

"You have nachos."

"I have fewer nachos than I started with. That's concerning."

"The concerning thing would be if you had more nachos than you started with. That would violate physics."

Nicky thought about this. "I would like to violate physics."

Sol closed his eyes. "He's going to hurt himself thinking."

"I think fine."

"You think adequately. That's not the same as fine."

Frankie emerged from the bathroom.

"Did I miss anything?"

228

"Reggie Miller is tired and we need more nachos," Bobby summarized.

"Is that analysis or opinion?"

"With this group? Both."

Frankie slid into his seat. "I had a thought while I was in there."

"I don't want to know about your bathroom thoughts."

"It's not a bathroom thought. It's a business thought that happened to occur in a bathroom."

"Still don't want to know."

"What if—"

"FRANKIE."

"Okay. Fine. No bathroom thoughts. Even though it was actually a pretty good thought."

The game resumed.

For five beautiful minutes, nobody argued.

They watched Jordan work. The way he moved. The way he saw the floor. The way he made the impossible look inevitable and the inevitable look easy.

"He's not human," Nicky said quietly. "He can't be."

"He's human," Bobby replied. "He's just... more."

"More what?"

"More everything. More drive. More skill. More will. Whatever the thing is that separates people who play basketball from people who are basketball, he has more of it."

Sol looked at Bobby. "That's surprisingly poetic."

"I have layers."

"You have opinions. Layers is generous."

"My opinions are layers. Each one builds on the last."

"That's not what layers means."

"It's what layers means to me."

Pippen hit a three.

The bar erupted.

Bobby stood up, arms raised, screaming something that was probably "YES" but sounded more like a wounded animal celebrating a successful hunt.

Vinny was hugging a stranger.

Nicky was crying.

Sol was nodding with what might have been approval or might have been gas.

Frankie was checking his phone, but even he was smiling.

This was it.

This was the thing that made all the rest of it bearable.

The jobs. The stress. The violence. The constant calculation of who was loyal and who was lying and how long until something went wrong.

For ninety minutes, twice a week, none of that mattered.

For ninety minutes, they were just fans.

Just guys in a bar watching a game they loved.

Just family.

"You know what I realized?" Bobby said during the next timeout.

"That Vinny's right about the soft playing?" Vinny asked hopefully.

"That we're going to remember this. Not the jobs. Not the business. This. Sitting here. Watching Jordan. Being together."

Sol lowered his newspaper. "That's unusually sentimental."

"I'm feeling sentimental. It's the playoffs. Playoffs make me sentimental."

"Everything makes you sentimental. The other day you got sentimental about a hot dog."

"It was a really good hot dog."

"It was a processed meat tube."

"A really good processed meat tube. There's a difference."

The Bulls won.

They always seemed to win when it mattered.

That was the thing about this team. About this era. About Michael Jordan and everything he represented.

When the moment was biggest, they rose to it.

When the pressure was highest, they delivered.

When everyone said it couldn't be done, they did it anyway.

Bobby loved that.

He aspired to that.

Even if his version of rising to moments involved significantly more Italian beef and significantly less athletic ability.

They walked out of Rosie's into the Chicago night.

The city was alive. Honking horns. Cheering crowds. That particular energy that only came when the Bulls won and everyone remembered at the same time how much they loved this team.

"Same time Thursday?" Nicky asked.

"Same time Thursday."

"I'm bringing better nachos."

"The nachos were fine."

"The nachos were adequate. I want better than adequate."

Bobby put his arm around Nicky. "You're a man of refined tastes, Nicky."

"I try."

"You succeed. At the nacho thing, at least."

"I'll take it."

They walked to their cars.

Five men. Linked by history. Bound by loyalty. Held together by something that couldn't be explained to anyone who wasn't part of it.

Sol fell into step beside Bobby.

"You know it's going to end, right? The Bulls. Jordan. This whole era. It's ending."

"Everything ends."

"And when it does? What then?"

Bobby looked up at the Chicago skyline. The buildings. The lights.

The city that had made him who he was.

"Then we remember it. And we tell stories about it. And we argue about whether they played soft or managed the clock. And eventually we die, and somebody else argues about it."

"That's bleak."

"That's life. The bleakness is part of the beauty."

"That doesn't make sense."

"It doesn't have to make sense. It just has to be true."

Sol was quiet for a moment.

"Thursday, then."

"Thursday."

"I'm bringing better nachos too."

"I thought Nicky was bringing better nachos."

"There's no rule against multiple people bringing better nachos."

"There should be. There should be a nacho limit."

"There are many things there should be, Bobby. We live in an imperfect world."

Bobby laughed.

Actually laughed.

A real laugh, not a performance.

Because Sol was right. The world was imperfect. The Bulls would end. Everything would change.

But not tonight.

Tonight, they were still champions.

And that was enough.

It had to be enough.

Because in the end, moments were all you got.

And this moment—walking through Chicago after a Bulls win, surrounded by his crew, arguing about nachos and destiny and the nature of athletic greatness—was a pretty good moment.

Bobby would take it.

He would remember it.

And when everything else was gone, he would still have this.

The night air. The city lights. The family he'd built from broken pieces and impossible loyalties.

The last dance.

While it lasted.

PART FIVE

LEGEND BORN

June 1998 The Last Day — Chicago The day before he flew to Utah, Bobby Bologna did a tour of his city.

Not officially. Not announced.

Just driving. Looking. Remembering.

He started in Bridgeport.

Drove past the house where he grew up. The church where he was baptized. The corner where he had his first kiss.

Sat in the car for twenty minutes just looking.

Not thinking about anything specific.

Just being present.

Then to the Loop.

Parked illegally and walked around the block where his first real office had been. Third floor of a building that no longer existed.

Demolished in the eighties to make room for something taller.

Bobby could still see it though.

Could still remember climbing those stairs. Feeling important.

Believing that everything was ahead of him.

Then to Lincoln Park.

His apartment. His neighborhood. The life he had built from nothing.

He stood on the sidewalk and looked up at his windows.

Wondered what the next person to live there would think.

Wondered if any trace of him would remain.

Then to Al's #1 Italian Beef.

His sanctuary. His temple. The place where he had made more decisions than any office.

He ordered his usual.

Ate it slowly.

Memorized the taste.

Then to Manny's Deli.

Another sandwich. Another memory.

Sol was supposed to meet him but got caught up with something.

Bobby ate alone.

Which was fine.

Sometimes alone was what you needed.

Then to Gene and Jude.

A hot dog.

No ketchup.

Obviously.

He stood at the wall and watched people come and go.

All of them hungry. All of them here for the same reason.

The simple pleasure of good food.

Then to Margie Candies.

A sundae.

Because you could not leave without something sweet.

He ate it slowly. Let the chocolate melt on his tongue. Closed his eyes and pretended he was twelve again.

Before everything got complicated.

Before he became Bobby Bologna instead of just Bobby.

A family came in while he was finishing. Father, mother, two kids. The father was wearing the kind of polo shirt that meant he worked in an office and had health insurance and would not die in a Salt Lake City arena. The mother was tired in the way of people who had spent the whole day saying no to small humans. The kids were arguing about ice cream flavors with the seriousness of people negotiating a treaty.

Bobby watched them.

He thought: I could have had that.

He thought: I did not want that.

He thought: Did I not want it because I really did not want it, or because by the time I knew I had a choice, the choice was already gone?

He did not have an answer.

He left a twenty on the counter for the family's order. Walked out before anyone noticed.

The sun was setting when he finished.

Orange and pink over a city that had given him everything.

He drove to the lakefront.

Parked.

Walked to the edge.

Stood looking at the water that had defined his entire life.

"I love you," he said.

To the lake.

To the city.

To the life he had lived.

"Whatever happens next, I love you."

The lake didn't answer.

But Bobby felt like it understood.

He drove home.

Packed for Utah.

Went to bed early because the flight was at dawn.

And somewhere in the darkness, as sleep took him, Bobby Bologna said goodbye.

To everything.

To everyone.

To the city that had made him who he was.

He did not know it was goodbye.

But some part of him must have felt it.

Because he slept well that night.

Better than he had slept in years.

The sleep of a man at peace.

The sleep of a man who had lived.

The sleep of a man who was ready.

For whatever came next.

CHAPTER 15

Salt Lake City — Courtside

Bobby Bologna had never been to Utah before and already did not trust it.

Too clean.

Too quiet.

Too many mountains judging him from every direction.

"Why does the air feel religious," he muttered as they stepped off the plane at Salt Lake City International Airport.

Vinny adjusted his jacket. "I think that's altitude."

Frankie—who had come despite his airplane anxiety, because missing history was worse than enclosed spaces—whispered, "I think that's God."

Nicky looked around the terminal. "Where's the ocean?"

Sol sighed. "There is no ocean near here. Or sin, apparently."

Bobby grinned. "Don't worry. We brought some."

The hotel was nice in that aggressive way that Utah hotels were nice—clean carpets, religious art in the hallways, a mini-bar that somehow managed to feel disapproving.

Bobby didn't care.

He was here.

He was actually here.

In less than six hours, he would be sitting courtside at what might be the most important basketball game of his lifetime. He would watch Michael Jordan do Michael Jordan things. He would witness history being made.

And he would do it all in a city that had never seen anything like Bobby Bologna and probably never would again.

"I need food," he announced. "Chicago food."

Sol looked at him. "We're in Utah."

"Utah has Italian restaurants."

"Utah has Italian-adjacent restaurants."

"Then we find the best one."

"Bobby, we're here for basketball. Can we focus on basketball?"

"Food is focus. I can't watch a championship game on an empty stomach. That's how bad things happen."

They found a restaurant that claimed to serve authentic Italian cuisine and served what was actually very nice food that was approximately Italian in the same way that Chicago-style pizza was approximately pizza.

Bobby ate anyway.

He wasn't hungry for food.

He was hungry for something bigger.

Something he couldn't quite name.

The Delta Center was a cathedral.

Not literally—it was a basketball arena in Utah, which was about as far from a cathedral as you could get—but the energy inside had that religious quality. Eighteen thousand people, all of them wanting the same thing, all of them believing that what happened in the next few hours would matter.

Bobby walked through the tunnels toward his seat and felt like he was approaching an altar.

"This is unreal," Nicky whispered.

"This is history," Bobby corrected. "Pay attention."

Their seats were perfect.

Not the absolute best seats in the house—those belonged to people with more money than Bobby could imagine—but close enough to see the sweat on the players' faces. Close enough to hear the shoes squeak on the hardwood. Close enough to feel like a part of something rather than just a witness to it.

Bobby sat down and took a breath.

He was here.

He had made it.

Whatever happened next, he had made it.

"I need a hot dog," Bobby announced.

Sol stared at him. "You just ate dinner."

"Dinner was hours ago."

"Dinner was ninety minutes ago."

"That's hours in basketball time."

Bobby flagged down a vendor and ordered two dogs with everything.

Utah everything, which was not the same as Chicago everything, but would have to do.

The first bite was not transcendent.

The second bite was acceptable.

By the third bite, Bobby had convinced himself it was good because he needed it to be good. The ritual demanded it.

"To health," he said, holding up his hot dog.

Nicky held up his own. "To health!"

Sol didn't participate.

Sol was watching the crowd, watching the exits, watching everything that could go wrong.

"Relax," Bobby told him. "Nothing bad happens at a basketball game."

Sol looked at him.

"Everything bad happens everywhere, Bobby. That's the nature of bad things."

"Not tonight. Tonight is sacred."

The game started.

Bobby stopped thinking about anything else.

The first quarter was tight—the Jazz were good, genuinely good, and Karl Malone and John Stockton were playing like men who knew this might be their last chance.

Bobby screamed at every call.

He celebrated every Bulls basket.

He suffered through every Jazz run.

Vinny got into an argument with the man next to him about a foul call and had to be calmed down by Frankie, which was like asking a fire to be calmed down by a smaller fire.

Nicky ate four hot dogs and showed no signs of stopping.

And through it all, Bobby watched Jordan.

Watched him move without the ball.

Watched him set up plays.

Watched him wait for his moment.

Halftime came and went.

The Bulls were down by three.

Bobby was nervous.

Not about the game—he believed in Jordan, believed in destiny, believed in the strange cosmic connection between his superstitions and the outcome of professional basketball.

He was nervous about everything else.

About the war with Tony Smiles.

About the warehouse incident.

About the way things had been slowly falling apart for months.

About whether this trip to Utah was confidence or stupidity, and whether there was even a difference anymore.

"Hey," Sol said quietly, during the halftime break. "You okay?"

Bobby looked at his oldest friend.

"I don't know," he admitted. "I feel like I'm watching something end. And I don't know if it's the Bulls dynasty or something else."

Sol was quiet for a moment.

"Everything ends, Bobby. The question is what you do with the time you have."

"That's very philosophical."

"You're not the only one who's been reading."

The third quarter started.

Bobby pushed away his doubts.

He had come here to witness history.

Whatever came after—the war, the consequences, the slow grind of a life spent always fighting—could wait.

Right now, there was only basketball.

Right now, there was only this.

He settled into his seat and watched Michael Jordan begin to take over the game.

It was beautiful.

It was terrifying.

It was exactly what Bobby had come to see.

The Flight — Chicago to Salt Lake Bobby hated flying.

This was not widely known.

He hid it well. Made jokes. Pretended the turbulence did not bother him. Acted like sitting in a metal tube thirty thousand feet above the ground was perfectly natural and not at all terrifying.

But he hated it.

Every moment of every flight was a small exercise in terror management.

"You look pale," Sol observed, as they boarded.

"I'm fine."

"You're gripping the armrest like it might escape."

"I'm preparing for takeoff."

"We haven't left the gate."

"I like to be prepared."

The flight was three hours.

Three hours of trying to read. Trying to watch the movie. Trying to do anything except think about the fact that they were suspended in the air by nothing but physics and faith.

Nicky slept the entire time.

How anyone could sleep on an airplane was beyond Bobby's comprehension. It seemed like a fundamental betrayal of survival instincts.

Vinny watched the movie without headphones.

Just stared at the screen while people talked and fought and fell in love in silence.

Sol read a book about accounting that looked even more boring than it sounded.

"You know what I hate about flying?" Bobby said, somewhere over Nebraska.

"Everything?" Sol guessed.

"The lack of control. On the ground, if something goes wrong, you can do something. You can run. Fight. Hide. Up here, you just sit. Wait. Hope the pilots know what they're doing."

"The pilots know what they're doing."

"Probably."

"Definitely."

"We'll agree to disagree."

The captain announced their descent.

Bobby felt the plane begin to drop and his stomach followed.

This was the worst part.

The knowledge that you were falling. The trust that someone would stop the falling before it became catastrophic.

He closed his eyes and thought about the game.

About Jordan.

About what it would feel like to watch history happen.

And somehow, that was enough to get him through.

They landed without incident.

Because flights almost always landed without incident. Because the fear was irrational. Because Bobby knew all of this and still couldn't make himself believe it.

"Solid ground," he said, stepping into the jetway. "Solid, beautiful ground."

"You're very dramatic," Sol observed.

"I'm alive. I'm allowed to be dramatic."

Salt Lake City looked like a different planet.

Mountains everywhere. Clean air that smelled like nothing at all.

People who smiled at strangers without obvious ulterior motives.

Bobby didn't trust any of it.

"Where is the grit?" he asked. "Where is the character?"

"Some cities are just clean, Bobby."

"Clean is suspicious. Clean means they're hiding something."

They checked into the hotel.

Nice place. Neutral territory. The kind of hotel that existed in every city and looked exactly the same no matter where you were.

Bobby stood at the window and looked at the mountains.

"I'm going to die here," he said quietly.

Sol looked up from his book. "What?"

"Nothing. Just being dramatic."

"You're being morbid."

"Same thing."

He didn't know he was right.

He didn't know that his casual comment would become prophetic.

He didn't know that the mountains he was looking at would be the last mountains he would ever see.

But some part of him must have suspected.

Because that night, he called his mother's grave in Chicago.

Left a voicemail with the cemetery that sounded crazy but felt necessary.

"Hey Ma. It's Bobby. I just wanted to say I love you. And I hope you are proud of me. And if I don't make it back from this trip, know that I died happy. I died watching something I loved. I died being exactly who I was."

He hung up.

Felt foolish.

But also felt better.

The game was tomorrow.

The dynasty was about to end.

And Bobby Bologna was about to become immortal.

He just did not know it yet.
None of them did.
That was the nature of fate.
You only understood it in retrospect.
And by then, it was already too late.

CHAPTER 16

The Shot

The fourth quarter of Game 6 of the 1998 NBA Finals was the greatest quarter of basketball Bobby Bologna had ever seen.

It was also, as it turned out, the last thing he would ever see clearly.

The Bulls were down by three with forty seconds left.

Jordan had the ball.

The entire arena—eighteen thousand Utah fans plus a handful of Chicago believers who had traveled halfway across the country for this moment—was on its feet.

Bobby couldn't breathe.

He literally could not take a breath.

His lungs had stopped working, replaced by pure anticipation.

"Come on," he whispered. "Come on, come on, come on."

Jordan drove toward the basket.

He was guarded, covered, seemingly trapped.

But Jordan was never trapped.

He elevated.

He released.

The ball arced toward the hoop with the lazy perfection of something that was always going to happen, that had been destined to happen since the moment the universe decided that Chicago deserved this.

Swish.

The Bulls were down by one.

Twenty seconds left.

Bobby grabbed Vinny's arm so hard that Vinny yelped.

"This is it," Bobby said. "This is the moment."

"You're hurting me."

"This is the moment, Vinny."

"You're really hurting me."

The Jazz had the ball.

Stockton to Malone.

The Bulls doubled.

Malone turned into the coverage.

And then— Jordan.

The steal.

The break.

The entire history of basketball condensed into one sequence of events.

Jordan crossed halfcourt.

Time slowed down.

Bobby could see everything with impossible clarity: the sweat on Jordan's forehead, the desperation on Byron Russell's face, the way the arena lights caught the red of the Bulls jersey.

Jordan stopped.

Crossover.

Russell stumbled.

Jordan rose.

The shot went up.

Time stopped.

For everyone.

For the eighteen thousand people in the arena.

For the millions watching at home.

For Bobby Bologna, standing at his courtside seat, hands raised toward the ceiling like he was trying to catch something falling from heaven.

The ball hung in the air.

Forever.

And then— Swish.

The Bulls led by one.

Five seconds left.

The Jazz couldn't get a shot off.

The buzzer sounded.

The Bulls won.

Chicago won.

Jordan won.

And Bobby Bologna, tears streaming down his face, let out a scream that came from somewhere deeper than his lungs, somewhere deeper than his bones, somewhere that had been waiting his entire life for this exact moment.

"YES!" he screamed. "YES! YES! YES!"

He was jumping.

He was hugging strangers.

He was crying in a way he hadn't cried since his mother died.

This was joy.

Pure, unfiltered, impossible joy.

The kind that comes once in a lifetime.

The kind that makes everything else worth it.

Sol was crying too.

Sol, who never showed emotion.

Sol, who calculated everything.

Sol, who had told Bobby this trip was a mistake.

He was crying, and smiling, and for one moment—one perfect moment—nothing else mattered.

Not Tony Smiles.

Not the warehouse.

Not the slow decline of everything they had built.

Just this.

Just the joy of being alive at the right moment, in the right place, watching the right thing happen.

Bobby reached for his hot dog.

He had ordered another one sometime during the fourth quarter—he couldn't remember when—and it was sitting in its paper tray, getting cold, waiting for the celebration.

He grabbed it.

Lifted it.

Took a bite.

The biggest bite of his life.

Because this moment deserved a big bite.

Because everything deserved to be big right now.

And then— He couldn't breathe.

Not in the good way.

Not in the anticipation way.

In the actual, physical, something-is-very-wrong way.

The hot dog was stuck.

Lodged somewhere between his mouth and his lungs.

Bobby grabbed at his throat.

He tried to cough.

Nothing came out.

He tried to breathe.

Nothing came in.

At first, nobody noticed.

The celebration was too loud.

The joy was too overwhelming.

Everyone was jumping and screaming and hugging and nobody was looking at Bobby Bologna, the man who had come all this way to witness history, the man who was now choking to death in the middle of it.

Sol noticed first.

Because Sol always noticed.

"Bobby?" he said. "Bobby, what's—"

He saw Bobby's face.

He saw the color draining.

He saw the hands at the throat.

"BOBBY!"

The celebration continued around them.

Jordan was being lifted onto shoulders.

Confetti was falling from somewhere.

The greatest moment in Chicago sports history was happening.

And Bobby Bologna was dying.

Sol grabbed him.

Tried the Heimlich.

Nothing.

"HELP!" Sol screamed. "SOMEBODY HELP!"

Vinny turned.

Saw what was happening.

His face went white.

Nicky dropped his hot dog—his seventh—and started crying.

Frankie just stood there, frozen, watching his boss turn purple.

Security came.

Then paramedics.

They laid Bobby on the floor, right there on the court, while the celebration continued around them.

They tried CPR.

They tried everything.

The confetti kept falling.

The music kept playing.

Michael Jordan was giving interviews somewhere.

And Bobby Bologna, the man who had believed in destiny more than anyone, was finding out what destiny really meant.

It took three minutes for him to die.

Three minutes of CPR and chaos and screaming.

Three minutes of Sol holding his hand and begging him to breathe.

Three minutes of the greatest celebration of his life turning into the worst moment of everyone else's.

And then it was over.

Bobby Bologna was gone.

Died courtside at the NBA Finals.

Died watching Jordan's last shot.

Died choking on a hot dog.

Died the way he lived.

Loudly.

Publicly.

In the middle of everything.

CHAPTER 17

Chaos

The next twenty-four hours were a blur.

The paramedics pronounced Bobby dead at 10:47 PM Mountain Time, which was 11:47 PM in Chicago, which meant he technically died on the same day as the Bulls' sixth championship, which would become important later for reasons of legend-building.

Sol stood over the body—because that's what it was now, a body, not Bobby anymore—and felt something break inside him.

Not his heart.

Something colder.

Something that had been holding everything together.

"We need to get him home," Sol heard himself say.

His voice sounded far away.

Like someone else was speaking through him.

"Sir," a paramedic said gently, "we need to process the scene. There are procedures—"

"He's going home," Sol said. "To Chicago. Tonight."

"That's not how this works—"

Sol turned to look at the paramedic.

Whatever was in his eyes made the man stop talking.

Vinny was silent.

This was unusual.

Vinny was never silent.

He stood against a wall, staring at nothing, his hands shaking in a way that suggested he was either going to start crying or start hitting things.

He did neither.

He just stood there.

Being quiet.

Nicky was definitely crying.

No ambiguity about it.

Full, heaving sobs that drew stares from people who didn't know what had happened and concerned looks from people who did.

"He was just eating," Nicky said, between sobs. "He was just eating a hot dog."

Frankie stood next to him, patting his back awkwardly.

"I know."

"He's eaten a million hot dogs."

"I know."

"Why this one?"

Frankie didn't have an answer.

The arena cleared slowly.

Most people didn't know what had happened.

They'd been too busy celebrating.

Too busy experiencing the greatest moment of their sports-watching lives.

A man had died fifteen feet from the court, and hardly anyone had noticed.

That felt fitting, somehow.

Bobby would have hated that.

Or maybe he would have loved it.

It was hard to say anymore.

Sol made phone calls.

To the funeral home.

To the lawyer.

To people in Chicago who needed to know before they heard it from someone else.

Each call was harder than the last.

Each time he had to say the words out loud, they became more real.

"Bobby's dead."

"Bobby died at the game."

"Bobby choked on a hot dog."

That last part was the hardest.

Because it was absurd.

Because Bobby Bologna—the man who had survived decades in organized crime, who had fought off rivals and dodged investigations and navigated politics that would have destroyed anyone else—had been killed by a stadium hot dog.

There was no dignity in it.

There was no meaning.

There was just meat and bread and a moment of joy turned into a moment of tragedy.

They flew back to Chicago the next morning.

Bobby's body was in the cargo hold.

None of them slept on the flight.

O'Hare was quiet at 6 AM.

The early morning light hit the terminals with that particular exhausted quality that airports always had, like the buildings themselves were tired of processing people.

They walked through the terminal in silence.

Past the Garrett Popcorn.

Past the Hudson News.

Past all the places that Bobby had probably walked through a hundred times, heading somewhere important, heading somewhere loud.

The car was waiting outside.

Same car as always.

Same driver.

Except Bobby wasn't getting in.

Bobby would never get in again.

Sol stopped at the curb and looked at the Chicago skyline in the distance.

The city where Bobby had been born.

The city where Bobby had built everything.

The city where Bobby would be buried.

"We have to tell people," Vinny said quietly.

"I know."

"We have to figure out what happens next."

"I know."

"Sol—"

"I know, Vinny. I know everything we have to do. I just need a minute."

They stood there for a long time.

Four men in expensive suits, standing on a curb at O'Hare, watching the sun rise over a city that didn't know yet that something had changed.

Something had ended.

And something else was about to begin.

What People Say By the next morning, everybody in Chicago had a story about Bobby Bologna.

And none of them were the same.

At Al's #1 Italian Beef, a guy named Tommy claimed he had been there the day Bobby cracked the counter.

"He was arguing about giardiniera ratios," Tommy said. "Got so passionate he leaned too hard. Crack. Right down the middle. And you know what he did? He laughed. Laughed like it was the funniest thing in the world. Then he ordered another sandwich."

This story was approximately forty percent true.

At Gene & Jude's, an older woman swore she had seen Bobby beat up a tourist for asking about ketchup.

"The whole line joined in," she said. "Even the staff. Bobby didn't start it. He finished it. There's a difference."

This story was approximately sixty percent true.

At Manny's Deli, the waitresses had a collection of Bobby stories.

"He tipped a hundred dollars on a fifty-dollar check."

"He once ate pastrami for six hours straight."

"He told my daughter to stay in school or he would be very disappointed."

These stories ranged from mostly true to completely invented.

Nobody cared.

At Portillo's, someone claimed Bobby had once challenged the manager to a hot dog eating contest and lost gracefully.

"He ate twelve," the storyteller said. "The manager ate thirteen. Bobby shook his hand and said may the best stomach win."

This story was completely false.

Bobby had never lost an eating contest in his life.

At Lou Malnati's, a busboy swore he had served Bobby his last Chicago meal.

"Deep dish. Extra sausage. He said it was perfect. Said he was going to Utah to watch the Bulls win. Said nothing could go wrong when you started the day with pizza like that."

This story was almost true.

Bobby had been at Lou Malnati's before the Utah trip.

But he had ordered thin crust, not deep dish.

The storyteller had changed it for dramatic effect.

A waitress at the same Lou Malnati's would later tell a different story to anyone who would listen.

"He proposed to a deep dish once. Got down on one knee. Whole restaurant clapped."

This story was approximately *five* percent true. He had once said the words "I love you" to a deep dish, but he had been seated and had not been entirely sober, and the restaurant had not clapped because the restaurant had been mostly empty.

Nobody held this against the waitress. In Chicago, embellishment was a *form of love.*

At a bar in Wrigleyville, a regular named Donny insisted that Bobby had once nearly fought a man for ordering a Bud Light during a Cubs game.

"Bobby looked at the bottle. Looked at the guy. Looked at the bottle again. Then he turned to me and said, 'You let this happen in your bar?'"

"What did you say?" the listener asked.

"I said it was a free country."

"And then?"

"And then Bobby paid for the guy's beer. Said anybody drinking a Bud Light during a Cubs game was already being punished enough."

This story was approximately eighty percent true.

The part about paying for the beer was real.

The part where Bobby called Bud Light "the official beer of *giving up*" was not in the official telling, but it should have been.

At Wrigley Field itself, an usher who had worked the bleachers for thirty years swore he once saw Bobby Bologna catch a foul ball one-handed while holding two Vienna Beef hot dogs in the other.

"Didn't drop a thing," the usher said. "Not the ball. Not the dogs. Not the onions."

This story was completely true.

It was, in fact, the *only* true story anyone ever told about Bobby Bologna.

Which was the funniest part.

The stories spread.

Grew.

Changed.

Each telling added details. Removed others. Made Bobby bigger, louder, more legendary than any man could actually be.

That was how legends worked.

Not through accuracy.

Through repetition.

Years later, people would tell Bobby Bologna stories to their children.

Some would remember his crimes.

Some would remember his kindness.

Some would remember only the way he died, which was either tragic or perfect depending on who was telling it.

But everyone would remember.

That was maybe the only point.

Bobby Bologna was dead.

But Bobby Bologna would never be forgotten.

And in Chicago, being remembered was the closest thing to immortality that anyone could achieve.

At the grave in Resurrection Cemetery, someone left a hot dog.

Nobody knew who.

Nobody asked.

It seemed right.

A tribute.

An offering.

A reminder that Bobby Bologna had lived exactly as he wanted to live.

And died exactly as he was always going to die.

Eating.

Loudly.

In public.

Chicago style.

THE LAST MOMENT

Delta Center — June 14, 1998 — 9:02 PM Bobby Bologna was not thinking about death.

This was important to understand later, when the stories circulated and the legends grew and everyone had an opinion about what Bobby's final moments must have been like.

He was not thinking about his enemies.

He was not thinking about his regrets.

He was not thinking about all the things he should have said to people or all the choices he should have made differently.

He was thinking about the hot dog.

It was a good hot dog. Not great—arena hot dogs were never great—but good enough. Mustard, onions, a little relish. No ketchup, obviously, because Bobby Bologna would die before he put ketchup on a hot dog.

Which, in retrospect, was ironic.

The game was tied.

Jordan had the ball.

Eighteen thousand people were on their feet, screaming, because everyone knew what was coming. Everyone understood that they were witnessing something that would be talked about for decades.

Bobby screamed too.

Not because he knew he was witnessing history.

Because he was happy.

Simple, uncomplicated happiness.

The kind that had been rare in his life. The kind that came from being exactly where you wanted to be, doing exactly what you wanted to do, surrounded by everything you loved.

Chicago was about to win.

And Bobby Bologna was there to see it.

He took a bite of the hot dog.

Too big a bite. He knew it even as he did it, the way you know you're making a mistake the moment you make it but can't stop because the moment has already started.

The hot dog lodged in his throat.

He coughed.

He couldn't cough.

The crowd surged forward as Jordan made his move.

Bobby reached for his neck.

Nobody noticed.

The strange thing was, he didn't panic.

Later, this would become part of the legend—Bobby Bologna, fearless to the end, facing death with the same bravado he'd faced everything else.

But that wasn't quite true.

It wasn't bravado. It was understanding.

Bobby understood, in that moment, what was happening. He understood that his airway was blocked and that he couldn't breathe and that the people around him were too focused on the game to see him struggling.

He understood that he was dying.

And his first thought—his honest, genuine, unedited first thought—was: At least I get to see the shot.

Jordan released the ball.

It arced through the air.

Bobby's vision was going dark around the edges, but the center was still clear. The center was the ball. The ball was everything.

Time stretched.

The ball hung in the air for what felt like forever.

And then it fell.

Through the net.

Nothing but net.

The Delta Center exploded.

Eighteen thousand people lost their minds.

And Bobby Bologna, dying on his feet, smiled.

He didn't feel himself fall.

He didn't hear the people around him finally notice that something was wrong.

He didn't see the paramedics who would arrive too late, or Sol pushing through the crowd screaming his name, or Vinny punching a security guard who was trying to hold him back.

All he saw was the scoreboard.

BULLS 87, JAZZ 86.

All he felt was victory.

All he knew was that Chicago had won.

And then everything went quiet.

And Bobby Bologna, who had eaten every meal like it might be his last, finally found one that was.

Some deaths are tragedies.

Some deaths are mercies.

Some deaths are just endings, neutral and inevitable, the period at the end of a sentence that was going to end eventually anyway.

But Bobby's death was different.

Bobby's death was Bobby.

Loud. Public. Completely inappropriate. Surrounded by food and sports and the city he loved.

If he could have written it himself, it wouldn't have been much different.

Maybe that was the real tragedy.

Or maybe it was the opposite of tragedy.

Maybe it was exactly right.

Maybe some people die the way they lived, and that's all you can ask for in this life.

Bobby Bologna died happy.

Bobby Bologna died a Bulls fan.

Bobby Bologna died in Chicago.

Even if the arena was in Utah, even if the coordinates said Salt Lake City, Bobby died in Chicago.

Because Chicago was never a place.

Chicago was a state of mind.

And Bobby Bologna had been in that state of mind since the day he was born.

He just finally stopped being in it.

One hot dog at a time.

PART SIX

AFTER

CHAPTER 18

The Funeral

St. Alphonsus Church was packed.

Standing room only. Four hundred people trying to fit in a space for three hundred.

Not because everyone loved Bobby.

Because everyone wanted to be seen paying respects.

The crew sat in front.

Sol in an expensive suit.

Vinny's jaw tight.

Frankie looking sick.

Nicky already crying.

Father Mike delivered the eulogy.

"Robert Filoni wasn't a perfect man."

Laughter through the congregation.

"He wasn't even a good man by most measures. He lived a life that brought harm as well as joy."

Silence.

"But he was a man who loved. His city. His friends. Food and basketball and Chicago in all its glory and flaws."

"Robert died watching something beautiful. Surrounded by joy. In a moment of triumph."

"There are worse ways to go."

"May God have mercy on his soul."

"And may we all be so lucky as to die doing what we love."

They buried him in Resurrection Cemetery.

The sun was shining. Which felt wrong.

Should have been gray and miserable.

But the universe never cared what Bobby thought was appropriate.

Sol stayed until the end.

Until the grave was filled.

Until he was alone with fresh dirt and new headstone.

"Goodbye Bobby," he whispered.

"I hope wherever you are, the beef is dipped and giardiniera is hot."

A small smile.

"To health."

Then he walked away.

Because that's what you did.

You buried your dead.

And kept going.

The Chicago way.

The Story Gets Out The story broke everywhere.

"CHICAGO MAN DIES AT NBA FINALS"

"COURTSIDE TRAGEDY MARS BULLS CELEBRATION"

"CHOKING DEATH DURING JORDAN'S LAST SHOT"

Channel 5 was first.

"Robert Filoni, known as Bobby Bologna, died at the Delta Center. Sources say he choked on a hot dog during celebration following Jordan's legendary shot."

The anchor paused.

"Filoni was known to police as an organized crime figure. Friends describe him as a passionate Bulls fan. He was forty-three."

Sports radio had a field day.

"Bobby Bologna was a real Chicago guy."

"I heard he ate seven hot dogs. Seven. Dedication."

"He died at the exact moment we won. Spirit went up with the confetti."

The myth was being born.

At Manny's Deli, Sol sat alone.

Gloria the waitress stopped by.

"You okay honey?"

"No. Not really."

"He was a good guy. Ate like a horse. Tipped like a king."

Sol looked at the pastrami.

"To health," he said quietly.

Then started eating.

Because that's what Bobby would have wanted.

And that's what Chicago did.

It kept eating.

CHAPTER 19

Tony Hears the News

Lincoln Park — June 15, 1998

Tony Smiles was having breakfast when he found out.

Eggs Benedict. Fresh-squeezed orange juice. The Tribune spread out on the table because Tony liked to read in the morning, even though most of what he read made him angry.

His phone rang.

"Yeah."

"Boss. You heard?"

"Heard what?"

"About Bobby Bologna."

Tony set down his fork. "What about him?"

"He's dead. Last night. In Salt Lake City. At the game."

Tony waited for more information.

"Choked on a hot dog."

"What?"

"Choked on a hot dog. During Jordan's shot. They're saying it was the excitement—"

Tony hung up.

He sat very still for a long moment.

Then he laughed.

The laughter lasted almost a minute.

Great, heaving waves of laughter that bent him forward in his chair and made his stomach hurt and brought tears to his eyes.

A hot dog.

Bobby Bologna—the man who had defied him, insulted him, stolen his handbags, and named a cat after him—had died choking on a hot dog.

It was perfect.

It was so perfect that Tony almost couldn't believe it.

He had spent months planning ways to handle Bobby. Contingencies. Strategies. Alliances that would isolate him. Pressure that would break him.

And then Bobby had gone and died on his own.

Eating.

At a basketball game.

Because of course he had.

Tony stopped laughing.

And something else took its place.

Something he didn't expect.

Bobby Bologna had been a problem.

Bobby Bologna had been an obstacle.

Bobby Bologna had been loud and brash and crude and everything that Tony Smiles hated about the old Chicago, the Chicago of stockyards and steel mills and men who measured respect in decibels.

But Bobby Bologna had also been real.

In a world of pretenders and posturers, of men who smiled when they didn't mean it (Tony knew this better than anyone), Bobby had been genuine. He said what he meant. He meant what he said. He loved his city and his crew and his food with an authenticity that was almost embarrassing in its nakedness.

Tony had hated him.

But he had also, in some strange way, respected him.

Because Bobby was the last of something. The last of a type that was disappearing. The last man in Chicago who didn't know how to be anything other than exactly what he was.

And now he was gone.

Choked to death on a hot dog.

While Michael Jordan hit the shot that would define a generation.

Tony pushed his breakfast away.

He wasn't hungry anymore.

"Sir?" His assistant appeared in the doorway. "Is everything okay?"

"Everything's fine."

"The Schaumburg people are asking about the timeline. With Bobby gone, they want to know if we're accelerating—"

"Cancel it."

"Sir?"

"Cancel the Schaumburg operation. All of it."

"But... we've been planning this for months. Bobby was the only thing standing in the way. Now that he's—"

"I said cancel it."

The assistant stared at him.

Tony didn't explain.

Because how could he explain that taking Schaumburg now would feel wrong? That swooping in on Bobby's territory while his body was still warm would be a victory that tasted like ashes?

Bobby would have done it. If positions were reversed, Bobby would have moved immediately, ruthlessly, without a moment's hesitation.

But Tony wasn't Bobby.

That was the whole point.

That had always been the whole point.

That night, Tony Smiles did something he hadn't done in years.

He went to a Italian beef place.

Not a nice one. Not one of the upscale spots that served fancy beef on focaccia with sun-dried tomatoes.

A real one. The kind Bobby would have approved of.

He ordered a beef sandwich, dipped, with hot giardiniera.

He ate it standing up, leaning forward so the juice ran down his arms instead of onto his shirt.

It was messy. It was undignified. It was everything Tony Smiles had spent his career trying to avoid becoming.

And it was delicious.

When he was done, the guy behind the counter nodded at him.

"You're not from around here."

"What makes you say that?"

"The suit. The watch. The way you looked at the menu like it was in a foreign language."

Tony almost smiled. A real smile. Not the performance.

"I knew someone who loved these places."

"Yeah?"

"He would have said this was the best beef in Chicago."

"It's not. The best beef is at Al's. But we're pretty good."

"He would have had an opinion about that."

"Everyone has opinions about beef. That's what makes it beef."

Tony put a hundred-dollar bill on the counter.

The guy stared at it.

"For the sandwich?"

"For the education."

He walked out into the Chicago night.

The city was celebrating. The Bulls had won. Jordan had cemented his legacy. Somewhere, probably everywhere, people were drunk and happy and convinced that Chicago was the greatest place on Earth.

Bobby would have loved this.

Bobby would have been somewhere in this city, surrounded by his crew, eating something excessive and proclaiming loudly that this was what life was about.

And Tony Smiles, alone on a sidewalk with beef juice on his fingers, realized something.

He was going to miss him.

Not the conflict. Not the competition. Not the problems Bobby created.

Just... him.

The loudness. The certainty. The absolute refusal to be anything other than Bobby Bologna from Chicago, Illinois.

"Goodbye, Bobby," Tony said quietly, to no one.

Then he got in his car and drove home.

Tomorrow, there would be business. Territory. The thousand small decisions that made an empire.

But tonight, just for tonight, Tony Smiles allowed himself to mourn a man he had never liked and would never forget.

Because that was Chicago too.

The city that never stopped eating its own.

But remembered them anyway.

CHAPTER 20

Sol Chooses a Side

Three Weeks After the Funeral Three weeks after the funeral, Sol Rosen sat in his apartment and stared at the wall.

This had become his routine.

Wake up. Coffee. Stare at wall. Try to figure out what came next.

The apartment was quiet. Too quiet. Sol had never minded quiet before, but now the silence felt like an accusation.

You should have done something.

You should have known.

You should have stopped him from eating that hot dog.

The phone rang.

It had been ringing constantly since Bobby died. People with questions. People with demands. People who wanted to know who was in charge now and what that meant for them.

Sol let it ring.

He was tired of being the one with answers.

The crew had scattered.

Vinny was still in the city, still angry, still looking for someone to blame. He had gotten into three fights in the last week alone, none of them productive, all of them expensive to clean up.

Nicky had gone quiet. He barely ate anymore, which for Nicky was like a bird forgetting how to fly. He just sat in his apartment, watching Bulls reruns, crying during the fourth quarters.

Frankie had retreated into his dry cleaning business like it was a bunker. He came out only when absolutely necessary and even then looked like he expected to be shot.

And Sol?

Sol was just tired.

The phone kept ringing.

Sol finally answered.

"Sol. It's Angie."

Of course it was.

"What do you want?"

"To talk. About the future."

"The future is something that happens to other people now."

"The future is something you can shape. If you're willing."

Sol closed his eyes.

"What did you've in mind?"

They met at a restaurant neither of them would normally choose.

Neutral ground. Unfamiliar territory.

A place where history couldn't ambush them.

Angie arrived first. She was always first.

Sol arrived second. He was always calculating.

"You look terrible," Angie observed.

"I haven't been sleeping."

"That's understandable. But also unsustainable."

"Everything is unsustainable. That's what I've learned."

They ordered food neither of them would eat.

The ritual mattered more than the consumption.

"I've a proposal," Angie said.

"I assumed."

"Tony is willing to offer protection. Real protection. For you and whoever from your crew wants to continue."

"In exchange for what?"

"Everything Bobby built. The routes. The connections. The relationships."

Sol laughed. It wasn't a happy laugh.

"So you want me to sell my friend's legacy."

"I want you to survive. Bobby is dead, Sol. His legacy died with him. What remains is just business."

Sol stared at his untouched plate.

She was right.

He hated that she was right.

But she was.

Bobby was gone. The empire was crumbling. The alternatives were prison, violence, or accommodation.

And Sol was tired of violence.

"I need time," he said.

"You've one week."

"That isn't much time."

"Time is a luxury. Survival is a necessity."

Angie stood to leave.

"Think about it, Sol. Think about what Bobby would want for you."

"Bobby would want me to fight."

"Bobby is dead because he couldn't stop fighting. Even with hot dogs."

She left.

Sol sat alone with cold food and impossible choices.

That night, Sol went to Al's #1 Italian Beef.

He hadn't been back since before Bobby died.

The place felt different now. Smaller. Sadder. Like the walls themselves were mourning.

He ordered two dipped with hot giardiniera.

Bobby's order.

The counter guy recognized him.

"Hey. You were Bobby's friend. I'm sorry about what happened."

"Thank you."

"He was a good customer. Always tipped. Always had opinions."

Sol almost smiled. "That sounds right."

"We're going to miss him around here."

Sol looked at his sandwiches.

Two. As if Bobby might still show up.

"Yeah," Sol said quietly. "Me too."

He ate both sandwiches.

Slowly.

Trying to taste what Bobby had tasted.

Trying to understand what Bobby had understood about food and life and the particular magic of Chicago cuisine.

The beef was good.

The giardiniera was hot.

And for a moment, just a moment, Sol felt connected to something larger than himself.

Then the moment passed.

And he was alone again.

The next morning, Sol made a decision.

He called Angie.

"I accept your proposal. With conditions."

"Name them."

"Vinny walks away clean. Nicky too. And Frankie. They get out without consequences."

"That can be arranged."

"And I want it in writing. Something that matters."

Angie paused.

"You don't trust us."

"I don't trust anyone. That's how I've survived this long."

"Fair enough. We'll put it in writing."

Sol hung up the phone and stared out his window at the Chicago skyline.

Bobby would have hated this.

Bobby would have wanted to fight.

Bobby would have said that accommodation was surrender and surrender was death.

But Bobby was dead.

And Sol was still alive.

And sometimes survival was its own kind of victory.

Even when it didn't feel like one.

Case Closed Detective Delaney heard the news on his car radio.

"Chicago man dies at NBA Finals..."

He pulled over.

Sat in silence.

At the station, Ruiz was staring at her computer.

"You heard?" Delaney asked.

"Bobby Bologna. Dead in Utah. Choking on a hot dog."

"You can't make this up."

Months of work.

Surveillance. Interviews. Building a case.

All suddenly irrelevant.

"What do we do now?" Ruiz asked.

"Close the file. Move on. The universe solved our problem."

"Just like that?"

"The most Chicago ending possible."

Ruiz almost smiled.

"He died watching Jordan hit the shot."

"Courtside."

"That's kind of amazing."

"It's kind of something."

Delaney closed the final folder.

Bobby Bologna. Gone.

Not with a bang. With a hot dog.

"His crew will fall apart," Ruiz observed.

"Tony Smiles will make a move."

"Things will get interesting."

Delaney nodded. "This city never calms down enough to be boring."

In the break room, he raised his coffee cup.

"To Bobby Bologna."

Ruiz looked at him. "You're toasting a criminal?"

"I'm toasting a Chicagoan. There's a difference."

"Is there?"

Delaney smiled. "Sometimes."

CHAPTER 21

Vinny Cannot Let Go

Vinny Capozzi wasn't built for grief.

He was built for anger.

And anger, unlike grief, had targets.

Two weeks after the funeral, Vinny went looking for someone to blame.

He started with the hot dog vendor at the Delta Center.

This required flying to Utah, which Vinny had never done before because Vinny didn't like flying and didn't like Utah and didn't like doing anything that required planning ahead.

But here he was.

Salt Lake City.

Looking for a man who sold hot dogs.

The vendor was easy to find.

Same spot. Same cart. Same oblivious smile.

Vinny approached with murder in his heart.

"You sold a hot dog to Bobby Bologna."

The vendor blinked. "Who?"

"The guy who died. During the game. The championship game."

Recognition dawned. "Oh. Yeah. That was terrible. I felt really bad about that."

"You felt bad?"

"Well, yeah. Nobody wants someone to die eating their food. That's bad for business."

Vinny stared at him.

This wasn't the villain he had expected.

This was just a guy. A normal guy selling normal food to normal people.

The anger that had carried Vinny across three states suddenly had nowhere to go.

"I'm going to kill you," Vinny said, but his heart wasn't in it.

"Please don't. I've kids."

"How many?"

"Three. And a dog."

"What kind of dog?"

"Golden retriever. Her name is Sunny."

Vinny closed his eyes.

He couldn't kill a man with a golden retriever named Sunny.

Bobby would have laughed at that. Would have said that even revenge had standards.

"You want a hot dog?" the vendor said.

"What?"

"On the house. You came all this way."

Vinny stared at him. The man who had killed his best friend was, at this exact moment, offering him a free hot dog. Out of what — guilt? Generosity? Some kind of Mormon thing?

"Are you serious?"

"I'm always serious about hot dogs."

Vinny realized he was hungry. He had not eaten since Detroit. He had been so focused on murder that he had forgotten about lunch.

"Mustard. Onions. No ketchup."

"Of course no ketchup. You from Chicago?"

"You can tell?"

"I can always tell."

The vendor handed him the hot dog.

Vinny ate it standing right there, twelve feet from the spot where Bobby Bologna had died, while a man he had flown across three states to murder watched him chew.

It was a good hot dog.

Not Chicago good. But honest.

"This is *humiliating*," Vinny said with his mouth full.

"Yeah," the vendor said. "Sorry about that."

A car pulled up at the curb. A woman rolled down the window. "Honey, are you almost done? Sunny needs to go."

Vinny looked.

In the backseat of the station wagon, a golden retriever was hanging her head out the window, tongue out, tail thumping, looking at Vinny with the unconditional love that golden retrievers gave to absolutely everyone, including murderers.

Sunny licked Vinny's hand through the window.

Vinny made a sound he had not made since he was nine years old.

It was somewhere between a laugh and a sob and a recipe for chicken parmesan.

He finished the hot dog.

Thanked the vendor.

Vinny walked away.

Flew back to Chicago.

Went to a bar in Bridgeport and drank until the anger turned back into grief.

Then he cried.

For the first time since Bobby died.

For the first time since maybe ever.

He cried because his friend was gone and there was nobody to blame and the universe was random and unfair and hot dogs were just hot dogs and none of it made any sense.

The bartender let him cry.

Poured him another drink when he was done.

"Bad night?" the bartender asked.

"Bad month."

"Someone die?"

"My best friend. At a basketball game. Choking."

The bartender winced. "That's rough."

"You know what the worst part is?"

"What?"

"He was happy. Right before. He was the happiest I had ever seen him."

"That doesn't sound like the worst part."

Vinny looked up.

"What?"

"Being happy right before you go. That sounds like the best part. Better than being miserable."

Vinny considered this.

It wasn't wisdom he had expected from a bartender in Bridgeport.

But maybe wisdom came from unexpected places.

Maybe that was the point.

Vinny went home that night and slept for the first time in weeks.

Deep, dreamless sleep.

The kind that feels like forgiveness.

In the morning, he called Sol.

"I'm done fighting."

"What changed?"

"I went to Utah."

"Why?"

"To *kill* the hot dog guy."

Silence.

"Did you?"

"No. He's a golden retriever named Sunny."

More silence.

"Vinny. That's the strangest reason I've ever heard for not killing someone."

"It made *sense* at the time."

Sol sighed.

"Come to my apartment. We need to talk about the future."

"Is there a future?"

"There's always a future, Vinny. The question is whether we want to be part of it."

Vinny hung up.

Looked out his window at the city.

Bobby's city.

His city now.

At least until it became someone else.

CHAPTER 22

Nicky Learns to Eat Again

Nicky Moretti hadn't eaten a hot dog the right way since Bobby died.

This was, for Nicky, a crisis.

Hot dogs had been his comfort. His joy. His reason for getting out of bed on difficult days.

And now he couldn't even look at them without remembering.

So for three weeks, in the privacy of his apartment, Nicky punished himself.

He bought hot dogs. He boiled them — not steamed, boiled, like a man with no soul. He served them on stale white-bread buns from the back of his pantry. And then, with both hands trembling, he did the thing.

He put ketchup on them.

A lot of ketchup. The cheap kind, from the squeeze bottle, in long sad red ribbons that pooled on the bun like crime-scene photos.

He ate them standing over the kitchen sink, because he could not bear to sit down for what he was doing.

It was penance. He didn't know what for. Maybe for being alive when Bobby wasn't. Maybe for not being there at the Delta Center to do the Heimlich. Maybe for being Nicky.

After every hot dog, he cried into the sink.

He was on hot dog number nineteen when his mother let herself in with her own key.

She stood in the doorway in her good coat and surveyed the scene — the open ketchup bottle, the boiled gray dogs in the pot on the stove, her grown son weeping over a bun.

She set down her purse with the kind of slowness that meant a storm was coming.

"Nicholas."

"Ma."

"Nicholas Anthony Moretti."

"Ma, please—"

"Is that ketchup."

Nicky tried to hide the bottle behind a paper towel roll.

"Don't you dare. Don't you dare hide it. Bring it here."

He brought her the bottle.

She took it from him with two fingers, like it was a dead mouse, walked it to the trash can, opened the lid, and dropped it in. Then she walked to the stove, picked up the pot of boiled hot dogs with both hands, walked it to the trash can, and tipped the entire thing in. Water and all.

She turned to face him.

"Get your coat."

"Where are we going?"

"My house. I'm making pasta. You're going to eat it. And tomorrow you're going to a Chicago hot dog stand and you're going to order a hot dog like a person from Chicago, and if I find out you boiled another hot dog in this apartment I will tell every woman at St. Hyacinth that my son committed a *hate crime* against his own people. Do you understand me?"

"Yes, Ma."

"Get your coat."

Nicky got his coat.

His mother noticed.

"You're getting thin," she said, during a visit. "That isn't like you."

"I'm not hungry."

"You're always hungry. You were hungry before you were born. I could feel you eating in there."

"That isn't how pregnancy works, Ma."

"You're telling me how pregnancy works? I was there."

His mother made pasta.

The good pasta. The kind that took all day. The kind that required fresh ingredients and old recipes and the particular magic that Italian grandmothers had been passing down for centuries.

Nicky ate.

Not because he was hungry.

Because his mother was watching.

But somewhere around the third bite, something changed.

The pasta was good.

Really good.

And for a moment, the grief lifted enough for him to taste it.

"That's better," his mother said, watching him eat. "Food isn't the enemy, Nicholas. Food is life. Your friend understood that."

"Bobby."

"Bobby, yes. He knew that eating was sacred. That sharing food was sharing love. Do you think he would want you to stop eating?"

Nicky thought about this.

Bobby, who had lived for food.

Bobby, who had opinions about everything from beef to bagels to the proper temperature of soup.

Bobby, who had died eating.

"No," Nicky said finally. "He would want me to eat."

"Then eat. Eat for him. Eat for yourself. Eat because you're alive and being alive means being hungry."

Nicky took another bite.

Then another.

And somewhere between the pasta and the bread, he found his appetite again.

The next day, Nicky went to Gene & Jude's hot dogs.

He stood in line.

His heart was pounding.

The menu hadn't changed. The smell hadn't changed. Everything was exactly as it had always been.

Except Bobby wasn't there.

And would never be there again.

Nicky ordered one hot dog.

Depression style.

Extra everything.

He took his food to the wall where they used to stand.

Looked at the empty space beside him.

"This is for you, Bobby," he whispered.

Then he took a bite.

And it was good.

Not just good. Perfect.

The same as it had always been.

The same as it would always be.

Because some things didn't change.

Some things stayed constant even when everything else fell apart.

And that was comforting.

That was maybe the most comforting thing of all.

Nicky finished his hot dog.

Ordered another one.

Ate that too.

By the third hot dog, he was crying.

But they were different tears now.

Not grief tears.

Something else.

Something that felt almost like gratitude.

"Thank you, Bobby," Nicky said to the empty space.

"For teaching me how to eat."

"And how to enjoy it."

"And how to be hungry for life, not just food."

He wiped his eyes.

Walked back to his car.

And drove home with something he hadn't felt in weeks.

Hope.

Small.

Fragile.

But real.

CHAPTER 23

The Choice

The FBI agent was named Morrison.

He had a forgettable face and a memorable offer.

They met in a windowless conference room on the fifteenth floor of the Dirksen Federal Building. Morrison had Frankie brought up through the parking garage with two other agents and a deputy U.S. marshal. Nobody who saw Frankie that morning would have known he was there. That was the point.

"Mr. Petrucci," Morrison said, sliding into the booth. "Thank you for meeting me."

"I shouldn't be here."

"And yet here you are."

Frankie stared at his coffee. He had ordered it but couldn't drink it. His stomach was in knots. His hands were shaking.

"We know everything," Morrison said calmly. "The money laundering. The fronts. The connections to Bobby Filoni. We have enough to put you away for fifteen years."

"Then why haven't you?"

"Because we don't want you. We want him."

Morrison slid a folder across the table.

"Witness protection. New identity. New life. All you have to do is testify."

Frankie opened the folder. Photographs. Documents. Evidence that proved Morrison wasn't bluffing.

"I have a wife," Frankie said quietly.

"She can come with you."

"She doesn't know what I do."

"Then now would be a good time to tell her."

Frankie thought about Bobby.

About the man who had saved his business, his marriage, his life.

About the debt he owed. The loyalty he had promised.

About the terror of what would happen if Bobby ever found out he was sitting in this booth.

"I need time."

"You have one week."

"That's not enough."

"It's all you're getting."

Frankie left the federal building with Morrison's card in his pocket and a decision he couldn't make in his heart.

He never called Morrison back.

Not because he was brave.

Because Bobby died before the week was up.

The day after the funeral, Frankie burned Morrison's card and every piece of evidence the FBI had given him. He stood over the flames and watched his almost-betrayal turn to ash.

No one would ever know.

Except Sol.

Sol knew everything.

Because Sol always knew everything.

Three weeks after the funeral, Sol showed up at Frankie's dry cleaning shop.

"We need to talk."

Frankie's blood went cold. "About what?"

"About a federal building downtown."

Frankie couldn't breathe.

"I didn't—"

"I know. You didn't flip. But you considered it."

"How did you—"

"I have people everywhere, Frankie. You know that."

Sol sat on the counter, looking tired. Not angry. Just tired.

"I should kill you. Or have you killed. That's what Bobby would have wanted."

"I know."

"But Bobby is dead. And I am not Bobby."

Sol looked at him with eyes that had seen too much.

"Walk away, Frankie. Take your wife. Go somewhere else. Start over. And never, ever talk about what you knew or who you knew."

"You're letting me go?"

"I'm giving you what you wanted without the betrayal attached. Consider it a gift."

Frankie moved to Florida three months later.

Opened a dry cleaning shop in Boca Raton.

Never spoke to any of them again.

And every night, before he fell asleep, he thought about what he had almost done.

And about the man who had let him live anyway.

EPILOGUE: TEN YEARS LATER

Ten years after Bobby Bologna died, a reporter from the Tribune wrote a retrospective.

"The Life and Legend of Bobby Bologna: A Chicago Story"

It ran in the Sunday magazine.

It got a lot of things wrong.

But it got the important things right.

SOL ROSEN:

By 2008, Sol had retired from everything illegal.

He ran a legitimate accounting firm in Skokie. Helped small businesses with their taxes. Occasionally consulted on matters that required discretion.

He never talked about the old days.

But he kept a photo of Bobby in his office. On his desk. Where everyone could see it.

When clients asked who that was, Sol would smile.

"Old friend," he would say. "We used to be in business together."

"What kind of business?"

"The Chicago kind."

Nobody asked follow-up questions.

VINNY CAPOZZI:

Vinny moved to Arizona in 2002.

The weather was better for his joints. The pace was slower. The memories were further away.

He ran a small Italian restaurant in Scottsdale. Made his mother recipes. Hired people who reminded him of people he used to know.

Once a year, on June 14th, he closed the restaurant and watched the video of Game Six.

The whole game.

Every minute.

By himself.

With a hot dog he could never bring himself to eat.

NICKY MORETTI:

The rumor about the hot dog stand in San Diego was true.

Nicky opened it in 2004. Called it Peanuts.

Served Chicago-style hot dogs to West Coast tourists who didn't understand what they were eating but could tell it was something special.

"No ketchup," Nicky would tell customers.

"Why not?"

"Because some things are *sacred*."

The customers usually accepted this.

The ones who didn't were politely but firmly asked to leave.

FRANKIE PETRUCCI:

Frankie stayed in Boca Raton.

His dry cleaning business was still there, in a strip mall between a bagel place and a podiatrist. Still losing a little money. Still laundering nothing except actual laundry.

His wife had divorced him in 2001 when he refused to talk about Chicago. He had gotten married again in 2003 — a kind woman named Susan who didn't ask questions. They had a daughter in 2005.

He named her Roberta.

Bobby, for short.

When Susan asked why, Frankie didn't have a good answer.

"I just like the name," he said.

She knew it was a lie.

She accepted it anyway.

Sol called him exactly once, in 2009, on Bobby's birthday. They didn't say much. At the end of the call, Sol said, "Bobby would have *hated* that you ended up in Florida."

"I know."

"That's the *funniest* part."

Frankie laughed for the first time since the funeral.

TONY SMILES:

Tony went to federal prison in 2005.

Tax evasion.

Not the dramatic ending he had imagined for himself.

He served four years. Got out. Tried to rebuild.

But the world had moved on.

Nobody smiled when they saw him anymore.

ANGIE MARINO:

Angie disappeared in 2007.

Some said she was in Italy.

Some said she was dead.

Some said she was still in Chicago, watching everything, waiting for the right moment to return.

Nobody knew for sure.

Which was exactly how Angie liked it.

THE CREW:

Sol, Vinny, and Nicky stayed in touch.

Not constantly. Not obsessively. Just enough to know the others were okay.

They met once a year. In Chicago. At Al's #1 Italian Beef.

Same order. Same booth. Same conversation about the old days and the new days and whether things had turned out the way any of them expected.

They always ordered an extra sandwich.

For Bobby.

They never ate it.

Just let it sit there.

A tribute.

An offering.

A reminder that some absences never stopped hurting.

THE CITY:

Chicago changed in the ten years after Bobby died.

The Bulls did not win another championship. Jordan retired for good.

The dynasty ended.

The neighborhoods shifted. Gentrification transformed places that used to be rough into places that had artisanal coffee shops.

But some things stayed the same.

The food was still good.

The winters were still brutal.

The people were still stubborn and proud and unwilling to apologize for being exactly who they were.

That was Chicago.

That was always Chicago.

And Bobby Bologna, wherever he was, would have approved.

ABOUT THE AUTHOR

Justin Lampert is an aspiring author, which is what you call somebody who has now written three books and continues to do it anyway. He has co-written others, the way some men have hobbies. He has a degree in History from DePaul University, where he learned that the past is mostly people making the same five mistakes in different *outfits*. His mother once said the degree would be very helpful. It was, in fact, *not at all helpful for any job he ever had*. It has been extremely helpful for writing books about Chicago.

He grew up in the city itself, not one of the suburbs that pretends to be Chicago by saying things like *Chicagoland*, and he remains, by his own admission, an aggressive and possibly clinical fan of everything Chicago: the sports, the food, the architecture, the politics (no — *those* politics), the music, the weather (yes — even *that*), and the deeply held cultural belief that ketchup belongs on eggs and absolutely nothing else.

He now lives in South Florida with his wife and son, where the weather is better, the food is *worse*, the sports are confusing, and the produce is suspiciously perfect all year round. He still puts giardiniera on everything. He still argues about pizza. He still believes the Cubs are going to win it all next year, and the year after, and the year after that, in perpetuity, until the heat death of the universe. By then, he assumes, they will probably finally win.

This is his third book.

He is already working on the fourth.

COMING NEXT IN THE LEGENDS DON'T DIE IN CHICAGO SERIES

Long before there was a Bobby Bologna, there was Chicago in the 1920s.

Speakeasies behind butcher shops. Bootleggers who took themselves *very* seriously. An entire generation of Chicago men who decided that the best way to handle Prohibition was to ignore it harder than anyone had ever ignored anything before.

Book Two takes us back to the era that *made* the city legendary — same wit, same food obsession, same complete disregard for personal safety, brand-new crew, slightly older suits.

You don't need to have read this one to read that one.

But you'll want to.

Coming 2027.

www.ingramcontent.com/pod-product-compliance
Lightning Source LLC
Chambersburg PA
CBHW070638260626
47161CB00007B/2750